THE SURVIVALIST

#26

COUNTDOWN

Books by Jerry Ahern

THE SURVIVALIST

#26

COUNTDOWN

JERRY AHERN

SPEAKING VOLUMES, LLC
NAPLES, FLORIDA
2014

THE SURVIVALIST
#26 COUNTDOWN

Copyright © 1993 by Jerry Ahern

ISBN 978-1-61232-289-6

**For more exciting
E-Books, Audiobooks and MP3 downloads visit us at
www.speakingvolumes.us**

Author's Note

For those who came in late . . .

In the latter part of the current era, John Thomas Rourke, Doctor of Medicine and former Covert Operations Officer in the Central Intelligence Agency, plied the trade at which he was most expert of all: he wrote and taught in the fields of survivalism and special weapons and tactics.

His motto was then and still is, Plan Ahead. To that end, although Rourke hoped that mankind would avoid all-out warfare, he planned for the opposite, investing virtually all his resources in the construction, fitting and stocking of an elaborately planned survival facility which he called the Retreat.

While Rourke was returning by commercial airline from a training exercise (in Canada for the Royal Canadian Mounted Police), the unthinkable occurred: global thermonuclear war.

Civilization stopped.

In the immediate aftermath of the Night of the War, Rourke became fast friends with a young magazine editor named Paul Rubenstein. What Paul initally lacked in skill, he compensated for with courage, resolve and the quickness and willingness to learn. The two friends set out across the ravaged landscape in search of John Rourke's wife, Sarah, and their then-young children, Michael and Annie, hoping to find them and bring them to the comparative safety of the Retreat.

Along the way, John Rourke and Paul Rubenstein saved the life of an enemy agent whose skills were a perfect match for Rourke's own, her name Major Natalia Anastasia Tiemerovna. Events soon forced Natalia to the realization that the government in whose name she had fought for so many years was the enemy of mankind. A woman of honor and conviction, she became Rourke's and Rubenstein's unswervingly steadfast ally and friend.

So began a chain of events which has lasted in print for approximately a dozen years as this is written and continued over the course of 625 years in the lives of what has come to be known as "the Rourke Family." The Rourke Family has survived holocaust, endured through cryogenic Sleep, and fought on in the cause of freedom and humanity. The children, Michael and Annie, have grown to adulthood; but, through the manipulation possible with cryogenics, they are chronologically the contemporaries of their parents, as well as of Natalia and Paul Rubenstein.

Three men and three women, they are the only remaining survivors from the twentieth century, in a far distant future disquietingly like the past.

Humanity is numbered only in the millions, but beginning once again to take hold of the planet, to mold nature to its will. The biosphere's wounds are nearly healed. But data surfaces concerning an environmental crisis of unprecedented magnitude, threatening to destroy the very fabric of the planet.

And, the spectre of global warfare looms once again. The enemy is a resurgent Nazi movement. At its head is Dr. Deitrich Zimmer, a man of unparalleled brilliance and skill, of unmitigated ruthlessness and malevolence.

The Family, John Rourke at its head, must fight to survive or die. And, if they fail, mankind will be nothing more than a lost chapter in the pages of time.

Jerry Ahern
Commerce, Georgia

Prologue

Almost-Sarah, or was she Sarah? She had Sarah's memories.

Was it only programming? Where did the input from another living being's memory begin and the reality of true memory start?

The gunfire. She recognized that plainly enough. It made her remember the birth of her third child, a little boy—or was she remembering . . .

It was clearly the sound of a pistol shot, nothing else.

And her husband's little office was suddenly a very vulnerable place, with too many windows, no secure door, very little potential for covered positions from which to return fire.

Sarah Rourke's right hand groped for the Trapper Scorpion .45 in the pocket of her German arctic parka, the garment draped over the back of her husband's chair.

11

The pistol's chamber was already loaded and she thumbed back the hammer as she stood.

Pain shot through her, from groin to chest.

She was cold and hot at once.

Fluid burst from her, spraying downward between her legs and onto the floor, her water bag broken.

Her knees went weak.

As she upped the safety on the .45 and doubled forward over the desk, choking back a scream, she realized the baby was coming early . . .

Sarah Rourke, her pistol clutched in her right hand, fought against the cramping which seized her, consumed her. She was dragging herself along the floor now, into the corridor, dragging herself because she could not walk. The first of the explosions had knocked her to the floor.

On her knees beside the corridor wall, she sagged, felt the movement of the baby.

It had to be a boy, racing to the sound of battle just like his father had always done, but not now!

She tried to get to her feet but could not rise.

Smoke filled the corridor, acrid-smelling, filling her lungs and the baby's bloodstream, too, she knew.

But the back door to the hospital, the emergency entrance, was only a few yards away, she told herself, only a few yards.

Where was John? Natalia? Where was Natalia?

Sarah Rourke leaned with her back against the wall, her legs squatted beneath her.

On one level of consciousness, she told herself that American Indian women—African women, women for centuries had delivered their own children this way.

But that level was very small and very far away.

Her fingernails gouged into the wall and she shrieked her pain to the flames around her, the smoke making her cough and gag, but the baby's head crowned, blood oozing along her thighs, her flesh ripping.

"John!"

The baby.

Something enormous was pushing through her, tearing at her, sending waves of pain through her body no matter how she tried to regulate her breathing.

"John!"

More pain than she had ever known, and then it was gone, and blood and fluid dripped from her, but her baby's head was out. She bore down with her shoulders, her rib cage, her pelvis, pushing as hard as she could, unable to move her hands to help herself lest she fall.

She drew herself in and pushed down.

Movement.

A shoulder. It had to be. She pushed. And she could feel her child alive and moving and she let herself slide down along the length of the wall as her hands grasped for the baby, drawing the child— her child, John's child—the rest of the way from her body.

As she raised the new life toward her—a boy—he simultaneously screamed and urinated.

13

"Very impressive, Frau Rourke."

Tears filling her eyes, she looked up toward the mechanical-sounding voice.

It had come to her through some sort of mask.

Her baby's body was slick and at the same time sticky, the umbilical cord still attached, blue and pulsing.

The man who had spoken to her had a gun in his hand. "This is for your crimes against National Socialism, Frau Rourke."

She screamed, "John!"

She saw a flash from the muzzle of the gun . . .

Did the possession of memories endow the possessor with the reality of the object or event remembered?

She was faintly aware of being in her husband's arms, but he wasn't her husband, or maybe he was. And she felt safe from the gunfire. But, didn't she want to kill this man? She could not remember that now.

Where was her baby boy, the child she'd birthed in the instant before what was almost death? For Sarah? For Almost-Sarah? Almost-Sarah, a clone of the original—or was she Sarah?

Were the memories hers or only stolen?

She felt tears in eyes that she was, as yet, too tired to open.

Chapter One

On one level, John Thomas Rourke was truly convinced that the woman whom he held cradled in his arms was, indeed, his wife. She not only looked and felt, even sounded like Sarah (in the instant that she had called his name before lapsing again from consciousness), but the womanly smell of her was distinctly Sarah Rourke. Yet, the doubt which Deitrich Zimmer had planted in Rourke's mind concerning her identity was something Rourke could neither escape nor ignore. And, if she were not Sarah, he might well be carrying the instrument of his death.

But there was no time for worrying about the situation now, too much to do. Another three dozen of Deitrich Zimmer's SS commandos were holding the top of the mountain where their helicopters had originally landed. No Trans-Global Alliance airpower was forthcoming, either, Commander Washington announced.

"And why is that?" Paul Rubenstein asked him.

Commander Washington's chocolate brown skin, already slightly greyed from the cold, became suddenly, subtly greyer. "There's been a nuclear attack on our forces located in Upstate New York," he said very softly. "No casualty count yet, General—Doctor Rourke—and Mr. Rubenstein, and no information at all except that it happened. No yield size, nothing. All we do know is that the detonation was probably an air burst, the most deadly technique for battlefield use."

Annie made the sign of the cross.

"Not only the most deadly," John Rourke said, almost as if speaking to himself, his mind focusing on the implications of Commander Washington's words rather than the surroundings, "but the most efficient, too. An obviously greater effect from blast—shock wave, heat wave, light—but mini- mized fallout, enhancing potential for the enemy's friendly forces to function in the battlefield environ- ment as quickly as possible after the detonation, and with some degree of impunity if the proper pre- cautions are taken. Before the Night of the War, the Russians actually trained for postnuclear battle- field combat. It would seem logical that our Dr. Zimmer and his Nazi hierarchy had their field forces doing the same."

Natalia, with her wounded left leg being attended to by a medic, was seated, leaning her back against the living rock which comprised the wall surface of the control center at the base of the Nazi mountain headquarters. She looked at Commander Washing- ton, then at John Rourke, then started laughing. It was a hollow laugh, the kind that sounded on the edge of tears or insanity.

Rourke was walking again, still carrying Sarah, nearly out the doorway, to the halftrack waiting outside; but, he just stopped. His wife—he would operate on the assumption that she was his wife, until and unless circumstances proved differently—lay somewhere between sleep and unconsciousness in his arms and the world was collapsing around them. Personal concerns, once again, had to be put aside. And, except for those five years he'd spent raising his son and daughter in the Retreat, he had known nothing beyond mortal conflict ever since the Night of the War. He was becoming increasingly tired of having no life other than that. Even those five years had been years of sadness, and fear, too, but there was true and profound satisfaction in taking two children and seeing them through their first steps into an adulthood such as no child had ever experienced before or since. Michael and Annie had been small children on the Night of the War, surviving into a future John Rourke could never have imagined.

"We'll need aircraft, then, in order to anticipate a wide range of contingencies," Rourke announced, his words a long exhalation of the exhaustion within him. He threw back his shoulders, his jaw setting, telling himself that it was time to go on, to do, to make things better than they were and that personal concerns mattered little if at all by comparison. "That means we neutralize the enemy personnel above, capture their machines if possible, meanwhile securing this base. If a general nuclear exchange results from the battlefield detonation to

17

which Commander Washington referred, this place might be our only sanctuary, the food and supplies here our only means of survival." Rourke looked at his son, telling him, "Michael, take your mother and—"

"I'm not leaving. I'll carry Mom to the halftrack, but I'm not going anywhere after that. I've got work to do here. She'll be cared for; we both know that. And, as soon as this facility is secured, we'll have her back here with us."

Rourke only nodded, respecting his son's judgement.

Before John Rourke could speak, Natalia said, "I'm not going to be very fast on my feet, John, but there is quite a bit I can do regardless of this." And she gestured to her leg wound. "Perhaps fly that helicopter the Nazis so kindly left us. My leg will work well enough for that."

And John Rourke started to laugh.

"I'm staying, too, Daddy," his daughter, Annie Rubenstein, announced. "I'm still fast on my feet." And she looked at Natalia and smiled. "We pretty much started out in all of this together and we'll keep at it until we finish it or die trying."

Paul hugged her.

"Fine," Rourke said at last. "Then, let's see if we can get Wolfgang Mann conscious, so he can help, too. As soon as he's got his faculties about him, we could benefit from having a real general to give us some advice as opposed to only an honorary one." Rourke considered the military rank conferred on him more than a century ago at Mid-Wake, however sincerely meant, as real a qualification for military leadership as being appointed a Kentucky Colonel, Before the Night of the War. And, Rourke looked pointedly at Commander Washington who had made reference to the rank. Washington shrugged his shoulders and smiled, as if to say, "Touché."

Michael took his mother from his father's arms into his own, saying, "She'll be all right, Dad."

John Thomas Rourke addressed all present, his voice little more than a whisper. "I think we have our work cut out for us, ladies and gentlemen." And, they did . . .

Climbing the cliff-face to the summit where the Nazi commando force held its fortified position was madness, in and of itself, the granite surface dangerous in the extreme. But, with enemy personnel above who might fire down at any second, the enterprise bordered on suicidal, Rourke realized. Yet, John Rourke had planned ahead.

Their greatest danger, both from the mountain itself and the armed men above lay in the final six hundred feet or so, where the angle as the summit was approached was too steep to be navigated on anything but all fours with climbing ropes to assist, yet level enough that it would be impossible to avoid detection by anyone who cared to look.

At that juncture, if they reached the approach to the summit alive, Natalia would utilize the captured Nazi helicopter gunship, and the remote video probes aboard the craft would be launched, the nonessential video apparatus removed, high explosives substituted in their place. With any luck, the

Nazi defenders would not realize what they were shooting at until they'd already shot, and the explosives would detonate. While this was going on, the distraction it would hopefully provide might mask the final stage of the ascent to the summit.

There was no proper climbing gear available, no crampons, nor even pitons to assist them, and their options among field expedients were limited. As Commander Washington's numerically superior force worked its way systematically through the structure, daring only to take the elevators to a command post established within two floors of the enemy base at the summit, a full machine shop was discovered. One of the men with Washington's command, Seaman First Class Clarence W. Wolverton, had had some experience as a machinist in civilian life and was immediately drafted into preparations needed for the climb.

Wolverton was relieved of his other duties. John Rourke took the fellow aside. "Wolverton, here's what I need."

"Aye, sir," Wolverton responded, pulling off his black balaclava, his grey eyes focusing intently on Rourke's own.

"I'll get as many men relieved to your detail as you require, Wolverton." The installation was being secured and the vaccine against the effects of *encephalitis lethargica,* which Rourke had used as a bioweapon in order to originally gain access to the facility, was being administered. With the exception of the two upper stories, just below the fortified Nazi position at the summit, the facility was almost completely stabilized. "The type of metal I'll need for the pitons should be a high grade of tool steel, resilient yet with enough surface hardness so that it can be hammered into rock. Bolts used in association with the elevator housings might be a good place to start. Those would have to be strong in order to handle the equipment-load weight-limits that are posted. Can you do it? And, fast? I know the equipment available to you may not be right for the job."

"Being perfectly honest, sir, I don't know. I'll sure try my damnedest."

"That's all I can ask, son," Rourke told the young sailor. "Get whatever men and gear you need; you have my full authority if anybody questions you."

"Aye, sir," and Wolverton snapped to. Rourke gave him a nod and Wolverton was off at a trot.

Rourke checked the black-faced Rolex on his left wrist. He had no idea how much time the preparations would consume, nor how much time he had left. He grabbed his parka and started for the doors leading to the outside and the helicopter where Natalia, resident explosives expert, was rigging the remote video probes.

Latest word from the field camp where Sarah had been taken for safety was that her condition was rapidly improving. Once the upper levels and the position on the summit were secured, Sarah could be brought back in relative safety. Wolfgang Mann's condition was improving rapidly, as well. In a few hours, although New Germany's premier general-oberst wouldn't be up and ready to fight, Mann should be able to offer military advice for the defense of the overrun Nazi headquarters complex.

That assumption was predicated, of course, on the further assumption that this Wolfgang Mann was the genuine Wolfgang Mann.

As Rourke ventured into the open, a bitterly cold wind cut into him and he pulled his parka closed around him, throwing up its hood as well. Rourke could not help but be reminded of how that wind would feel as they made their way along the face of the mountain.

With heatlamps to warm the position, Commander Washington's senior radioman was attending his equipment, trying to raise anything he could find on a Trans-Global Alliance frequency in search of information and air support.

Rourke nodded as he passed the man. "Any luck?"

"Nothing yet, sir, except a hell of a lot of static."

"Carry on."

What about Emma Shaw? Rourke bit his lower lip. There was a significant likelihood that she was somehow involved in the nuclear incident; therefore, there was an equally substantial chance that she had been killed. "Damn it," Rourke rasped.

He kept walking, quickening his pace as he neared the captured Nazi helicopter where Natalia was preparing the explosives. As Rourke reached it, he hammered his fist on the portside fuselage door, then waited. The door slid open, one of the SEAL Team personnel behind it. "Good evening, sir."

"Yes, good evening."

Rourke stepped up and inside, the SEAL sliding the door closed behind him, then passing him, rejoining Natalia and one of the German Long

22

Range Mountain Patrol commandos aft. Two of the remote video probes were partially disemboweled on the deck before them and surrounding these were coils of multicolored wire and bricks of plastique. "How's it going, Natalia?"

Without turning around to look at him, she said, "This is not all that difficult, really, just time-consuming, John. The same electronics which allow manipulation of the video can be utilized to trigger the explosives, should that be necessary. Or, at least in theory they can be."

There was too much "theory" to this entire operation, Rourke thought. "Fine, let me know, then."

"Right. Any word on Sarah?"

"She's coming along nicely."

"Good."

"How's the leg?"

"It only hurts when I laugh," she told him bravely.

"Fortunate we don't have much to laugh about, then, isn't it?"

Her wounded leg was outstretched and, only to someone who knew Natalia as well as John Rourke did, it was clear that she was in at least moderate pain. Switching over to Russian, which neither of the two men with her could be expected to understand, she said, "Michael asked me to be his wife, John."

Answering her in Russian, Rourke told her, "That is wonderful for both of you."

"It is insane, John. Michael and I love each other and what we have is something I have never known before. Yet, I will be your daughter-in-law, and I

23

cannot forget the feelings we shared before any of this happened. Am I doing the right thing? I think that I am."

"I know that you are." Rourke told her, smiling. "You and Paul are the best friends I have ever had, could ever have. Paul is my son-in-law, you will be my daughter-in-law. And no man could ask for better."

"I will always love you, Ivan, you know that."

"And I will always love you, Natalia Anastasia," John Rourke told her. Then, taking a cigar from beneath his once-again open parka, he said in English, "One of you gentlemen close up after me, please," and John Rourke threw aside the door, the cigar clamped tight in his teeth. He stepped out into the night after pausing for an instant to roll the striking-wheel of his battered Zippo windlighter beneath his thumb, then plunge the cigar's tip into its blue-yellow flame.

The wind seemed colder.

That was to be expected.

Chapter Two

The aircraft was well into its reserve tanks, and Emma Shaw had practiced all the fuel-economy measures that she could think of. The hand-operated semaphores were long since replaced by what appeared to be a battery-operated electrical unit. She was certain that no power was available on the base as yet. Radio, except between the aircraft themselves, was still out.

As she swept a lazy circle—mostly glide—around the main runway, mentally scoring her chances for a deadstick landing and finding them less than satisfactory, she spied another aircraft identical to her own and those of her squadron. It was taking off into the wind. As it did so, her radio began to crackle. "This is Communicator One calling Bulldog Leader. Do you copy? Over."

"This is Bulldog Leader, Communicator One. Reading you loud and clear. Over."

"Bulldog Leader, this is Communicator One. All ground-based electrical systems are still out. Do you copy that? Over."

"Affirmative, Communicator One."

"Am switching to LRF Nine, Bulldog Leader. Will continue on that frequency. Stand by. Over."

"Bulldog Leader standing by, Communicator One. Reading Lima Romeo Foxtrot Niner. Over."

Emma Shaw switched her ship-to-ship onto Limited Range Frequency Nine. Communicator One's voice was harder to understand, the signal weak, but that was by design. The LRF frequencies were used only when there was significant danger of ship-to-ship communications security being compromised. But why had Communicator One said that all base electrical systems were still out? This was valuable data to an enemy considering attack. "Bulldog Leader, negative all base electrical systems are out. I say again, negative. All systems, including long-range scanning, approximately eighty-five percent operational. All additional fighter aircraft have been ordered away to regroup. Cargo lifters more than ninety-five percent incapacitated. Impossible to evacuate base at this time. Do you copy, Bulldog Leader? Over."

"Roger that, Communicator One. Both squadrons under my command are flying on vapor only. Do you copy, Communicator One? Over."

"Affirmative, Bulldog Leader. Your fuel-consumption rates have been calculated. Aerial refueling impossible under impending combat conditions. Minimum thirty-six bogeys visible on long-range scanning, ETA seven minutes forty-three seconds. Do you copy? Over."

"Roger, Communicator One. We do not have

enough fuel to engage or flee. Over."

"Roger that, Bulldog Leader. You are instructed to order down Bulldog Pups lowest on reserve fuel tanks while balance of your two squadrons maintain defensive posture. As soon as refueling is accomplished, the remainder of your squadrons are to land and refuel. Any problems with that, Commander Shaw? Over."

"Wilco, Communicator One. Beginning compliance now. Bulldog Leader Out."

"Good luck, Commander. Communicator One, Out."

Emma Shaw switched away from LRF Nine to regular ship-to-ship. "Bulldog Pups, this is Bulldog Leader." She ordered down to hard deck for refueling those aircraft within her squadrons which were lowest on reserve fuel, assigning the remaining aircraft to stay on her wings in modified defense formation, then designating priorities for those aircraft to refuel in turn. "Any questions? Over."

"This is Bulldog Pup One to Bulldog Leader. Wilco that, Bulldog Leader. I'll be taking a coffee break myself. Bulldog Pup One Out."

"This is Bulldog Pup Two, Bulldog Leader. Wilco your instructions. I'll stay with you so that we can grab some java together and see what happens next. Do you copy, Bulldog Leader? Over."

Lieutenant Tom Larabee, one of the most happily married men she'd ever met, was always pretending to flirt. Half laughing, despite their rather dire circumstances, Emma Shaw told him, "This is Bulldog Leader. I'm getting wet just thinking about being with you, Bulldog Pup Two. Out."

27

There would not be time enough for all aircraft in her two squadrons to refuel and get airborne again before the arrival of the enemy fighter aircraft; Emma Shaw knew that. Six minutes and forty-five seconds remained before the thirty-six bogeys would be in combat range. Their longer-range weapons could already have been fired against ground-based targets, would soon be in range to acquire preliminary fixes on airborne targets. Emma Shaw estimated that fewer than two minutes of aerial combat would drain her tanks dry and, if she were lucky, she'd drop like a stone and die in the crash as opposed to getting blown out of the sky.

That was the kind of luck that she did not need.

Chapter Three

Paul Rubenstein was not given to doodling, but as he stood before the imposing shape of the mountain summit, he drew in the snow, with the toe of his boot, the mushroom-shaped cloud characteristic of a thermonuclear detonation.

Mankind was, he was now firmly convinced, incapable of learning from past mistakes. The best scientific minds in both the Trans-Global Alliance and the enemy camp—Eden and her Nazi allies— freely admitted that even one nuclear blast might bring about the destruction of the atmosphere, obliterating all human and animal life as was almost the case six hundred and twenty-five years ago when this all began.

He was an accidental survivor. That was how Paul Rubenstein had always viewed himself. Although he was born and raised an Air Force brat, he never had any martial training of any sort until after falling in with John Rourke in the aftermath of the Night of the War. He'd volunteered to march across the desert with this strangely commanding man he'd met among the complement of passengers, stayed with him, learned from him, became very proficient at the ways of warfare simply out of the demands of survival.

As a child, it was somehow implicit that all super-heroes—outside of men like Moses and Joshua—were Christian, but that had never bothered him, because he had no aspirations to go about the world righting wrongs with anything more violent than a passion for right and contempt for prejudice. Nor did Paul Rubenstein consider himself at all heroic now. Albeit that he fit the mold not at all—he was tall enough, but never more than slightly built, and from childhood up until his awakening from the Sleep that first time he had aways needed glasses—he merely did what he had to do, in order to keep himself on good terms with his conscience and to keep himself and his friends alive.

John, on the other hand, was the hero through and through. Unlike many so-called heroes, how-ever, John's heroism was intrinsic to John's being. John Rourke could be nothing else, and herosim became him well.

After all the fighting, all the killing, all the struggles, mankind was once again brought to the brink of total annihilation by stupidity and greed.

John liked to look at the stars. Paul Rubenstein felt that if anyone looked at the stars right now, it would be likely the stars could be seen laughing back at the suicidal folly below . . .

*   *   *

Michael Rourke had nothing to do but clean and check his weapons, which he did, field-stripping the last of the two Beretta 92F 9 mm's which he carried. Removing the magazine, then clearing the chamber, he let the slide move forward, depressing the disassembly latch, swinging it downward, then pulling slide and barrel forward off the frame.

He set to work on the interior diameter of the bore with a soaked patch. Now that he had asked Natalia to marry him and Natalia had accepted—his question and her response were implicit between them for some time—he had to consider the future, if there was one.

Either one of two things would occur as a result of two distinct chains of events, neither of which he could predict. Human life would either be obliterated or there would be peace, at least of a sort.

In the case of the former possibility, there would be no future about which to worry. If, however, the nuclear detonation which had already occurred did not, in and of itself, signal man's doom nor precipitate increased nuclear combat which would, this war at least would eventually end. Michael Rourke doubted not for a moment that, if the war ended, the side of the angels would somehow come out victorious. The Trans-Global Alliance, if for no other reason than the fact that it stood opposed to neo-Nazism, was definitely the side of the angels. As his father, John Rourke, had once said, "The good guy always wins. It may seem as though evil is victorious at times, but in the end, evil will always fail and right will eventually prevail. Such a victory might take longer to be achieved than any of us will ever live to see, than any of us might even imagine; but, in the final analysis, there can be no other way."

A bit optimistic, perhaps, but without such optimism there would be no reason beyond sheer stubbornness to do anything other than give up. Aside from the war itself, there was the nagging issue of Doctor Thorn Rolvaag's discoveries concerning the suboceanic rift. The planet might already be doomed by a volcanic anomaly.

So, if mankind were not wiped clean from the face of the Earth, there would be details to which he must attend: making a home, supporting his wife, finding something productive to do with his life, making the world a better place for the children whom he and Natalia would bring into that world together.

Somehow, the thought of normalcy was unnerving to him. He had never lived in a time of peace. Even Before the Night of the War, there was the constant sabre-rattling of the two superpowers, something about which not even a small child—as he had been—could remain wholly ignorant. Barely to the age of understanding, his sister two years younger still, the Night of the War came and, in the morning of its aftermath, he killed for the first time, plunging a boning knife into the kidney of a man who was about to sexually assault his mother. Not long after that, he'd killed again in defense of what was right. It was not, thank God, exactly habit, but it was something to which he had become at least somewhat accustomed.

Michael Rourke supposed that he was fortunate, born without the sort of liberal excuse for a conscience which would have totally traumatized

32

him. His conscience was not an excuse, but the real thing. From what he'd seen in videos, read in books, heard related by his father and faintly recalled from his own memories of the time Before the Night of the War, it was fashionable in some quarters to believe that violence of any sort, even in defense of human life, was somehow intrinsically evil.

If, however, a man or woman stepped so far outside the human community as to rob another human being of his life or dignity, killing that man or woman was, however regrettable, not something of great moral import, considered in full context.

What was of moral import and cause for great sadness and soul-searching was the fact that a human being could sink to such a level that he or she had to be destroyed because he or she was no longer truly human, only preyed on the human community while pretending to be a part of it.

Michael Rourke's father had told him once when they were alone in the Retreat, Annie already asleep for the night, "Had the Night of the War never come, Michael, it's sad to say that the eventual outcome for humanity might have been little different. The economy of the United States, like the economies of other nations, was already severely strained. The possible solutions to ecological concerns, such as the depletion of the ozone layer, global warming, and overpopulation, were staggering even to consider.

"We've talked about the issue of global warming before, Son. Did you ever consider what might have happened, say, if there had never been the Night of the War and the scientists who predicted global warming had turned out to be right?"

33

"I don't know, Dad. I mean, it would have been hotter everywhere and that would have meant farming problems and like that, and the oceans rising."

"Take the ocean-level rise, considering only the economic consequences of that one potential result of the global warming hypothesis, should it have come to pass. According to some computer models at the time, a significant rise in global temperature would have raised ocean levels—by the melting of the icecaps and some glaciers—to a point where much of the Eastern seaboard of the United States—not to mention other places—would have been flooded.

"Consider New York City, all right? Before its destruction During the Night of the War, it was the most heavily populated city in the United States. It was the financial capital of the Western World, perhaps of the entire world. Innumerable businesses were run from New York City, financial decisions made there which shaped the future of mankind. Now, how much do you think it would have cost to move New York City? Either that or build a sea wall around it, and all down the rest of the East Coast? To save all the other important cities?"

"I don't—I don't know, Dad."

"Trouble was, Son, if anybody did know, no one was telling. And that was just one of the problems facing humanity. There were diseases, there was poverty, there was international aggression—the catalog was almost endless. And fewer and fewer people wanted to be bothered by the problems. It was better to bury oneself in self-indulgence, shut

34

the mind away in ephemeral pleasures and just wait for the inevitable cataclysm.

"In some ways, Michael," his father had said, "the last half of the twentieth century was an era of renewed involvement, but only by a comparatively small segment of the population. Some people, out of ignorance or greed, aligned themselves with causes which were deleterious to mankind's welfare. There were those who supported the abrogation of their own civil liberties and their possible subjugation into serfdom by fighting for the destruction of the Second Amendment. There were others whose translation of a genuine concern for the welfare of animals led them to destroy or interfere with medical research which could have saved human lives. Still others were so narrow-minded in their own religious beliefs and so convinced that their conception of morality was the only correct conception that they fought to have government codify religion and dictate every aspect of human existence, totally denying freedom of choice and individual moral responsibility.

"But, at least, however benighted, self-destructive—dumb, okay?—at least they were doing something, even if it was stupid. And there were many more people, who worked with remarkable diligence in true service to mankind, helping to solve problems rather than make more problems, fighting to alleviate suffering, working to spread freedom of choice. But those who chose to be involved—for good or for bad—were the minority as opposed to the vast majority of people who did nothing at all except kick back. And the minority who worked diligently to inform, to educate, to uplift their fellow man and to enhance human dignity were numerically overwhelmed; but, they kept trying in the face of incalculable odds.

"So, in a way, Michael, it all might have ended anyway. To paraphrase T. S. Eliot, mankind just went out with a 'bang' rather than a 'whimper,' but in either case the result might just as well have been the same."

Perhaps, Michael Rourke thought, his hands moving as if with a will of their own as he reassembled his pistol, mankind had a death wish. And, however the events in which he and his Family were embroiled were to turn out, the ultimate destiny of mankind was indelibly written in the fabric of time: the inevitable destruction of all by the many despite the valor and compassion of the few.

Chapter Four

The bullet wound across his left tricep was deep, but Tim Shaw had been able to stanch the bleeding. His right arm, which had numbed as if broken when the Nazi's knife had cut him, pained him greatly but, not counting the discomfort, the limb was fully functional.

He sat in the little clearing in the high mountain woods beside the already livid body of the man who had tried to kill him. But he didn't ponder the Nazi's death. What was done was done and, in this case, of terrific advantage. Instead, he considered his own problems. The loss of blood from his wounds, especially the gunshot, was severe enough to drastically limit his strength and endurance. When he'd first hit the ground from the tree, he'd thought he'd broken his back. Evidently, he had not, but he was sore beyond belief and might have suffered some serious damage.

Every time he moved, Tim Shaw was in pain.

There was always the hope that his son, Eddie,

37

hadn't paid any attention to him and even now had the Honolulu SWAT Team combing the mountains for him; but, that was a slim chance indeed. And, because of his own stubbornness, he had no means of radio communication.

This fight with the Nazi saboteur who was behind the bloodbath at Sebastian's Reef Country Day School and so dedicated to mayhem and murder was to have been *mano a mano*. It had been that. The Nazi was dead, but Tim Shaw didn't survive the encounter in exactly perfect shape either.

With considerable difficulty, Shaw stood up. He looked down at the dead man by his feet. "Hope the worms don't get sick on ya, pal." And then he started to walk.

It would be slow, but he told himself he'd make it . . .

Thorn Rolvaag's eyes scanned beyond the hastily erected coastal defense battery and out to sea. Kilauea was still erupting, but the eruptions beneath the sea were what concerned him.

The volcanic vent was widening in an easterly direction, taking it toward the North American plate. Although no computer model could predict with exact certainty what would happen then, Rolvaag was convinced that the odds lay in favor of the vent splitting, going in both directions along the boundary of the plate, slicing through the so-called Ring of Fire, the volcanoes surrounding the Pacific Basin, and precipitating a chain of volcanic eruptions which would be of biblical proportion.

That would almost certainly mean the end of the world.

It would mean the death of his wife, his children, the destruction of everyone and everything which he held dear. And there was only one slim chance that the relentless, inexorable expansion of the vent could be halted. For that, he would need to utilize nuclear energy in a way which had not been discussed since the dawn of the Nuclear Age almost seven hundred years ago.

In those days, propaganda had stressed the peaceful uses of atomic energy. And, indeed, there were many possibilities, few of them used except in medicine and in the generation of primitive fission-based electrical power. But, at the time, "the bomb" was touted as a means by which harbors could be cut with almost surgical precision, the face of the land altered at a fraction of the cost, time or labor involved with more conventional means.

That potential was never realized. Yet, if the Earth were to be saved, that potential would have to be harnessed. He could vent the volcanic energy a little bit at a time. He could wall up the rift, diverting it gradually by degrees. He could save the planet from destruction.

Maybe.

But, there would be no chance at all without virtually every nuclear weapon available in the current world arsenal. Unlike the days Before the Night of the War, when thousands of nuclear warheads existed in the arsenals of both super powers, when two thousand nuclear warheads alone could have been found on the Eastern coast of what was then the United States along the Savannah River, there were comparatively few today.

Best intelligence estimates allowed Deitrich Zimmer's Nazi forces and the forces of Eden a combined total slightly in excess of five hundred warheads. The vast majority of these were, however, low yield, comparatively clean tactical devices, battlefield weapons, ideal for Rolvaag's purposes. New Germany possessed somewhere around one hundred, almost all tactical. The present-day United States—which largely consisted of Mid-Wake and Hawaii—had approximately two hundred, of these more than eighty percent submarine-launched ballistic missiles within the tactical power range. The only Intercontinental Ballistic Missiles in the U.S. inventory were antiques, converted from captured enemy stockpiles, the vast majority of which had been destroyed under controlled conditions.

No one power, not even the United States and New Germany combined (the only two nuclear powers within the Trans-Global Alliance), possessed sufficient nuclear warheads to get the job done.

The larger weapons in each nation's inventory would be useless. And, there was no time to build or convert what he needed. Without the full cooperation of Eden and her Nazi allies, there would not be sufficient battlefield-power warheads to stop the volcanic vent from growing, from destroying the planet.

Thorn Rolvaag looked out to sea, powerless unless a miracle were to take place . . .

*   *   *

Over the course of time, there were many secrets hidden in the Himalayas. More than half a millenia ago, some scientific researchers had felt that a possible missing link between man and his simian ancestors might be found surviving in the icy Himalayan vastness. If a yeti ever existed, or did still, Deitrich Zimmer truly didn't care.

His secret was more important.

It was here, in the Himalayas, that his most secret and most impregnable fortress lay, its entrances and defenses known to only a trusted few, its location known only to those who had built it and supplied it.

He sat at his desk, his son Martin pacing back and forth before him. "Why can't we release the clones?"

"For a very simple reason. Physically identical duplicates of John Rourke and his Family would be of no use whatsoever without proper programming and mental conditioning. Sarah Rourke, your mother, was available to us, as was Wolfgang Mann. Your natural father, John Rourke, your brother and sister, Michael and Annie, and the Jew, Rubenstein, and the Russian woman, Major Tiemerovna, have not been available to us. Since we have not recorded them, their clones are useless to us.

"You must have patience," Zimmer told Martin. "As was once said, 'All things come to him who waits.' That is not a bad piece of advice. Our plans progress quite well. And, I did not even have to use my own clone." It had been a near thing, his pilot barely able to land the command aircraft before falling over at the plane's controls.

"You used one nuclear weapon. Why not hit hard and fast right now?"

Zimmer smiled indulgently at the boy. "Because, Martin, I want the Trans-Global Alliance to do what I want it to do, not to vanish from the face of the Earth. That is the entire purpose of my plan. And, you know that."

"What are we going to do with the remains?"

"Ah, yes, the remains," Deitrich Zimmer said, nodding his head. "We are searching for viable cells even as we speak. They should be obtainable. Then, you will be quite pleased. Sit down, relax. All is well."

Chapter Five

John Rourke had planned ahead. When he and the Family first left Pearl Harbor, Hawaii, to rendezvous with Deitrich Zimmer in what devolved into an abortive attempt to make an exchange for Sarah Rourke, John Rourke anticipated a wide variety of contingencies and planned accordingly for them. One of those was that he would somehow wind up weaponless.

In light of that, he had visited the Lancer showroom just prior to leaving the islands, one of the purposes behind that visit to purchase (but the management would not charge him, insisted on gifting him with the items instead) two of Lancer's superlative duplicates of the SIG-Sauer P-228. Natalia already had one of their 226s, and it was faultless to the last detail, identical to the original.

Although never a great fan of the 9mm Parabellum cartridge as compared to the .45 ACP, from an objective basis he knew the ballistic performance was, if the gun were properly loaded, nearly identical between the calibers. From Lancers, Rourke additionally secured a supply of thirteen- and twenty-round magazines, plus a substantial stock of Lancer's equally excellent duplication of the only 9mm Parabellum load he'd ever really liked, the Federal 9BP 115-grain jacketed hollow point.

At the corporate range in the basement of the facility, Rourke ran two hundred rounds through each pistol, testing the spare magazines as well. As he had come to expect from Lancer replications, just as he would have expected from the original guns manufactured over six centuries ago, performance was flawless.

To accompany the pistols, he secured another of Lancer's duplications, this a double-rig copy of the special-purpose shoulder holster designed exclusively for the 228 pistols by the designer of the Tri-Speed adjustable shoulder holsters. Made of waterproof black ballistic nylon and lined with waterproof black doeskin suede, the holsters were fully ambidexterous and could be dismounted from the shoulder harness to be worn fully concealed on the belt, if desired. Acquiring two double-magazine pouches as well and packing the rest of the magazines in a black musette bag (if he lived, he would lend the Lancer people one of his Milt Sparks Six-Pack magazine carriers to duplicate), he handed over the guns, the holsters, the magazines and a supply of extra ammunition to Commander Washington, asking the SEAL Team Leader to bring them along for him, just in case.

Although Rourke's usual weapons were available to him, now was "just in case."

He dismounted the holsters from their harness, partially removed his wide trouser-belt and threaded one of the two holsters to his left side, one to his right, threading in one of the double magazine pouches between them, twenty-round magazines in place. When they reached the mountain's summit, if they did, the combat would be close-range and fast, with no time for such luxuries as reloading.

John Rourke, during a class he had taught once in Hostage Rescue Unit tactics, had once been asked, "Aren't you carrying too many guns, sir?"

In those days, Before the Night of the War, he always wore at least two handguns, frequently three and sometimes four. His twin stainless Detonics .45s were always with him unless he was in an environment where being so armed was physically impossible. These days, the number varied even more greatly. He'd answered the question then, the same as he would have answered it now were it asked. "There are persons who carry guns, and then there are gunfighters. To the gunfighter, who works close in and fast, there is almost invariably a lack of time. Some people called it the New York reload, a second gun. But it could just as easily have been called a Chicago reload or anything else. The old gunfighting lawmen knew that a second gun was essential equipment for staying alive.

"In the days of single-shot pistols, even though the arms themselves were relatively large, it wasn't at all uncommon to carry several guns because of the time consumed with reloading, even though everyone else had the same difficulty. Even though most gunfights entail fewer than a half dozen shots, there are those rare times when a heavy volume of fire is required in the minimum amount of time." He remembered making one of his rare attempts at humor, adding, "Besides, all that weight on the body helps keep you trim." There had been polite laughter, more than he'd really expected.

The pitons which Wolverton had crafted for them seemed serviceable enough, if only the metal from which they were formed had not become brittle. He'd know when he reached the rock face, if they had.

Natalia's expropriated Nazi gunship was ready to go airborne, Annie with her.

Michael and Paul flanked John Rourke now as he approached the face they had chosen to climb. Commander Washington was in charge on the ground, two of his SEAL Team personnel, Moore and Jones, along with one of the German Long Range Mountain Patrol commandos, Schmidt, along as well for the climb to the summit.

Rourke was free of armament save for the pistols he wore—six semiautos and the little S&W .38 Special revolver—and his now-customary three knifes. Paul had his German MP-40 submachine gun slung tight to his side, his two Browning High Powers in their usual carries. Michael had his two shoulder-holstered Berettas and his four-inch barreled S&W .44 Magnum revolver, a bullpup-stocked energy rifle slung at his side.

Rourke addressed the five men with him. "Assuming all goes well and we reach the summit, it's almost certain that we'll be instantly detected. If for some reason we are not, then so much the better, of course. We should remember that the men topside are Nazis, and we should remember it well because our mission is to kill as many of them as possible as quickly as we can. The more of their equipment which remains intact, the better off we are. We don't want any of their helicopters getting away, either.

"Are there any questions?"

Jones, a ruddy-faced fellow with a tuft of carrot red hair visible under his parka hood, asked, "Begging the general's pardon, sir, but how many of them do you think there are up there?"

Rourke smiled. "There are six of us, and that should be sufficient. Suit up gentlemen." They would take the ropes in moments, as soon as Natalia signaled she was ready. Rourke shoved back his hood and started pulling the black toque over his head . . .

Natalia Tiemerovna gave one last look toward the gauges on her panel. Then she looked through the helicopter's bubble toward the mountain's base. She shook her head, exhaled. Annie, sitting beside her, said, "They'll be all right."

"We love all three of them, don't we?"

Annie laughed softly. "They know it."

Natalia only nodded. John, Michael and Paul, along with the three volunteers from Commander Washington's force, waited, ready to move. The six men were stripped of their arctic parkas, attired in black combat boots, black BDU pants, black sweaters and black hoods, these latter with a window at the center of the eyes, but the eyes covered with snow goggles. They looked like they should be freezing, but to a man they would be wearing thermal gear beneath their outer clothes— she'd been with Michael when he'd donned his, telling him that he looked cute.

Annie asked, "Are you ready to signal them?"

"No, but I suppose that I have to." She turned on the cabin lights, then turned them off, then on, then off, then on, then off again.

There was an answering series of flashes from one of the six men at the base of the mountain, then within seconds they started the climb.

Chapter Six

Paul Rubenstein wrapped his fists around the rope and started with his right foot against the rock surface. Perhaps a hundred yards above him, John Rourke and the German commando, Schmidt (who was also an experienced climber) had let down two ropes, so he, Michael and the two SEAL Team men, Moore and Jones, could follow. By the time they reached the location of the first tie-off, John and Schmidt would be well along toward the next level, perhaps already have attained it.

John had planned the climb as a general—he was one, after all—might plan a battle; but, in this case, the terrain and the enemy were one in the same . . .

John Rourke's left foot was levered into a niche of rock, the rock coated with slick ice, as was the rope Rourke trailed behind him. His right foot perched on one of the improvised pitons, Rourke reached up, another of the pitons in his left hand, a heavy-headed hammer—not a proper climber's hammer, but a substantially sized claw hammer from the machine shop—in his right.

The hammer was ice-coated and, as he struck at the piton, ice flew from it and the rock surface. Involuntarily, John Rourke averted his eyes, but the snow goggles he wore were shatterproof. He struck the piton again, then again, then once more. The piton was in as deep as it would go. Slipping the hammer into an improvised loop on his pistol belt, then locking it in place with a hook and pile strip, Rourke took solid hold of the piton and tugged.

It held; at least so far.

Playing his body weight between the crack in the rock surface and the piton on which his booted right foot rested, he simultaneously pulled with his arm and pushed with his leg.

Because of the uncertainty of the equipment, the horrendous visibility (it would have been impossible to tell if it were night or day, the sky a black nothingness and wind-driven snow swirling about him) and his unfamiliarity with the rock surface, he was taking the climb in the slow, painstaking way, relying as little as possible on the rock face, as much as possible on the pitons.

Standing to his full height now, his safety line looped into the last piton he'd driven, Rourke reached to maximum comfortable extension, retrieved his hammer and began to stake another piton into the living rock.

The piton was driven, tested, and Rourke pulled himself up, moving like a spider along an only partially finished web, his left foot up to the next piton, his right foot searching for purchase in the rock, the last piton he'd driven was at waist level now.

He looked to his left, for Schmidt. The German commando was perhaps fifty feet below him, but apparently doing well. Rourke paused for a breath, exhaled, eyeballed a likely spot for his next piton, then retrieved his hammer. He would repeat the process until he reached the next likely place to pause and was nearly out of pitons. As Paul, Michael, Moore and Jones followed, they would extract the pitons Rourke and Schmidt had left behind, then secure them into the rope so Rourke and Schmidt could haul them up and begin again.

John Rourke kept moving . . .

Annie had learned to do two things at once at a comparatively early age, sitting in front of a television screen and watching one of the many video tapes her father had suggested that they watch, while at the same time working on her embroidery. If the tape required intensive viewing, she would crochet, something she could do without looking at all, really. She crocheted now, her eyes on the mountain wall, the blizzard raging around the tied-down helicopter.

She didn't know what she expected to see. She knew what she did not want to see: A body falling from the mountainside.

Natalia smoked, stared, made the occasional comment, then stared some more.

The shawl Annie crocheted would be a present for

51

her mother, when her mother eventually awakened.

And, after her mother awakened, everything would end for their Family as a true family. Annie Rourke Rubenstein knew that her mother would leave her father, over the death of Martin, the son who had been born to Sarah Rourke an instant before Deitrich Zimmer shot her, kidnapped and raised a Nazi by Deitrich Zimmer.

To save the lives of Paul and Natalia and a wounded man, Annie's father fought with Martin and Martin fell to his death through the open door of a helicopter into a river of volcanic lava below.

Martin was dead.

So was the marriage between her parents.

Eventually, Sarah Rourke and Wolfgang Mann would get together; Annie knew that. And, when that happened, for her father's sake, she hoped that he would find happiness with Emma Shaw.

But Wolfgang Mann, a truly fine individual, heroic and strong, she would never call "father," nor Emma Shaw, equally heroic, "mother."

They would all be good friends—civilized.

The Rourke Family would cease to exist.

Annie's eyes stared into the night. Annie's fingers worked the hook and the yarn. Annie's soul ached. When this was over, she wanted Paul to make her pregnant.

Chapter Seven

John Rourke's clothing crackled as he moved, ice forming on his arms and legs each time he paused, the ice on the granite surface of the mountainside thick and slick, making each movement more incredibly dangerous. He was cold, and not just on the outside.

There were those who contended that men and women who involved themselves in dangerous activities knew no fear. Perhaps that was true, but Rourke doubted so. When there was time for it, the men and women he'd known Before the Night of the War, and since, who had displayed conspicuous courage in times of great danger had all known fear as well.

Fear was a normal human response. Those who had to go on in spite of fear merely became skilled at conquering it. John Thomas Rourke did not know how skilled or unskilled he might be in that regard, but the cold feeling in the pit of his stomach was something he had known before and, if he lived, would know again—fear. He went on, clambering along the ice-slicked rock face, the wind howling, strong now, vision obscured by the swirling of the snow. The only way that he would know he had reached the steeply angled summit would be by the orientation of his body to the ground.

The only plus to the miserable weather conditions was that the enemy would be less able to detect the assault visually. Electronic sensing equipment was another matter, however.

John Rourke kept moving, driving in a piton, pulling himself up, getting a fresh foothold, equally precarious to the last, then driving in another piton.

At what he gauged as perhaps a hundred yards below the angled summit, Rourke found a rock chimney. He knew its location from previous reconnaissance of the mountain face, and discovering it less than a yard above him now meant that he was, indeed, close to the summit, but he was also a good one hundred feet to the north of his originally planned route.

There were two choices now confronting him. He could rope his way laterally, back a hundred feet or so and thus return to the planned route. Or, he could climb the chinmey. Schmidt was still well below him, the other climbers—Paul, Michael and the two SEAL Team men, Moore and Jones, further below still. Everyone else would have to rope back, too. And that, under the circumstances (both atmospheric and topographic) could be insanely dangerous.

If they came up through the chimney, the burden for the men below him would be easier, and—of considerable importance under the deteriorating conditions—protect them from the elements. But the climb for him would be tougher in one respect. As he automatically squinted against the driving sleet and snow in order to view the chimney through his goggles now, despite their protection, he could see that the chimney surface was glass-slick from ice. If he used the methodology he had employed so far successfully, however tediously in the earlier portion of the climb, attacking the chimney would mean leaving the men exposed, unmoving, possible sniper bait and certainly at the mercy of the elements. If he climbed in the accepted fashion, he would save time but dramatically increase his own chances for disaster.

He could barely see the four men below Schmidt, Schmidt spiderwebbing his way upward a piton at a time.

Rourke made his decision.

He started snaking down a rope to Schmidt . . .

Icing conditions were worsening rapidly. "Will you be able to take off in this?" Annie asked her.

"I don't know, Annie. But, I'm not going to wait until the last minute to find out," Natalia told her.

Vicious crosswinds assaulted the open ground before the mouth of the entrance into the mountain. Natalia felt genuine sympathy for the men of Commander Washington's force who had to endure the wind unprotected. Visibility was obscenely bad. Before she went airborne, Natalia fully intended to construct some ruse by means of which she could

55

entice Annie out of the helicopter. There was no sense in both of them risking their lives in the assault on the mountain summit. In a worst-case scenario, Michael and Paul and John might be killed as well, which would mean that Sarah's family would all be taken from her. That would be too much to ask any person to endure if it could be avoided.

Natalia once again activated the helicopter's de-icing system, asking Annie, "Monitor de-icing for me, will you? I want to check my gear just in case we have to ditch."

"Sure thing."

Natalia looked to her weapons. Her customary twin stainless four-inch L-Frame Smiths, 686s with American Eagles on the barrel flats, were holstered in the double-flap rig which rode just below her natural waist. The Bali-Song knife, rather than pouched in the leg of her jumpsuit along her left thigh, was in the pocket of her parka.

Her left leg was moving better; and, if circumstances forced her to, she could move reasonably normally on it. The German painkiller was doing its work well.

In addition to the revolvers, beneath her open parka was the Ken Null shoulder holster with the suppressor-fitted Walther PPK/S. She had one other handgun with her, a Lancer copy of the SIG-Sauer P-226 9mm. This rested on the map console beside her, but would be shoved between her pistol belt and her abdomen once she was airborne.

Natalia looked over Annie's shoulder. The de-icing system, at least according to the panel readouts, was performing as it should.

The true test lay in the flying, which she would begin shortly enough . . .

Paul Rubenstein made a cradle for himself out of two sixty-inch lengths of 2500-pound test nylon webbing, anchoring the ends to pitons, thus allowing his body to rest as he waited on the cliff face, nothing below but darkness and certain death should he fall.

He had gone over the details of the climb with John Rourke, and knew now full well that the delay in reaching the summit had to have been caused by John's somehow missing the intended path, easy enough to do in near-zero visibility.

There was a rock chimney which had appeared in the recon photos. If John were climbing that now, in order to make up time and get the rest of them off the cliff face sooner, he was at considerable risk. The chimney of rock would be ice-slicked and deadly.

For the billionth time since he'd stopped smoking years Before the Night of the War, Paul Rubenstein wished he hadn't. But he laughed; even John's old Zippo windlighter would have been hard-pressed to keep a flame in this.

Chapter Eight

The sole of John Rourke's left boot slipped and he started down the chimney, hands groping for a hold, gloved fingers slipping over the ice-slicked black granite, outcroppings of rock pummeling him.

He thrust his right foot outward and locked his leg. He'd either break his leg at the knee or stop. With a bone shuddering lurch, he stopped.

John Rourke exhaled, closed his eyes, inhaled, his hands—palms outward—already wedged against the rock on either side of him. Rourke assessed his body for damage, not finding any readily apparent; he opened his eyes once again, then looked up. Some fifty yards of the rock chimney still needed to be traversed, counting the yardage he'd lost when he slipped.

He paused, wedging himself more securely, then finding a piton. He took the hammer from the improvised loop at his pistol belt, slightly altered his position and tried taking a swing. There was little room for movement of his arm, but with great difficulty he was at last able to anchor a piton.

He roped into it, insurance against another fall. There was the temptation to work his way upward the rest of the way by using pitons, but he was at least out of the killing wind. Paul, Michael and the others were not.

Exhaling hard, then inhaling, Rouke started up once again, wedging himself, then pushing, then wedging again. Rock chimneys were climbed this way, by alternately wedging and then freeing the body, but not usually with ice so slick as this. He kept moving.

When he judged he had gone another five yards, he stopped, anchored another piton, then roped into it. Insurance again.

And, again, he began to climb.

Once he reached the top, he would let down rope, and the others could climb along the rope after him, joining him at the slope before the summit. Once the first of the five were up the chimney, Rourke would set to driving pitons along the slope and webbing rope, but as silently and unobtrusively as he could.

He would be in sight of the enemy if they cared to look.

The matter of electronic countermeasures was something for which he could not compensate, why timing would be critical with Natalia's chopper flight. But there was a fact which he had to face, that Natalia might not be able to get airborne in these terrible winds and visibility. If she could not get airborne and launch the explosives-laden remote video probes she had aboard, there would be no distraction to mask the last phase of the assault.

And the fight would be there, on the slick, sloping granite above the cliff face.

The thought made John Rourke even colder.

He kept climbing, stopping again in order to drive another piton, roping into it, then moving on once more. The volume of firearms he carried on his body had, at times throughout the climb, been burdensome. But, once he reached the summit, he would be glad for them, perhaps more than he realized.

Rourke kept climbing, glancing above through the swirling snow and into the impenetrable darkness.

There was a chance that the climb had already been detected, that the Nazi commandos in position on the summit were merely waiting to strike.

He could not dismiss that thought, try as he might. Rourke just kept climbing . . .

Thirty-six Eden fighter aircraft closed from the west on the crippled base as Emma Shaw, her engines near to flame-out, had been forced to land.

The refueling process seemed to be taking an eternity, but while it was in progress her V/STOL was being fitted with additional forward missile pods on both wings. The added weight would slow her down, but only for a little while. She would lose the missiles quickly enough.

"Ready, Commander!" Her canopy was already closing as Emma Shaw returned the thumbs-up signal and started taxiing for the field. The sky overhead was filled with explosions, missiles and aircraft streaking everywhere, her own two squadrons and the enemy aircraft at times nearly colliding, it seemed, as she observed. And darkness with heavy overcast made things worse. Despite the electronics with which her aircraft was equipped, she was the kind of pilot who preferred to actually fly, not ride.

The field over which Emma Shaw taxied her V/STOL fighter was already pockmarked with craters and, if she were not careful, she'd intersect with one and her aircraft would be crippled. Landing, if she had that opportunity, would be dangerous in the extreme.

At last she turned into the nearest runway; there were no tower orders to worry about. Emma reminded herself that she was used to taking off from carriers, whether on the surface or beneath it, and that runway distances here on land were a luxury.

To have made a vertical takeoff under combat conditions would have been suicidal, leaving herself crippled for precious seconds. "Oh, shit—here we go," she hissed through her teeth, starting to throttle out.

An enemy aircraft swept over the field, strafing it just ahead of her. A service vehicle overturned, its fuel supply exploding, with burning synth-fuel spraying across the field. She kept increasing speed.

Her fists were balled so tightly on the yoke that she could feel every stitch in the seams of her gloves.

A missile exploded to her left, blackening a portion of her canopy and—she hoped—doing no other damage.

Two enemy fighters were zeroing in toward her from the far side of the field. One of her own squadron was on their tails, but Emma Shaw could not help.

Or, could she? she wondered.

"Let's pretend this is a carrier," Emma Shaw snarled, then throttled full out. "This is Bulldog Leader, Bulldog Pups. Momma's comin' back home to get those nasty bullies. Cover me!"

Her own squadron member launched a forward-firing missile, catching one of the two enemy aircraft in the starboard wing, the enemy plane's wing ripping away, the aircraft cartwheeling through the air, flames spraying in its wake as the synth-fuel in its wings caught.

Emma Shaw pulled up hard on the yoke, her aircraft's nose rising just enough to make her airborne in a steep climb from the tarmac. She banked, flattening out, streaking over the wrecked enemy aircraft, joining the pursuit of the second Eden fighter. "Time to lighten up," she hissed, launching a portside forward-firing missile.

The enemy aircraft vaporized and Emma Shaw hauled back on the yoke, starting to climb into the darkness . . .

Annie Rubenstein was worried about Natalia's leg, because Natalia had asked for more pain medication. The drug's effect should have held on for at least another few hours, Annie thought. Bundled to the nth degree against the cold, face swathed in scarves, and hood wrapped tightly around her head (and, for once in her life, grateful that she was wearing trousers), Annie stepped out of

63

the chopper and into the night, instantly chilled to the bone despite the layers of clothing she wore.

She wedged her body against the wind, bending into it as she walked toward the entrance to the mountain fortress that had been Deitrich Zimmer's Nazi headquarters in North America. Natalia had said, "I'm going to get another dose of that pain killer. My leg's bothering me a little and I'm afraid it will cramp when I'm flying the helicopter. Wait here, will you Annie?"

"You shouldn't walk on it then!"

"Well, I don't want to get any of the men inside to come for it. The weather is just so awful."

That was when Annie volunteered; and, as she reviewed the conversation, she stopped still in her tracks.

She turned around. The helicopter was automatically releasing the guy lines which had anchored it against the wind. Rotor speed, which had been minimal a few seconds before, was increasing.

"Natalia!"

But the helicopter was already beginning to rise out of the snow, buffeted crazily in the winds, Natalia obviously fighting to keep control, the machine lurching, slipping, rising, then slipping laterally again. "Natalia! Don't!"

Annie started running, back toward the aircraft, knowing that it was useless, but shouting, "You can't do this alone, Natalia!"

Her friend, soon to be her sister-in-law, was suddenly lost in the blackness above.

64

Chapter Nine

John Rourke rolled over onto his back, caution be damned, happy for an instant to be out of the chimney.

He took a deep breath, then rolled over again, snatching one of the twin stainless Detonics Score-Masters from its holster at his hip.

He lay on the slope, the ice was thick and slick here. Had he tried to stand, the action would have been hopeless. As his eyes scanned as far as he could see, through the darkness and the swirling snow, he spied no enemy personnel. Far in the distance, there were several light sources. He presumed these were the enemy aircraft, or perhaps the landing-pad control facilities.

Reholstering his pistol, Rourke twisted himself around, taking from a musette bag at his side the last remaining pitons, grabbing for the hammer as he glanced once over his shoulder, then beginning to drive the pitons into the living granite.

He set a triangularly shaped pattern, where the

weight which would be on the rope would be shared relatively evenly by the pitons, rather than only on the one bearing the bulk of the tension.

Rourke secured his rope, weighted it with the last piton, then began snaking it down through the chimney. Merely to have dropped it would invite the rope to snag on the rocks or on one of the pitons he had set into the chimney's face along the way. Several times, he was forced to coil upward, then re-release the rope, but at last, after he had let out the entire length, he felt a previously determined series of tugs, indicating that someone had the rope and was ready to use it.

Rourke wedged himself as best he could, looking over his shoulder again. Should he be discovered whilst aiding the next climber, there would be nothing that he could do. If he let go of the rope, there would be a substantial chance that the pitons alone might not hold.

He tugged back in code on his end of the rope, then felt the rope go taut under his hands.

Someone was on the way up . . .

Paul Rubenstein had volunteered to go first.

Schmidt, the most experienced climber, was the logical man to be last, in case anyone got in trouble along the way.

Well into the chimney now, with the surface around him like jagged glass, Paul Rubenstein only smiled. He would have marveled at any ordinary man having been able to do this; for John, such was to be expected.

Hand-over-hand, he worked his way up the rope . . .

The helicopter's controls were not to her liking. The Nazi machine lacked finesse, responsiveness. And, with the severe crosswinds and drastically limited visibility, such was more than an inconvenience.

Natalia's eyes scanned the summit of the mountain, from which she was now approximately three miles distant. It was an amorphous darkness, only marginally distinguishable against the night. But there would be a flare fired when the last of the climbers had reached the summit.

When she saw it, she would go in.

She waited . . .

John Rourke edged along the ice-slicked surface of the slope, his body spread-eagled for maximum friction, a piton in each hand, his fists balled on them, ready to hamer them down to stop him from sliding over the edge if need be—if they would do that.

A solitary length of rope trailed after him. Rourke looked back toward the chimney. Another length of rope trailed after Paul, the younger man doing the same thing, clawing his way across the ice-slicked slope just below the summit, positioning pitons, roping into them, moving on, making a web along which the other four men could follow in the final assault.

Rourke kept moving . . .

Annie pushed the scarves away from her face as she touched Commander Washington's shoulder.

"Yes, Mrs. Rubenstein?"

"You're going up, toward the summit from the inside, correct?"

"Yes ma'am. Most of my people are already in position. As you know, enemy personnel are suspected of holding the two top floors. We intend to do something about that. And, it might also assist your father and husband and brother up there on the summit. I have Major Tiemerovna's helicopter under observation. As soon as she moves in—meaning that she'll have gotten the flare signal from your father's team—we move in."

Annie swung her M-16 forward on its sling. "I'm going with you."

"But, Mrs. Rubenstein, if your father or your husband—"

"They'd approve. I'm going with you."

Commander Washington's dark eyes lit with a smile. "Yes, ma'am."

"Give me two seconds to get rid of these things," she added, starting to strip away her arctic gear . . .

Emma Shaw barrel-rolled the V/STOL to port, two Eden fighters streaking past her, following the contrails of their missiles.

As she pulled out of the roll, she brought her fighter's engines to full power, climbing after the enemy aircraft. The two pods of additional missiles she had carried were fired out, their racks jettisoned. She was lighter, faster, but almost out of missiles, too.

Leveling out, her eyes alternated between the electronic headsup on her canopy windscreen and the darkness surrounding her.

She knew how combat would be on the dark side of the moon. It would be like this.

At three o'clock, she saw one of the two aircraft she'd followed, its propwash glowing against the night. Headsup was signaling her that her aircraft had been acquired by an enemy heat seeker. Emma Shaw smiled, in that same instant spying the second aircraft. She banked hard to port, half rolled, dove, the heat seeker on her tail, her nose aimed toward the second enemy aircraft.

The second enemy aircraft was going into evasive maneuvers that Emma Shaw had seen before. She anticipated their result, banking hard to port, throttling back, then dropping her landing gear as she leveled off. Airspeed and altitude began dropping almost instantly as she skipped over the air. She was right over the second enemy aircraft. The heat seeker would contact in thirteen seconds according to the computer—she missed Gorgeous, her computerized companion in the Blackbird. This computer voice had no personality at all.

The second enemy aircraft was picking up speed. Emma Shaw retracted her landing gear as she increased speed, matching the second enemy aircraft, dangerously close to it. Four seconds until impact from the heat seeker. Three.

Emma Shaw throttled back almost to stall speed, dropping landing gear once more, neither the enemy aircraft just below her nor the heat seeker having time to change course.

There was always the chance that when the heat seeker struck the enemy fighter, the blast would destroy her as well, but she had to take that chance. One second before impact, Emma Shaw retracted landing gear once again, throttled out and rolled.

The blast almost rattled her canopy, but the enemy aircraft was going down in a red-and-orange fireball.

"Yo! Bulldog Leader! Great one, Emma!"

"This is Bulldog Leader, Bulldog Pups. Keep killin' those bad guys. Bulldog Leader out."

She had to nail the aircraft which had fired on her.

Chapter Ten

Paul Rubenstein's hands ached, but he grasped the last of his pitons in his left fist, the hammer in his right, then spiked the piton into the granite, making each blow count, because each blow made a sound, and even though the wind howled, there was always the possibility, however slight, that the noise might be detected.

As Paul Rubenstein roped on, he tried spotting John on the far side of the slope, but the darkness and the swirling snow made that impossible. When he'd at last gotten to the height of the chimney, to take over for John on the rope for the next climber, John told him, "Give it ten minutes from now." Their watches were already synchronized. "Then fire the flare pistol for Natalia."

Paul Rubenstein looked now at the face of his wristwatch.

He judged that some two minutes remained.

He leaned back, unlimbering his submachine gun. His position was approximately one hundred yards away from the perimeter of the mountaintop landing pad, the nearest enemy personnel perhaps that close, perhaps even closer.

By now, Michael, Jones, Moore and Schmidt would be on the slope, starting to work their way out along the ropes that he and John had laid, readying themselves for the assault.

Paul Rubenstein estimated that he had perhaps fifty yards of crawling to do, unaided by a safety line, before he'd be able to stand upright, then attack.

Once he fired the flare, he would begin the crawl, as would the others.

By the time they reached the point where, theoretically, it would be possible for them to stand and fight, Natalia should be in position, her explosives-laden remote video probes launched and zigzagging their way over the enemy position, hopefully diverting attention from the first few seconds of the assault which would be the most dangerous.

One minute remained . . .

Natalia's eyes were fixed on the mountaintop, the Nazi helicopter hovering some two miles off. She glanced at the Rolex on her left wrist, previously synchronized with John's watch and the watches of the other men. Once the flare was fired, which should be at any time now, she would have one minute to get the helicopter gunship into position and activate the remote probes.

It would take that long, John had judged, for the men to scramble over the remaining portion of the summit slope and get themselves into position.

The flare which would be fired would of course, alert the enemy defenders that something was about to happen, but if she stayed to the schedule there would be virtually no time for reaction.

She returned her full attention to the summit, although she had not once fully let her eyes leave it. And, the gunship's sensing equipment was preset to alarm her when the flare fired. She would rather trust her own senses than something mechanical.

And then she saw it, so faint that, had she not anticipated the flare being fired, she might never have noticed it.

Natalia started her machine toward the summit, arming the remote video probes in the same instant, then arming her weapons systems. If one of the Nazi helicopter gunships which remained on the summit were to get airborne, her job would be to prevent it from getting away, regardless of what that required of her . . .

John Rourke was moving on knees and elbows, a Detonics ScoreMaster in each hand, the guns beginning to coat with ice from the instant he drew them from the full-flap holsters at his sides.

He was counting seconds. Natalia would be prompt, and the moment the first of the remote probes was launched, John Rourke wanted to be in position, because each second he delayed was a second more allowing the Nazi defenders here at the mountain's summit to realize that the probes were a diversion.

Despite the fact that he had roped his way as close as he dared, and that the slope was vastly less steep here, just crawling was a challenge. He fell, spread-eagling once, then continuing on.

Lights were visible from the control station for the mountaintop helipad, as were running lights from the helicopters. Four of these, he judged. That would be enough to get Commander Washington's entire force away from the mountain, if none of the machines were too severely damaged, and if there were someplace left to go.

The stupidity, the arrogance, the calculated viciousness of Deitrich Zimmer's utilizing a battle-field nuclear weapon was beyond comprehension. A few such detonations and the precarious atmospheric envelope—which had been steadily returning since the Great Conflagration when the atmosphere ionized and burned—might again be destroyed.

Forty-two seconds had passed since Paul fired the flare. Natalia would be three-quarters of the way to her position, her remote probes ready to launch.

The ground was more level here, and Rourke risked moving more rapidly. He was within twenty yards of the helipad, the nearest of the Nazi machines some ten yards beyond that. Nazi personnel were not, so far, in evidence, but he could still only discern lights, not anything in greater detail because of the darkness and the snow.

Rourke kept moving.

Fifty seconds . . .

In six seconds, her gunship would be on station.

74

The probes were ready to launch. She could make out light patterns on the summit, from structures and from machines like her own. That would mean that her own running lights, had she used any, would have been noticeable as well.

Four seconds.

The instant that she launched the probes, she could be tracked. Three seconds. She flipped back the safety cover for the launch switch. The first finger of Natalia's right hand flicked downward.

Chapter Eleven

John Rourke rose to his full height and started cautiously forward, ice-creepers lashed to the soles of his boots. Paul and Michael wore sets of creepers as well, and the other three men wore improvised versions of the same thing. It was one of the curiosities of this new age that, with all the added ice and snow coverage because of drastically reduced global temperatures as a result of the thinning of the atmosphere and the subsequent escape of heat into the blackness of space, no one manufactured ice-creepers. He had been introduced to them by his old friend Jerry Buergel, years Before the Night of the War. Often, they had proved invaluable, providing steady footing under otherwise intolerably slick conditions.

Had John Rourke been possessed of any entre-preneurial inclinations, a business opportunity of rare potential would have awaited him, assuming of course that the entire planet would not be destroyed as a result of Deitrich Zimmer's unconscionable use of nuclear weapons.

But, because of Deitrich Zimmer's insane ambitions, there were other matters more pressing for John Rourke's mind to ponder at the moment.

The video probes which Natalia had launched glided overhead toward the Nazi gunships.

It would only be a matter of seconds before the reaction started.

It was better not to wait.

He was within ten yards of the rear wall of the control building for the helipad. It was logical to assume that many of the Nazi commandos would be huddled inside it against the storm, while only a few unlucky souls waited in the cold and wind.

John Rourke holstered his pistols, securing the flaps more as a retention device than as protection, the guns already ice coated. Instead, he drew the Crain LS-X knife, its twelve-inch blade worked to a near razor hone.

Rourke quickened his pace, eyes scanning the night for some sign of human activity. And, he found it. Still standing, but huddled along the north wall of the building in the full force of the wind was a sentry.

The man's head was turning upward, eyes evidently attracted to the movement from the remote video probes. It was important to silence the man before he could sound the alarm that, a few seconds later, John Rourke would be eager for.

Rourke, because of the ice-creepers, was able to cautiously jog over the ice, toward the control building's wall, out of sight of the sentry, and seeing no one else in the immediate vicinity.

Quickly, Rourke moved along the wall, with the back of his gloved left hand smudging snow away from his goggles.

Where the two walls met, Rourke paused, took a deep breath, then wheeled around the wall.

The Nazi sentry was just activating his transmitter as Rourke reached out with his left hand, closing it hard and fast over the man's toque-swathed face. He snapped the man's head back, exposing the throat to the primary edge of the knife, cutting deep in order not only to kill but to silence.

The man's body twitched, then slumped. Rourke dragged him back around the corner, quickly wiping the blade clean on the fellow's arctic gear, then resheathing. Under more relaxed circumstances, Rourke would have made a quick search for papers of potential intelligence value and disabled the weapons he was leaving behind. There was, however, time for neither.

Rourke stood, reaching to his sides for the ScoreMasters.

He thumbed back the hammers, raising the safeties, keeping the edges of his thumbs just beneath the safeties as an added precaution.

He reached the far side of the building. There was already movement, men running from their machines, sentries appearing from hiding places taken against the elements, the video probes doing their work.

Rourke glanced around the corner of the building, seeing the main entrance. He turned the corner, approaching the entrance, then taking the kick-boardless steps two at a time. There was a small porch at their height and Rourke stopped there, inhaled, placed one of the ScoreMasters beneath his left armpit. He pulled his snow goggles down to his throat; they would fog over instantly when he entered the warmth inside. Then, Rourke turned his right hand on the knob. The door flew open with the pressure of the wind in the same instant that Rourke retrieved the second handgun.

John Rourke stepped through the door.

There was a radioman seated on the far side of the room.

Rourke shot him in the mouth as the fellow turned to shout a warning. An officer to Rourke's left was dressing, picking up his rifle. As the man thrust the rifle toward Rourke, Rourke fired, putting him down with a single 185-grain jacketed hollow point into the chest.

Another man on the left side of the single, large room, was securing the hood of his parka. Rourke shot him in the chest as well.

A man to Rourke's right shouted something that was inaudible in the still-echoing reverberations from the shots. Rourke shot him in the throat.

There was movement everywhere in the room now. Rourke was firing his guns into the Nazi personnel, mostly officers. A double tap into the chest and throat of a man leveling an energy rifle toward him, another into the throat and left cheek of a man racing for the door. He leveled both pistols toward a man courageously charging at him with only a folding camp chair as a weapon, firing a round from each pistol. With only standard seven-round magazines in place, plus a round each in the pistols' chambers, exactly three rounds remained in each pistol.

Rourke fired out the ScoreMaster in his left hand, putting down two more men. As he worked his way counterclockwise into the room and away from the door, Rourke thrust the pistol, slide locked back over the empty magazine, into his pistol belt, in the same motion sweeping his left hand back to the Professional Gear holster at his left side beneath the sweater. He popped the thumb break, freeing one of the two SIG-Sauer P-228 9mms, stabbing the pistol toward a young officer trying to escape through the still-open door. Rourke fired a double tap, putting him down, pitching the body through the open doorway and onto the snow-covered porch.

The wind tore through the room, maps and other documents scattering about in cyclonic patterns.

Rourke fired the last three rounds from the ScoreMaster in his right hand, one into the chest, the next into the throat, the third and last into the head of a man charging toward him with an energy rifle in each hand. One of the energy rifles discharged, blowing out a chunk of the wall behind Rourke.

The wind instantly entered.

John Rourke belted the emptied ScoreMaster and drew the second SIG, firing into the far corner of the room where a senior noncom was shouldering a conventional caseless projectile rifle.

Rourke stood there, everyone in the room other than himself dead.

He moved quickly toward the doorway, thumbing down the hammer for the pistol in his right hand, with the trigger finger of his left hand doing the same.

Gunfire was everywhere on the helipad, a video probe exploding in midair, whether from enemy gunfire or by remote detonation he could not be certain. Across the helipad, near to one of the Nazi gunships, he could barely make out in the momentary glow a small battle raging. Rourke stepped out onto the porch, killing two Nazi commandos who were racing toward the shelter, then moving down the steps, onto the fringe of the expansive helipad.

Rourke took cover beside the steps, then slipped one of the SIGs beneath his armpit, drawing one of the twenty-round spares from beneath his sweater and making a tactical magazine change, pocketing the partially spent magazine in his BDU pants. He did the same for the second pistol. Twenty-one rounds in each handgun, Rourke waited for a break in movement on the helipad, then darted from cover, toward the helicopter on the far side of the pad.

He could see Schmidt, firing a captured Nazi weapon from the cover of a concrete-block bunker.

Rourke kept moving, running as quickly as he dared across the ice. Another remote video probe exploded, shards of white-hot metal and burning insulation showering the helipad, in the glow of the explosion the battle beside the helicopter once again visible. Michael and Paul, he thought, locked in close-quarters combat with perhaps a half dozen men or more, Michael trading shots with four of the men, Paul fighting hand-to-hand.

John Rourke quickened his pace beyond common-sense restriction, nearly slipping twice, keeping his balance and moving toward the helicopter.

Energy weapons were being fired now, their blue-white bolts flashing over the ground like chain lightning. Moore went down, legs blown from under him, but the man still moving, firing his weapon.

Rourke wheeled toward the source of energy fire which had brought the SEAL down, found two men firing the energy-weapon equivalent of a machine-gun from the wrong, open side of a bunker.

Rourke changed direction, running toward the enemy personnel at an oblique angle. As soon as they spotted him, wheeling the weapon toward him, Rourke stabbed both pistols toward the Nazi commandos and fired, spraying the target area in order to bring the men down. The man operating the gun fell away, dead or injured, his assistant trying to shove the body aside in order to operate the gun. Rourke fired as he closed, putting a half dozen shots into the second man.

Rourke dropped to cover beside the energy weapon, looking for Moore. Jones had him, the two men firing as they moved to cover.

Rourke stabbed both pistols into their holsters, securing the thumb breaks, then twisting the energy machine gun free from its tripod.

The weapon was heavy, a good twenty pounds or more as he judged it. But, it would be likely to have a full charge and, despite the cold, most of that charge should remain. Enough, at least, for the work he had to do.

Rourke peered over the lip of the bunker, toward the center of the field, then looked toward the helicopter where Paul and Michael were embattled. Rourke scrambled out of the bunker, firing a burst of the energy weapon toward a knot of Nazi commandos who were, in turn, firing on the position to which Jones had taken the downed SEAL, Moore. Rourke fired again, then again.

Energy weapons were very similar in "mission" to conventional small arms, the hand-held models firing lower-power charges, the shoulder weapons higher-power charges, and the crew served small arms such as the machine gun he now operated, firing heavier charges at longer duration and capable of more sustained fire before a recharge.

Rourke fired again toward the men firing on Moore and Jones, killing or wounding another three.

He turned his attention once again toward the helicopter where Michael and Paul were still fighting what seemed to be a growing number of Nazi personnel, judging from the flashes of energy weapons.

Rourke was moving again, the energy weapon in his hands held at hip level. He fired indiscriminately toward enemy personnel, bringing down as many as he could. The helicopter beside which Paul and Michael had taken cover was all but surrounded by enemy personnel. John Rourke decided to correct that condition, circling widely across the helipad, encountering a pocket of resistance near a service vehicle. Rourke fired at the two men huddled there, one of the energy bolts striking the vehicle's synth-fuel tank, the tank exploding, a black-and-orange fireball belching upward into the night, everything below it red tinged, glowing.

Another video probe detonated overhead, brilliantly illuminating the field for a few seconds. He could see clearly now, Paul and Michael surrounded on three sides, their only means of withdrawal the slope itself.

Rourke glanced back across the field. The wounded SEAL, Moore, was firing an energy weapon from cover, while Jones and Schmidt, with captured heavy-capacity energy weapons in hand, advanced across the field.

Rourke neared the closest of the enemy personnel who were firing on Michael and Paul.

Rourke fired on them, spraying long bluish-white trailers of plasma energy in a zigzag pattern over five of the Nazi commandos, bringing the men down, as their bodies tossed as if they were discarded toys of some gigantic and malevolent child, clothing and flesh smoldering. Enemy fire came toward him, Rourke diving for cover behind another service vehicle. But, remembering what had happened to the last one when its fuel tank was struck, Rourke paused there only briefly, scrambling away toward a concrete bunker.

Energy bolts and conventional caseless small-arms fire poured toward him, peppering the ice-slicked tarmac surface of the helipad as he ran. He jumped, landing in the bunker beside two dead men.

Rourke pried the fingers of one of them from the pistol grip of his energy rifle. Without looking up over the lip of the bunker, Rourke stabbed the weapon over the top and turreted it from side to side, firing as fast as he could pull the trigger, spraying anything that might be moving toward him.

Discarding the weapon, Rourke shoved the energy machine gun over the lip of the bunker and fired a long charge, cutting down three enemy personnel who were storming toward the bunker. Rourke tucked down, enemy small-arms fire impacting the lip of the bunker, chunks of ice and concrete spraying everywhere. Energy bolts rippled over the bunker in wispy, blue-white clouds.

Energy weapons had no recoil, of course. And, an idea instantly came to mind. He flicked the energy machinegun's selector switch into the "safe" position.

Rourke reached into a pocket of his BDU pants, finding the shoulder harness from the dismounted Professional Gear holsters for the SIGs. The harness was made from 2500-pound test nylon webbing. He twisted one tail of the four, first removing the buckle at the end. Working several inches of the webbing into cord shape, then sliding this through the energy machinegun's trigger guard, he utilized a triglide slider from the harness to secure the loop he had made.

Rourke drew the shoulder harness toward the rear of the bunker, then dropped the loose ends. One of the dead men in the bunker had another energy rifle. Rourke used this as a wedge against the buttstock of the energy machinegun. Despite the fact there was no true recoil as such, there was vibration.

Hurriedly, Rourke reloaded the two SIGs with the remaining two twenty-round magazines, then holstered them. He grabbed one of the dead men under the armpits and dragged him forward, propping the body up behind the energy weapon, so only a little bit of the torso would show and part of the helmet. Then Rourke moved toward the rear of the bunker once again. His eyes scanned across the bunker floor. Nothing that would be of use.

He went to the other dead man, found the man's still-sheathed bayonet and looped one of the loose ends of the harness around the hilt, tightening the triglide on the loop.

Rourke gauged the distance, put the selector into the burst-control position, then hammered the knife into the floor of the bunker.

Immediately, the energy weapon began firing. On burst control, it would fire three bolts, pause, then fire three bolts again.

As the weapon began firing, he couldn't help but smile. Here, at last, was the small arm that all of the pitifully naive antigunners of the twentieth century would have pointed to with glee—with a little help, it could shoot by itself.

Chapter Twelve

As the energy machine gun began firing its second burst, Rourke was already moving, the Score-Masters reloaded and holstered, the two SIG-Sauer P-228 9mms with their twenty-round magazines in his fists.

He squinted against the swirling snow.

Another remote video probe exploded, but this time impacting near the center of the helipad, claiming at least three of the enemy force that he could see, perhaps more.

Gunfire from the battle within a battle near the helicopter was intense, and he was close to it. The portion of the enveloping enemy force which he had neutralized had not yet been replaced, but Rourke did not run through the hole. Instead, he ran behind the line of enemy personnel, determined to cut another hole in that line.

Rourke encountered enemy personnel sooner than he anticipated, two men rising up from behind a rank of crates, the men themselves about to storm forward to another position of cover in the same direction as Rourke ran. Rourke wheeled half right, both pistols at chest height, both pistols double-tapping, one of the two men down dead. As the second man spun toward him, firing his conventional caseless assault rifle, Rourke dropped to his right, hitting the icy ground and sliding, gunfire tearing into the helipad surface near him.

Rourke spread-eagled, slowing, stopping, firing both pistols again, catching the enemy commando in center of mass, the man's body jackknifing into itself, then falling back into a fetal postition.

Rourke was to his knees, to his feet.

Seventeen rounds left in each pistol, a tactical reload—had freshly loaded spares been available—would not yet have been necessary. He ran forward, thumbing down the hammer-drop on the pistol in his right hand, belting it under his pistol belt, then grabbing up the nearer assault rifle of the two dead men.

The Nazi assault rifle in his right fist, the other SIG in his left, Rourke ran forward as fast as he dared, considering the footing.

Michael's and Paul's position was about to be overrun, Rourke's son and his friend outnumbered at least four to one. Rourke veered at a right angle toward the strongest portion of the enemy line, the attention of the eight Nazi commandos concentrated on Michael and Paul.

That was their mistake.

Rourke dropped to cover in the position the eight commandos had just vacated, two dead men there, another one displaying several gunshot wounds.

Only barbarians made war on the wounded. Rourke relieved the wounded man of his weapons, taking the assault rifle and bandolier of spare magazines for himself, then telling the injured man in German, "You will not be harmed unless you interfere."

The man nodded his head, eyes filled with hate and anger, but reason getting the better of both emotions. Rourke had two assault rifles now, dropping to cover, behind the crates which had served the Nazis. Belting the second SIG after working the hammer drop, he brought one of the assault rifles to his shoulder and opened fire into the backs of the eight advancing commandos. Two down, then a third, the remaining five wheeled toward him as he tucked down.

There was the familiar sound of Paul's German MP-40 submachine gun, pistol shots as well, even the roar of Michael's .44 Magnum revolver. Bullets and energy bolts tore into the crates behind which Rourke stayed crouched. He stabbed the second assault rifle around the corner of the crates and sprayed it.

As answering fire came, he raised up, firing long, ragged bursts from the other rifle, this one to his shoulder. He brought down two more of the enemy personnel.

The remaining three fled, Paul standing now, firing his submachine gun from the shoulder, stock extended. Michael held his dully gleaming Smith & Wesson in both fists, tongues of flame licking from the muzzle of the .44.

Rourke didn't waste time or ammunition, changing magazines in both captured assault rifles, slinging the bandolier to his shoulder, then shouting over the roar of gunfire, "There's a wounded man here, disarmed. Make sure he's cared for!" And Rourke was up and running, toward the center of the helipad and the last vestiges of battle.

For six men, they had done well, taking the enemy with a decent measure of surprise, so far at least none of the Nazi gunships visibly having suffered any substantial damage.

Natalia's helicopter slipped over the field, closing.

John Rourke shouted to Paul and to Michael, "Follow me!"

Chapter Thirteen

A half dozen or more Nazi commandos had taken refuge on the far side of the helipad, armed with energy weapons, conventional caseless small arms and some explosive ordnance. Rourke, Paul Rubenstein, Michael Rourke and Schmidt huddled near the control building, Jones and Moore with them as well. Aside from the heavily armed holdouts, the helipad was secured—for the moment. Commander Washington and his men would be fighting their way up through the two top levels of the mountain's interior and it was likely in the extreme that the Nazi defenders there would retreat toward the helipad when pressed. It was also very likely that the Nazi commandos were aware of what had already transpired on the mountaintop helipad and would be ready for a wide range of contingencies. Without the element of surprise, six men, one of whom was seriously wounded, would have no chance at all.

Natalia would have detected the tactical situation

by now and be preparing to respond, to neutralize the still-fighting Nazi personnel, thus enabling a better defense for the mountaintop against the inevitable backwash of Nazi personnel.

"Incoming!" Jones shouted, Rourke throwing his body over Moore's body in order to protect the injured man from the grenade or whatever it was.

It was a grenade, as Rourke looked back Michael taking an energy rifle, swinging it to his shoulder and firing, the grenade exploding while still airborne.

"Good trick-shooting," Rourke remarked, less than pleased that his son had exposed himself to enemy fire, happy at his son's success.

Rourke returned to what had occupied his attention before the grenade had been fired toward them—and it was a rifle grenade, of that Rourke was certain. Moore, both legs injured by an energy blast, was very badly burned and already into shock. The small medical kit in Rourke's musette bag carried an adrenalin shot, and Rourke administered that now because of the man's heart rate, along with a B-Complex shot. But, without the opportunity for stablizing him under more complete medical facilities, Moore might well die, at the very least lose his legs.

Rourke looked skyward.

Natalia's gunship was strafing the enemy position, but the position was well fortified, energy machine guns, rifle grenades, even a mortar. The energy machine guns could reach up for Natalia's helicopter without great difficulty. But, if she utilized a missile in order to neutralize their position, she would risk destroying two of the Nazi helicopters which were on the ground. The enemy position's proximity to the helicopters was the rationale behind Rourke and the men of his strike force not assaulting the Nazis on the ground.

But, it was time for that rationale to be re-appraised. "Schmidt!"

"Yes, Herr Generaloberst!"

"You have medic training, correct?"

"Yes, Herr Generaloberst!"

"We have to do something about our friends over there. Try to keep Moore here stablized while we do. I'm worried about shock."

"Yes, Generaloberst."

"Carry on." And Rourke looked to Jones, Michael and Paul. "Jones, I want you to keep the men over by the helicopters occupied; a little gunfire, that sort of thing, just so that their attention is kept on you rather than us."

"Aye, sir."

Rourke looked to Michael and Paul. "So, what do you have in mind, Dad?" Michael asked him, smiling.

Paul, a wicked grin crossing his lips, said, "Yeah, Dad, what?"

Rourke nodded, forcing a smile. After all, he was Paul's father-in-law. "Natalia can keep them occupied. Jones can make them think we're interested in trading shots with them. That leaves the three of us the opportunity for action." Rourke gestured toward the control building. "We can get inside and out again, without them seeing us. There's a hole in the wall on the far side from us, but they won't know that. If we're lucky, the enemy personnel know our

95

numbers, will figure that we're all accounted for. We get out through the hole in the wall, then work our way down to the ropes we webbed along the slope. We move across, getting up on their right flank. We wait for Natalia to make another strafing run, and when she does we close with their position and end this thing. Any questions?"

"Just run up and kill them," Michael said, then shrugged his shoulders. "Sounds straight-forward enough. If they don't spot us out in the open."

"Details, details," Paul said, grinning.

"No explosive ordnance, because we can't risk those two helicopters," Rourke added.

Paul nodded, starting a weapons check. Michael was already picking up a Nazi assault rifle—he was out of ammunition for his M-16.

Rourke crouched beside Moore, checking the man once again, telling Schmidt, "As soon as Major Tiemerovna is able to land, get Moore aboard her machine and out of here to medical assistance. Have her ferry up personnel who are helicopter qualified to get these machines to safety below, and bring along any reenforcing personnel she can muster. Meanwhile, you and Jones cover us. If we're successful, we'll take up positions near the entrances to the elevator shafts." Those were on the far north side of the helipad, near another control structure. "Got it?"

"Yes, Herr Generaloberst."

"John'll do just fine, really," Rourke told the German Long Range Mountain Patrol commando, clapping him on the shoulder.

"Yes, Herr Generaloberst."

96

Rourke merely shook his head, then made a quick check of his own weapons. Incoming enemy fire was of moderate volume, which meant they were waiting to see what would happen next. The magazines for Rourke's personal weapons were all reloaded. He had acquired two Nazi assault rifles, and he took up a bandolier of magazines as well, the bandolier nearly full.

"Ready?"

"Ready," Paul answered. Michael merely nodded.

Rourke rasped, "Jones, cover us." And Rourke started for the steps in a dead run.

Chapter Fourteen

This was some of the most intense fighting Annie had ever experienced, firefights starting, ending, starting again only seconds later as, foot-by-foot it seemed, Commander Washington's combined force of SEAL Team personnel and German Long Range Mountain Patrol commandos took the second-highest level of the Nazi command complex. The fierceness with which the Nazis fought was doubly understandable. They were SS, as were all of Deitrich Zimmer's elite forces, and they were conditioned to believe that, if captured, they would be subjected to hideous, mutilating tortures in order to extract intelligence data from them, then be summarily executed. Trans-Global Alliance prisoners were not tortured for any reason, nor killed, but instead given food, shelter and medical treatment equivalent to that afforded Trans-Global Alliance fighting personnel. If it proved necessary to extract intelligence data from prisoners reluctant to give it, this was accomplished by means of state-of-the-art drug therapy, and such prisoners, when the war would eventually end, by direction of a joint resolution of all Trans-Global Alliance leaders, would be provided certification that the obtaining of any and all data from them was involuntary.

The fighting ceased for the moment, the enemy personnel regrouping on the top level of the facility. Annie Rourke Rubenstein crouched beside Washington, the black SEAL Team commander. He was holding a caseless assault rifle in both fists. Annie's Detonics ScoreMaster was in her right hand, the Beretta 92F in her left.

There were dead bodies lying strewn along the stairs and over the railings as she peered upward toward the top level. She ducked back. "How'll we get them out of there? If we assault from the stairwells, we'll be cut to pieces."

"Agreed, Mrs. Rubenstein. But, we don't have much choice. Since we don't know exactly what's on the top floor, using explosives might cause more problems than it would solve. Even if we had lethal gas, which we don't, it's a violation of General Orders to use it. And remember, they don't operate under restrictions like that. Conventional chemical weapons wouldn't do any good against their gas equipment. And, we can't wait around for their exposure to *encephalitis lethargica,* if they've been exposed, to catch up with them and put them out of commission. So, it has to be a frontal assault. And yes, we'll take heavy casualties. If your father's tactical genius is hereditary and you've got an idea, now's the time to share it, ma'am."

Annie leaned back against the wall, setting her

100

pistols in her lap, running her hands back over her hair. It had been French-braided, a technique she had learned from Natalia, and by now probably looked a mess, she thought. "What about a coordinated attack from above and below? That would minimize casualties, wouldn't it?"

"Yes, ma'am, and if your father, your husband and your brother have been successful, it might just be the solution. If not, we have no choice. Either way, there isn't a lot of time. The men we're fighting aren't going to wait forever. They'll try something, even if it means sacrificing their own lives en masse. But, we can give it a shot." He called out to one of his SEAL Team personnel, "Collins."

"Aye, sir!"

"Get in touch with Major Tiemerovna's gunship. Get a status report on what's going on at the helipad. I need information, fast."

"Aye, sir!"

Annie hoped it would be fast enough.

Chapter Fifteen

John Rourke, with Michael and Paul just behind him, was well past the midway point along the ropes. In another comparatively few yards, they would, quite literally, Rourke thought, "have reached the end of their rope." There would be a distance of some one hundred yards which they would need to navigate without the benefit of a safety line to assist them, the rock there just as slick and just as steeply inclined as the surface they traversed now.

They were roped each man to the other, so that in the event that one man began to slide away to his death, the other two would have a chance to save him. Conversely, should two men get in trouble, they would seal the third man's doom.

But, John Rourke had planned ahead. One of the many martial-arts disciplines with which he had become familiar Before the Night of the War dealt with the art of the Ninja. To master and perfect such arts required the devotion of a lifetime. But, he had learned the use of climbing claws.

When Wolverton crafted the pitons and the ice-creepers, Rourke also had him make three sets of crude, but effective—he hoped—claws similar to those of which Rourke had learned the use long years ago. Nearing the end of the rope, Rourke paused, soundlessly signaling to his son and his friend that it was time to don the claws.

Rourke buckled one claw set to his right palm, another to his left. He buckled on the claws for his right knee and his left. There was a danger to using the claws, that being that they would slip on the ice. But, without the use of the claws, he and his son and his friend would surely perish.

Rourke reached out with his clawed left hand, found purchase and applied pressure, then pulled. The claw held and he was able to move, spiderlike, his right knee next, then his right hand, then his left knee.

As he looked back, Paul and Michael—neither man had ever tried the use of the climbing claws—seemed to be doing reasonably well, not nearly so bad as Rourke himself had done the first time he had tried them so long ago.

Rourke kept moving . . .

From above, despite the darkness and the swirling snow, she could see it all, through the gunship's chin bubble. She watched, but not dispassionately, what was taking place, as if it were an adventure film unfolding before her on some unimaginably vast movie screen; she was rooting for the good guys to win, and when the film ended, if they won, she would be the woman who swooned in the arms of her couragous lover. She wasn't a swooner of course, but she was thinking figuratively.

Natalia Anastasia Tiemerovna (she had many times tried the name Natalia Rourke just to see how it sounded, how it felt) could do nothing to truly assist her lover and his father and his friend, except make periodic forays against the enemy position toward which they moved now in stealth, hoping to keep the attention of that position's defenders as a cover for movement.

To have launched a missile against the Nazi defenders would have precipitated the destruction of two helicopters, and, these would be needed in order to get friendly forces evacuated, should that be possible.

It was time to make another run, but as she was about to begin, a signal came in on the field communicator, its strength very weak because it was not designed for use between ground and air. "This is Major Tiemerovna. Your signal is weak. Say slowly. Over."

"Ground to Tiemerovna. Status required on Operation Madness. Over."

Operation Madness was the codename Paul had picked for the assault up the mountainside against the summit.

"Operation Madness approximately ninety percent completed. Cannot accurately predict conclusion. Over."

"Ground to Tiemerovna. Can you stand by for further communications? Over."

"Negative, Ground. I am commencing a run. Over."

"Ground to Tiemerovna. Can you reestablish contact after your run? Over."

"Affirmative, Ground. Wilco. Tiemerovna out."

She started the run . . .

Their rate of travel was maddeningly tedious, and the wind lashed at their bodies. Rourke looked back from checking on Paul and Michael and began again to move; but, each time he did so, wind gusts assaulted him as if they were human enemies, intent somehow on tearing him away from the slope to fall to his death below.

The safety line, by means of which he and Paul and Michael were tied together, would have little effect except to damn Paul and Michael as well should the wind literally hurl him over the side. He kept moving, at least another twenty yards to crawl with the aid of the climbing claws. And, should the defenders of the Nazi position look his way during some ephemeral cessation of the wind, when the blowing snow did not mask his body, he would be seen, shot from his precarious position without even the hope of returning fire. To operate a firearm of any sort while wearing the climbing claws would be impossible.

Above him, John Rourke could just discern that Natalia was making another strafing run on the enemy position.

Rourke kept going . . .

Annie Rubenstein made a final check of her M-16.

With Natalia's report that the final Nazi position still remained to be taken, Commander Washington no longer had the option of waiting for a simultaneous attack from above and below.

With each moment that passed, chances increased that a more sizable Nazi force would reach the headquarters complex and crush them.

Like her father, John Rourke (she hoped), Annie Rubenstein had planned ahead. "If you don't mind my input, I have an idea, Commander."

"All ideas welcome, Mrs. Rubenstein."

"What if we make an explosion down here, something which sounds really loud but isn't really big at all? Well, what we could do then is convince the Nazis that we've had some sort of catastrophe and we're withdrawing, but a bunch of us stay behind, wearing gasmasks and everything, and armed to the teeth. When the Nazis probe the floor, we don't do a thing, but wait for them to come back in force. Then we hit them. Do you think that would work?"

Annie had learned from Natalia that when a woman was making a statement to a man, she was often better off phrasing it as a question, as if she were asking his approval for the idea rather than telling him it was a good idea. That way, when he agreed, and supplied some sort of detail—as Commander Washington did now . . . "We could use smoke grenades, really confuse the hell out of them when we attacked, then our guys could storm back up here to back us up" . . . he could credit himself with the idea, or at the least its refinement to practicality.

"That would really do it, wouldn't it?"

"It just might, Mrs. Rubenstein. It just might," Commander Washington told her.

She merely folded her hands in her lap and said nothing else . . .

At last, John Rourke reached safety; but, that was relative. He would be able to stand, be able to feel confident that he would not be swept over the edge of the escarpment to his death, but he was fewer than twenty-five yards from the enemy position and had just noticed that, contrary to what he had thought, in addition to the defenders of the actual position, there were at least two men posted well away from the main body, perhaps for potential use as snipers.

One of these men was so close to him now that the slightest sound might alert the fellow to his presence. Rourke signaled to Michael and Paul to remain where they were.

While Rourke quickly debated his next move, as silently as he could he began to undo the knotted rope from his body. The claws would have to come off, but the buckles and hook and pile fasteners with which they were secured might make a betraying noise. Because the wind had suddenly died.

Snow was falling in greater quantity now than before. Had the circumstances been different, the mere size and texture of the flakes would have been exquisitely beautiful, the lazy rhythm with which they tumbled downward almost mesmerizingly soothing. It was as if he were inside one of those tiny glass globes which were so popular as Christmas

108

decorations in his youth, the globe containing a holiday scene, snow falling when the globe was picked up, turned over, and then set down again.

But, instead, he found himself in immediate peril.

The nearer of the two Nazi outer guards was starting to turn around. In an instant, he would see that he was not alone, would open fire, thus sounding an alarm as well.

There was nothing for it, no other choice.

John Rourke drew himself up into a crouch. If he attacked the fellow, all of the attention the noise would bring would be focused on him alone, allowing Paul and Michael to get to safe ground, free themselves of the climbing claws and utilize their weapons.

Rourke sprang at the man in the same instant that the Nazi raised his rifle to fire.

Chapter Sixteen

John Rourke hurled his body weight against his foe with full force, his hands held palm outward, to make use of the climbing claws as weapons. His right knee, claw-fitted as well, rammed into the Nazi commando's chest in the same instant. The technique of utilizing three of the four limbs as simultaneously striking weapons with the full force of the body behind it was something he had learned Before the Night of the War from his old friend Ron Mahovsky. When done properly, defense against the maneuver was impossible.

There was more than a shout of pain or surprise from the man as their bodies impacted; it was a scream, primal and final, Rourke's left claw slashing open the carotid artery, the right stabbing downward toward the heart, the claw attached to Rourke's knee gouging toward the sternum.

Rourke rolled away as the second outer guard shouted, then brought his rifle to bear, firing toward Rourke's position. But John Rourke had the body of the dead man, using it as a shield, letting go of it only as he was able to take better cover. Bullets ripped into the dead man's upper body. Rourke drew back deeper into cover, tearing away the bloodied climbing claws from his hands, swinging one of the Nazi assault rifles forward on its sling, stabbing it over the crates behind which he'd taken cover, then returning fire.

There was no thought of aiming, only making noise, and hence perpetuating the diversion in order to give Paul and Michael time to find cover and bring their weapons into play. Rourke ducked down for an instant, removing the climbing claws from his knees as well.

Harassing fire poured toward the Nazi position from beside the control building, Jones and Schmidt firing alternately, in random rotation.

Rourke looked back, Paul and Michael in motion, safe from the treacherous slope, closing from behind on the Nazi position into which Schmidt and Jones fired.

Rourke snatched a fully loaded magazine for the Nazi assault rifle from the bandolier he'd slung crossbody, rammed it in place. The second rifle in his left fist, Rourke eyeballed the terrain, selecting his next spot of cover. It was a dicey choice, a service vehicle with forklift attachment, dicey because it would have a synth-fuel tank which, if struck properly by a bullet or an energy blast, would explode. But, there was no choice.

Rourke waited for another volley of shots from Schmidt and Jones, and, as they fired, threw himself into as rapid a run as he dared over the ice, launching himself toward the yellow service vehicle, hitting the ice-coated tarmac behind it and sliding. Kneeling behind a wheelwell, the engine block and as much of the vehicle's body as possible between him and enemy fire, Rourke caught his breath as enemy small-arms fire tore into the vehicle's coachwork, energy bolts rippling across the hood, arcing as one bolt after another struck, the vehicle crackling with electricity.

Michael and Paul should be nearly into position.

Rourke pushed himself up into a crouch, both rifles fully loaded, selectors set to auto. He disliked burst control mechanisms on automatic weapons, preferring to rely instead on his own sense of touch.

He inhaled, exhaled, inhaled again, then darted from cover behind the service vehicle toward another, identical vehicle closer still to the enemy position. This time, he didn't wait for harassing fire to cover his movements because, over the cacophony of gunfire, he'd heard the hollow sound of a mortar being dropped down its firing tube. Fewer than five yards from the service vehicle behind which he'd initially taken cover, the mortar struck, Rourke thrown to the tarmac, fiery debris raining down around him as a secondary explosion—the service vehicle's synth-fuel tank—went up.

Rourke rolled onto his back, momentarily stunned, energy bolts weaving through the snow-filled air toward him, impacting the icy tarmac.

Rourke shook his head to clear it, got to his knees, his feet, ran, gunfire and energy bolts impacting the tarmac near his feet, gunfire rippling across the hood of the second service vehicle as Rourke dove to cover.

113

He could hear small-arms fire originating from behind the enemy position now. It would be Paul and Michael. Because of the mortar, they might have been forced into opening fire prematurely in order to divert attention away from him. Rourke looked toward the vehicle's cab above him. And, as he looked, he could see its ignition key still in the switch, a fob with a swastika dangling from it.

Rourke clambered up, into the yellow service vehicle's cab, safing the two assault rifles as he moved. Crouching as low as he could behind the dashboard, Rourke turned the key. The engine groaned in the cold, not catching. Rourke pumped the accelerator, then tried turning it over again. And, the engine caught.

John Rourke's gloved hands moved over the controls, searching for the forklift controls themselves. He found them, the fork rising. Rourke cut the wheel into a hard right as he released the emergency brake and geared up, the vehicle hesitating, its tires breaking free of the ice, then gaining momentum, rolling ahead.

Bullets whined over the body, energy bolts flickering across it, the entire interior of the cab bathed in bluish-white light. For an instant only, his mind was drawn back to the memory of the cryogenic chambers, the gas used inside them of the same, almost ethereal color.

The enemy fire was intensifying. A mortar was launched, exploding only a few yards from the vehicle Rourke drove, its concussive force nearly overturning it. Rourke drove on, stabbing one of the assault rifles through the still-open door, firing, spraying out the magazine in three- and four-round bursts.

A rifle grenade struck the hood, bounced away, exploded, as Rourke was cranking the wheel left and away from it.

He was within mere yards of the enemy position now, the Nazi commandos on their feet, firing almost point blank. His windshield, long since shattered, totally collapsed, showering him with shards of safety glass. Rourke didn't swerve. A man had a hand-thrown grenade ready to toss, but a burst of gunfire from behind cut him down.

One of the Nazi commandos ran toward the cab, jumping toward it, half in through the open doorway as Rourke stabbed the now-empty rifle's muzzle into the man's face, driving him back.

Rourke was surrounded now, emeny personnel on all sides. And, it was time to exit the vehicle.

Rourke wedged the butt of the remaining Nazi assault rifle against the accelerator pedal, then jumped, hitting the ice-slicked tarmac hard, rolling. A man lunged toward him with a bayonet. Rourke rolled away, drew one of the ScoreMasters and fired point-blank, then again and again, the enemy commando going down dead.

Gunfire surrounded Rourke on all sides as he drew the second ScoreMaster. The yellow service vehicle was still going, plowing forward through the enemy position, overturning the enemy defenses, enemy personnel running from the blades of the forklift. Rourke fired out the pistol in his right hand, putting down one of the Nazis who was trying to board the vehicle.

Stabbing the spent full-size Detonics into his pistol belt, Rourke drew one of the two SIG-Sauer P-228s from beneath his sweater. Then, he advanced.

Paul and Michael were closing from the far side of the enemy position, their weapons firing at point-blank range into the Nazi defenders.

Rourke kept moving, putting down a man who was attempting to dismount an energy machine gun from its carriage. Rourke went on, firing a succession of double taps from the SIG into one of the commandos who was firing toward Michael, killing the Nazi.

As Rourke turned toward another target, the man threw up his hands in surrender.

Rourke aimed the SIG at the Nazi's head, ordering, "On your knees, hands clasped behind your head. You will not be harmed." The few surviving personnel were following this man's lead, laying down their weapons, raising their hands. Gunfire had ceased. And, John Rourke suddenly thought: Was there a Geneva Convention anymore? No matter, men of honor did not need rules of morality imposed upon them.

Chapter Seventeen

The Nazi personnel were moving into position on this level more rapidly than Annie would have anticipated, almost as if they were being chased.

The smell from the explosives still permeated the air around her, slightly sweet and slightly sickening in the confined space.

Dead Nazi commandos, dressed in SEAL Team uniforms, were placed at strategic locations about the main corridor, to further enhance the notion that the explosion was an accident and that these were its victims. Annie, Commander Washington beside her, lay prone inside an air shaft overlooking the level's main corridor. If she moved at all, the ductwork would reverberate like a drum being beaten, so, despite the fact that her legs were beginning to cramp a little, she remained perfectly still, as did Washington.

All told, sixteen persons—all of them men except for herself—mostly SEALs, some members of German Long Range Mountain Patrol units, were secreted about the level, waiting for Commander Washington to trigger, by radio signal, smoke bombs which had been planted at strategic locations throughout the corridor and in some of the larger rooms.

The level seemed to be utilized for planning, military and otherwise. There were maps, wall-mounted vid screens, even tables with fully fleshed terrain segments set upon them. The contents would be a treasure trove of intelligence data, once this level and the top floor just above were secured.

Thoughts of her father, her husband and her brother came to her and she pushed them away, telling herself that if any of them were in truly mortal peril she would have felt it. She did not confide this to Commander Washington, merely telling him just before they'd taken hiding, "Don't worry; I'm sure my father and husband and brother are all right. They'll probably have the helipad secured in short order."

"I hope you're right, Mrs. Rubenstein," was all Washington had said in response.

Now, all they could do was wait until enough of the Nazi personnel were in position to give this ruse some chance of working.

Chapter Eighteen

His weapons freshly loaded, John Rourke looked up. He sat in the cockpit of the only one of the Nazi helicopters which had so far been cleared of potential demolitions. None were found. Natalia's gunship had ferried Moore to proper medical attention below and brought back with it a small force of Commander Washington's SEAL Team personnel and some of the German Long Range Mountain Patrol commandos. Natalia and these men filled the fuselage section of the chopper, along with Paul, Michael, Schmidt and Jones. Natalia, like John Rourke, sat. She was massaging her left thigh.

Rourke addressed the assembly. "We have to assume that Commander Washington has some plan in the works. This problem we're having with radio communications isn't helping matters. The interior of the structure is almost impossible to work with, absorbing almost all radio signals. And, a considerable amount of our radio equipment was fried during the electromagnetic pulse, as we discovered. Thank God the Nazis had these helicopters wired against it.

"The fact remains," Rourke went on, "that Commander Washington may well need our help; but our very assistance could screw up his plans beyond measure. The horns of the proverbial dilemma, Natalia, gentlemen. How's Wolfgang doing?"

He looked at Natalia as he spoke. She answered, "The last time I checked—about a half hour ago—he was responding well. We should have him back on his feet in another few hours at most, perhaps considerably sooner."

"Good, but we could use his military background now. Any suggestions?" Rourke asked.

"Herr Generaloberst, I request permission to speak." John Rourke granted it with a wave, the pomposity of such military formalities something he found silly but realized he would never be able to change. "The remote video probes aboard these machines, Herr Generaloberst, they are capable of quite precise manuevering. Such probes could be launched at lowest speed on manual control and sent down inside the structure, thus perhaps providing us with the necessary intelligence data upon which a plan of action might be based, Herr Generaloberst."

"Brilliant idea, Schmidt. You're in charge of it and get it underway immediately."

"Yes, Herr Generaloberst!"

Rourke nodded. He looked at Natalia, asking, "How bad is that leg now?"

"I'm fully capable, just not fully comfortable,

John. What do you have in mind?"

"Paul, you assist Schmidt with the video probe. Michael, you and Jones take charge of getting together a small party of men to follow us down into the stairwell. Cobble together shields from the scrap materials around here. There are helicopter parts stored up here, I think, for service. See if there are any body parts. Those could serve as shields against most small-arms fire and deflect energy bursts, at least to a degree. Natalia and I will make what used to be called a soft penetration down into the structure below." He looked at Paul again, asking, "Can you wire us up something that would work like a field telephone?"

"I think so."

"Good. The remote probe goes ahead of us. If it spots anything terribly unfriendly, let us know. If we spot anything it doesn't, we'll do the same." And, Rourke looked at Natalia. "You sure you're up to this?"

"One of the movies on videotape at the Retreat, with John Wayne and Ward Bond? Do you remember it?"

"They made quite a few together."

"Based on the Louis L'Amour novel? The Western? Ward Bond is driving a wagon and everyone is being chased by Apache Indians. When John Wayne asks Ward Bond—"

Rourke smiled, telling her, "I know—you were born ready. All right, let's get this operation moving, people."

Chapter Nineteen

She would normally have been the last one down, shepherding her squadron through the landing, but the damage sustained by her aircraft had made such a choice impossible.

Hauling back on the yoke, bringing up the V/STOL fighter's nose, she brought the machine into the hover mode, still uncertain whether or not she had full operational capabilities for the portside engine. But, she had no choice other than vertical landing, with machine gun bullets pockmarking the wing, damaging her flaps and the field itself so littered with fallen aircraft that, even had her plane been in perfect condition, there was no place for a conventional landing.

Emma Shaw's aircraft was partially crippled, all her armament gone except for the pistols that she carried (of absolutely no use to her while she was airborne), the surviving members of her squadron circled the field while she made her attempt. If she failed, the ground-crew personnel would be getting her out of the wreckage with a vacuum cleaner, she realized.

Too many of her people had gone down, lost, but all thirty-six of the enemy fighter planes were destroyed in the air, and so preoccupied that they never had a chance to do most of their intended damage to the airfield.

Her aircraft shuddered and bucked, starting to go out of trim, at last the questionable engine was coming around in full rotation. And, she started down, half holding her breath.

Touchdown.

As quickly as she could, she hit the release and started her canopy rearward. She punched the seat restraint release, was up and clambering out of the machine, the smell of burning insulation a harbinger of fire. She jumped from the cockpit to the wing stem, then down to the tarmac, running.

Fire and other emergency vehicles were closing on her craft.

Emma Shaw pulled off her helmet, bending forward slightly and shaking free her hair. "Oh, shit, I never want another day like this one!" She turned back and looked at the just-landed V/STOL, foam already being sprayed over the damaged wing, technicians starting to pour across the machine. The crew chief was slowing up, already starting to climb out of his tow vehicle as she ran toward him. "Chief, signal whoever the hell's running that electronic semaphore out there and get my people down."

"You got it, Commander. How you doin'?"

"I've been better," she told him honestly. She was

starting to dig into the pockets of her flightsuit for cigarettes and a lighter, found both and lit up, coughing after being so long on oxygen. She shook her head again, turning her eyes skyward. Light snow was falling. She could hear the chief on his radio. Apparently, the service and emergency equipment radios were still functional, as were ship-to-ship communications between the members of her squadrons. She inhaled again, letting the smoke out through her nostrils, the light-headedness starting to pass.

The wind was icy cold, but she loved it, the sensation of feeling that she was still alive. And, Emma Shaw thought about John Rourke, wondering if he were alive. She loved him, which was insanity, but her family was given to mental aberrations she thought, smiling. Right now, her dad was probably chasing crooks down some alley in Honolulu . . .

Tim Shaw just shook his head. "The bastard couldn't play it straight, even once." Moving through the woods which covered the slope were three heavily armed men. Shaw recognized their type, Honolulu street punks. They weren't out enjoying the wonders of nature, either. The Nazi Fifth Columnists utilized local street thugs as "soldiers," he had learned, and these men were obviously some of them. Whether the man Shaw had defeated one-on-one had brought them along as backup or whether some Nazi superior had thought

125

of it, didn't really matter. They were here, between him and where he had to go.

His right arm was feeling pretty good, really, all things considered. On the down side, his left tricep was still hurting like hell and his back—Tim Shaw didn't want to think about his back at all, because he might have done significant damage. When he turned the wrong way, hit a bump on the slope or breathed too deeply, he was in pain such as he had never known before. These days, of course, medical science had licked cancer, the crippling diseases such as muscular dystrophy and multiple sclerosis, congenital diseases such as Epstein-Barr and sickle-cell anemia and organ transplants and reconstructive surgery were so advanced that virtually no one alive was forced to spend life in a wheelchair or on crutches, but all of that notwithstanding, the prospect of having to face radical surgery just in order to be restored to his former generally good health was not only daunting, but pissed him off.

The Nazi child-killer would get his revenge.

Meanwhile, the three men approaching had to be dealt with.

Unlike the paranoid times about which he'd read—the days Before the Night of the War—when one saw a man or woman carrying an assault rifle these days, it was a sign of good, common sense, not some omen of evil intent as such had been perceived in that bygone era. Everyone who chose to be was armed, and most of these carried firearms concealed, occasionally openly. That was only good sense as well.

126

Certainly, there was crime, but that was a part of the human condition. Yet, there was less crime per capita than ever in human history, and violent personal crimes, such as muggings and rapes, were lower still by comparison. There would always be the unscrupulous who wished to prey upon the weak, but because people were armed for their defense, the weak were fewer and farther between, prey harder to come by.

Toward the last days Before the Night of the War, according to what Tim Shaw had read, every media source imaginable was finding some way or another to brand firearms ownership as being tantamount to madness. That there seemed to be some almost deliberate program to disarm the American people in those wildly misguided days appeared obvious through the twenty-twenty hindsight of history. For what purpose, Tim Shaw could not hazard a guess.

These three men approaching him did not fill him with misgivings because they were armed, but because of the way they moved, carried themselves, their overall demeanor. He had been a street cop all of his adult life, and he had learned that although it was morally wrong to make lasting judgements based upon appearance and the subtleties which could not properly be put into words, such temporary character assessments were, in reality, subliminal cues for staying alive.

As if they wore flashing electronic signs, these men bore the words "punk" and "criminal" and "badass" just as surely.

The immediate problem was how to deal with

them. He could not just sit someplace and wait for them to pass in hopes that they would remain ignorant of his presence, nor could he take potshots at them when they passed. The former ploy would be naively dangerous, the latter morally unacceptable just in case he was misreading the subliminal cues.

Tim Shaw summed up his thoughts in a single word, "Shit."

Chapter Twenty

There was no light, except for the smoky, grey haze below, this from the tactical deployment of gas and the aftermath of fires, these likely originated by the explosions of gas cannisters and shells as well. There was a faint hum—from the video probe which flew ahead of them—and this and the sounds of his own breathing were all that could be heard. When one wore a gas mask, one was very aware of one's breathing, rather like wearing scuba gear, Rourke thought. Or, at least, *he* was.

There was a substantial possibility that the "bad guys" might win this one. Not the battle, because at this juncture its ultimate resolution was in little doubt. Instead of losing the battle, the "good guys" might lose the war. If Thorn Rolvaag were correct, and every nuclear warhead which could be had was needed to counteract the growing fissure beneath the Pacific Ocean, there was a substantial chance that such weapons might not be available, and the world would end.

If, by some miracle, those warheads in the arsenals of the Trans-Global Alliance might be enough to save the planet, then no threat of nuclear retaliation would remain against Eden and the Nazi forces; and judicious tactical use of such nuclear weapons by the enemy, if indeed it did not precipitate the destruction of the planet, would neutralize resistance.

He smiled, laughing silently under his breath. Natalia, beside him, asked, "Were you laughing?" He wore a bone transmitter along his jawbone, the limited-range device unaffected by the problems they'd been having with some other forms of more conventional radio communication.

"Yes, I was laughing," Rourke whispered back.

"At what?"

"At the madness, Natalia, the sheer madness. We've been at this same war, essentially, for six hundred and twenty-five years, and we've come full circle, but the irony of it all is that the nuclear weapons which once destroyed the planet are now the only things which might save the planet. But, if we use them to save the planet, we stand a very real chance of losing the war and all we've fought for."

"Do you ever wish things had been different before?"

Although the reference was, on the surface, a bit obtuse, he understood her remark perfectly. "But we would have been on opposite sides."

"I hope you and Emma Shaw find a way of being together. She not only loves you, she worships you."

Rourke was also tired of forcing himself to hold in his feelings, as he had always done, for some "higher purpose," whatever that happened to be at the time. But, for what he promised himself was the last time, he said nothing.

One level of his consciousness, indeed, began to focus on Emma Shaw. Natalia was wrong. Emma did not "worship" him, and he would have rejected such had it been evident. But, she genuinely loved him and, more than any woman he had ever met, seemed also to genuinely understand him. He'd met a number of men over the years who had confided, "My wife (or girlfriend) just doesn't understand me, so I'm leaving her." What adults of either sex did with their personal lives was no business of his, and he'd always tried to avoid the ofttimes formulaic descriptions of why relationships fell apart.

There was nothing formulaic about his relationship with Sarah. They had always loved each other, always would, he knew. But they had never liked each other as friends. With maturity, John Rourke had realized that there was no real love simply having love without the friendship.

Sarah, if indeed this woman he had carried from a hospital cell was Sarah and not one of Deitrich Zimmer's insidious clones, would leave him. She was in love and friendship with Generaloberst Wolfgang Mann, as was Mann with her. The death of Martin, his and Sarah's third child, even if it had not really been Martin, but another of Deitrich Zimmer's clones, would be the catalyst, but not the reason.

He was reminded of the story about the young student in a world-history class asked by his professor to discuss the causes of U.S. involvement

131

in World War II, responding by discussing the attack on Pearl Harbor and official U.S. desire to support desperately besieged European nations. Of course, the causes of World War II could be traced with ease to the Franco-Prussian War of 1870, and the attack on Pearl Harbor by the Japanese directly linked to anti-United States sentiment engendered by Theodore Roosevelt's pro-Russian mediation of the peace following the Russo-Japanese War of 1905. Although the Japanese militarily won, their victory was negotiated away and the resultant bitterness was the seed from which the Pearl Harbor massacre eventually sprang.

Martin was his and Sarah's "December 7, 1941"; their divergent philosophies and the bitterness these bred were their Franco-Prussian and Russo-Japanese wars.

Rourke and Natalia neared the base of the stairs at the first landing, the probe hovering above the landing, returned from a foray well ahead of them. Paul's voice was coming through the cord-supplied radio receiver in Rourke's other ear. "John, I'm pulling back the probe. You and Natalia freeze. There's a Nazi force massing in the stairwell leading to the next level down. Michael and I'll follow you down."

Rourke switched to the second microphone, this one hook and pile attached to the borrowed flak jacket he wore. "No, Paul. We're just checking things out. Keep the probe where it is, and you and Michael stand by, get some other personnel ready, too. But nothing until you hear from Natalia or from me, or haven't heard from us for a long enough

132

period of time that you think we're in trouble. All we want is intelligence at this point."

"You guys be careful, huh?"

Rourke smiled in spite of himself, "Well, we were planning on being reckless, but since you insist—just hang in there." He put the microphone back, then spoke into the unit which connected him to Natalia. "Could you get most of that?"

"Uh-huh—so? We keep going?"

"Maybe a little faster. Let's stay sharp."

She only nodded as Rourke looked at her.

Rourke reached the landing, glanced upward toward the video probe and shot a wave to Paul and Michael, then started down the stairwell, one of the captured Nazi assault rifles in his right hand, the second slung at his left side.

He moved with the classic methodology he had practiced so often when teaching special weapons and tactics, all motion deliberate, each footfall calculated for position, the body coiled like a spring, ready for response, his rifle locked tightly to his side, head moving side to side. Behind him, when he caught a glimpse of her, he could see Natalia, performing her own function within the "two-man" team, her focus of attention the stairwell behind them and side to side, even though there was virtually no chance of difficulties in those directions. Her weapon was held at a ready high port.

They reached the base of the second flight, Rourke quickly taking up position on the right side of the doorframe, not having to cross in front of the opening in order to do so, merely vaulting over the rail to the flight below, then moving back up to

133

the landing. Natalia was half on the stairs and half on the landing, to the left of the door. The door was fully open. Rourke leaned near it, edged toward the opening.

Natalia took a mirror from one of the utility pouches on her flak jacket, silently extending the deployment handle that was integral to it, adjusting the angle, locking the mirror in place, then manipulating the mirror. This consumed several seconds, and she studied what she saw in the mirror for several seconds more. With any luck, she would have a reasonably clear view of the far end of the floor which they were about to enter, Rourke knew. The other side of the doorway would be up to him.

She shook her head, beginning to disassemble the mirror.

Rourke dropped to his knees, Natalia bringing her rifle to an assault position. He set down his rifles, went prone and edged forward on knees and elbows, slowly, only an inch or so at a time, at last getting his head into position where he could see the far wall of the corridor on Natalia's side. Dead bodies, some smoldering debris, casings from gas bombs, these in jagged fragments, strewn among the dead who lay on the floor or collapsed over desks, slumped against walls. The dead wore Nazi uniforms, which was encouraging.

Rourke edged back, stood, retook the assault rifles and flattened himself beside the open door.

It wasn't necessary to tell Natalia, "Cover me." He merely nodded and she nodded in return. The rifle which was in his right hand, muzzle up, was flush along the right side of his body, the rifle in his left hand, muzzle down, flat against his left thigh and calf. Rourke edged still closer to the opening. His back to the door itself, but not touching it, he nodded once more to Natalia as he flexed his knees, then on the count of three, took a half step into and through the opening on his right foot, the muzzle of the rifle in his right hand snapping downward, the rifle in his left hand rising forty-five degrees, snapping downward again as he pulled back.

He saw only the same.

He spoke into the bone contact microphone. "Dead Nazis."

"The same. But there's some activity near the center of the corridor. I caught a glimpse in the mirror of someone disappearing into what looks like a second stairwell."

"What Paul was talking about. All right. I'm out first, you cover, then we leapfrog it."

"Right," Natalia responded, nodding.

Rourke jumped through the open doorway.

Chapter Twenty-One

The first shots came unexpectedly, but Annie Rubenstein had learned that lesson in her first gunfight a very long time ago: enemy fire always came unexpectedly, no matter how long anticipated it was. She was up and moving before the next burst, Commander Washington beside her. Her M-16 spitting short bursts, she picked a quadrant that she could easily cover and started killing everything in sight wearing a Nazi uniform.

And, there were numerous targets from which she could choose, the corridor suddenly full, the Nazi personnel who had passed by seconds earlier rushing back into the exponentially growing fray.

No gunfight was without incredible danger, but this sort of fight was the most dangerous of all, bullets and energy bolts flying everywhere, much of the firing at near point-blank range, living targets almost impossible to miss with each shot or burst that was fired. Annie drew back, retreating as the superior numbers of Nazi personnel swarmed forward. Commander Washington beside her was struck, she did not know where, but doubled over, nearly falling.

Annie shifted her assault rifle to her left hand, her right arm going out around Washington's back. "Lean on me!"

"No, leave me, ma'am!"

"Lean on me, damn it, Commander!" His left arm draped wearily across her shoulders. His rifle had fallen to the floor, but in his right hand he held a pistol, firing the weapon in double taps.

They were caught in a crossfire, the Nazi personnel who had been entering the corridor pushing them toward the Nazi personnel who had already passed by. Annie's rifle, held awkwardly against the sling since she'd shifted firing hands, was empty and she let it fall away between her body and Washington's. She grabbed the Beretta 92F from the holster at her left hip, thumbed the safety up into the firing position and fired point-blank into the face of an SS trooper thrusting his bayonet toward her chest.

She twisted left, the pistol extended at the end of her arm, her finger twitching twice against its trigger, a double tap into the chest and thorax of one of the SS officers. He fell over dead at her feet as she backed along the corridor, Washington still at her side. He was changing magazines in his pistol, awkwardly done one-handed.

An energy bolt rippled across the corridor wall beside her head. Involuntarily, she averted her eyes. Something clubbed her left arm, numbing her to the bone, the Beretta falling from her grasp. Com-

138

mander Washington snapped, "Avert your eyes, ma'am!" She twisted her head away, her eyes closed for an instant, floaters of blood from the pain in her arm washing over them, Commander Washington's pistol firing, then again and again.

As she opened her eyes, Washington let go of her. She slumped back against the corridor wall. Her left arm, useless, pressed across her abdomen, Annie Rubenstein drew the Detonics ScoreMaster from the holster at her right side. She thumbed back the hammer, her right first finger snapping back against the trigger as an SS trooper charged toward her, one round from the .45 putting him down to his knees, his body twisting back. Nazi personnel were everywhere, many of Commander Washington's people down, the rest of them bottled up as were she and Washington.

And, Annie Rourke Rubenstein realized quite suddenly that in all likelihood, she would never have Paul's baby, never grow old with him, never do anything beyond what could be done with the seven rounds remaining in her pistol, that she would be dead in the next few seconds.

Chapter Twenty-Two

John Rourke went through the doorway leading into the alternate stairwell, two flights below him on the next level's landing a half dozen SS personnel, all trying to crowd through the doorway into the next level, the sound of gunfire and energy bolts emanating from the space beyond.

Natalia almost screamed into the bone transmitter, "I am right behind you, John!"

He didn't answer her, talking instead into the wire-connected transmitter which linked him to Paul Rubenstein and Michael. "There's a firefight down here! Get in behind us fast, but watch out for us because we might be in the middle of it. Use the video probe to guide you. Bring all the personnel you can. We underestimated remaining enemy forces. Hurry!"

Rourke tore the wired radio system from his ear and from his vest, useless to him now, then flipped over the railing onto the next lower flight, dropping into a crouch as he did so, his left hand letting loose the second rifle, reaching out for one of the gas grenades from one of the musette bags at his side. Albeit that positioning grenades on the vest made them fast into action (not to mention looked macho), there was enormous danger potential, should one of the grenades, attached only by its pin, pull loose. He preferred the slower but surer way. Ripping the pin from the grenade Rourke flipped it into the midst of the men gathered near the doorway, shouting simultaneously, "Heads up!"

As the men wheeled toward him, Rourke was already fisting his assault rifles, arcing them upward on their slings, thumbs flipping ambidextrous safeties into full auto position, index fingers touching triggers.

He sprayed the assault rifles into the knot of men, their bodies falling into the rising cloud of gas. Natalia flipped over the railing from above and landed beside him, a little less than graceful. "The damned leg wound," she said as he glanced toward her.

He said nothing in response.

Rourke ran down half the flight's length, then jumped into the cloud of gas, coming down in a crouch, both rifles' safeties flipped back into the auto mode the instant his feet touched the floor of the landing.

He reached the doorway, Natalia beside him, shouldering past him. "More gas, John!" There were grenades in each of her tiny, gloved fists, and she flipped them simultaneously into the corridor beyond, one to the right, one to the left. Rourke was into the corridor in the next instant, just beyond the

142

doorway a small war was in progress, gunfire—both cartridge arms and energy weapons—everywhere. A blue-white energy bolt streaked past his face and Rourke wheeled toward its origin, firing a short burst from the assault rifle in his right hand in response.

And he heard something which chilled him. "Daddy!"

Natalia streaked past him, dropping to her knees and skidding along the corridor floor as she sprayed out her assault rifle into a veritable wall of men in SS uniforms. "John!" No radio now, just a scream. Natalia went flat, Rourke firing over her into another phalanx of SS personnel. The first shout he'd heard was from his daughter, and as some of the SS personnel fell back, some dead, others wounded, still others retreating, Rourke could see Annie.

She was wrestling against a man in Nazi uniform perhaps one and a half times her size, the man holding a pistol, just as she did. But the slide of her pistol was locked open, the gun empty. Commander Washington lay sprawled on the floor beside her, dead or unconscious.

Natalia rolled toward the left side of the corridor, a fresh magazine in her assault rifle. John Rourke's guns were nearly empty, and he shouted to Natalia, "I'm going past you! Watch out!" Rourke threw himself into a headlong lunge along the corridor, past Natalia, knowing that he was neutralizing any effectiveness her fire might have had, but having no choice. He emptied the assault rifle in his right hand into two SS men lunging for him with fixed bayonets. He let the weapon fall to his right side,

143

already reaching for a pistol.

An SS officer fired an energy weapon from Rourke's left, the energy bolt missing Rourke's face by inches. Rourke returned fire, zipping a ragged swath of bullets across the man's abdomen and chest. This second assault rifle was empty as well.

The first of the two SIG-Sauer P-228s was in Rourke's right hand, a twenty-round magazine loaded, the second coming into his left.

He didn't shoot, instead hurled his body mass into the man fighting with his daughter, Annie. Rourke's right arm curled around the man's neck and, as Rourke literally tore the SS man away from his daughter, Rourke bulldogged the man to the floor, the muzzle of the pistol in Rourke's left hand less than an inch from the man's left temple as Rourke pulled the trigger.

Involuntarily, despite the eye protection afforded by the gas mask, Rourke averted his eyes against the spray of blood and brain and bone. "Get out of here! That way!" Rourke shouted to his daughter.

"Commander Washington is—"

"I'll get him. Run!" Rourke wheeled away from her, expecting (under the circumstances) to be obeyed unquestioningly. As his feet settled, elbows locked to his sides, a pistol in each hand, John Rourke opened fire into every man that he saw wearing a Nazi uniform.

He was not fighting, he realized on a very basic level deep within him, only killing. And he had learned that well in more than six centuries.

Chapter Twenty-Three

Paul and Michael and a dozen fresh men from Washington's command entered the corridor within sixty seconds that seemed like an eternity. The fighting ended within another sixty seconds, the Nazi personnel trapped between the survivors of Commander Washington's original force and the reinforcements.

Washington himself was alive, but comatose, severe loss of blood putting him in serious risk of his life.

The unit's medic—an M.D. with skills more modern than John Rourke's own—was caring for him even as Rourke sat down to reload his weapons, Annie crouched beside him.

"Thank you."

He looked at his daughter, realizing how she had meant what she said, but chastising her nonetheless. "That's the sort of thing you never have to thank me for. You and Michael and your mother—and Paul, too—you're my life. You know that, so thank me if I hold your chair or help you with your coat, but don't thank me for saving your life. Do you understand?"

"Yes. I love you, Daddy."

Rourke put down the freshly loaded SIG-Sauer P-228 and folded Annie against him within his right arm, touching his lips to his daughter's hair, then to her forehead. "And, I love you, too, little one."

Annie kissed his cheek. Rourke held her for a long moment that was, when it ended, far too short. He'd always laughed at the men who felt it was macho to lament having daughters in favor of sons. He counted himself blessed that he had one of each.

A daughter, unlike a son, was never too old to kiss her father, or hug him, never too self-possessed to hide tears which needed to be shed, never too much a woman to still be a little girl when needed. "I love you very much," Rourke whispered again, his voice suddenly hoarse sounding to him. He let go.

Michael approached, loading a fresh magazine into a Nazi assault rifle as he said, "Mom's on the way back here. We're secured. Colonel Mann—I mean Generaloberst Mann—"

"You might start calling him 'stepfather,'" Natalia supplied, standing beside Michael, supporting herself against him as she elevated her left foot and rubbed at her recently wounded left thigh.

John Rourke just looked at her, saying nothing.

Michael went on. "Wolfgang Mann is up and around, seems—literally—himself. There's no way to tell, of course, if he's another clone or what, but I spoke to him on the jury-rigged field telephone system with the ground level and he really sounds like the old Wolfgang Mann. Know what I mean?"

146

"I hope you're right," John Rourke said, nodding his head. "We're going to need him if we have to hold out here, and he could be enormously useful in terms of countering Deitrich Zimmer. They knew each other, and Wolf, of all of us, is the most qualified to outguess Zimmer if anyone is."

"Commander Washington's radio man says he thinks he's picking up something, but doesn't know what, yet. Could be Allied traffic, could be enemy, but at this point in time just to know that there's something on the air after an electromagnetic pulse is encouraging."

"Agreed. Have him keep you posted on progress with interpreting the traffic." Rourke looked past his son, seeing his friend Paul marshaling the Allied commando unit to see to the SS prisoners. Rourke looked back at Michael, saying, "You and Paul make certain we've got whatever defense posture we can muster, just in case." He turned his attention to Natalia, telling her, "You've got the air force, Major," and he smiled. "Get us ready to get the hell out of here if we need to or if we have the open option. Those helicopter gunships should be as well fitted as we can make them, and have all the fuel aboard they can carry."

"I'll see to it, John," she answered, smiling. "And why don't you take five minutes and rest, hmm? Just a suggestion, 'General,' but one I think you should consider."

"Suggestion noted, Natalia," Rourke smiled . . .

Tim Shaw smiled. Although the snow from the

147

broad-leaved jungle ferns all but covered him and he was no longer merely in pain—with his back and his other injuries—but he was cold as well, and he was in the best possible position to do what he had to do to the three men coming up the mountainside.

To have yelled out, "Police!" and expect anything but answering gunfire, if these men were allied to the Nazi saboteurs, would have been insane. Instead, he would play it by ear, waiting to see if the men would miss him entirely. He had left a subtle trail, not something easily followed. If they tracked him, he had decided, they were bad guys. Good guys wouldn't be looking for a trail, wouldn't bother tracking him. If they were bad guys, they'd die, or he would.

That was the way of it.

Even though he was surrounded by trees and rocks, this was just like the city, and what would happen here if they were bad guys would go down the same way that it would on the street. Live or die, the easy way to measure success or failure.

The .45 Government Model in his right fist, the little snubby .38 Special Centennial in his left, his back screaming at him, his left tricep hurting like a burn, his teeth gritted, Tim Shaw waited . . .

There were six V/STOLs in all, five of them still airborne, the sixth completing a perfect landing despite the ice spicules and snow driven on the relentless, merciless wind.

John Rourke waited in the wind, the hood of his parka up, an assault rifle across his back, gloved hands in his pockets, his right hand beside the butt of the little Smith & Wesson revolver he had taken to carrying as a hideout. Three truly perfect hideout guns were created during the twentieth century, the American Walther PPK .380 ACP, the Seecamp DA .32 ACP and the second edition Smith & Wesson Centennial .38 Special, all three stainless steel and all three carrying the maximum cartridge for the minimum package. He had used them all and liked them all, but always a revolver man despite the practicality of the autoloaders he habitually carried, he had chosen the Centennial when he'd determined that even in the situation of open combat a small hideout gun could make the difference between life and death.

But he doubted he would need a gun now. No enemy personnel were in range of the mountain's "liberated" sensing equipment (as well as it worked) and he already knew who would be exiting the aircraft.

The canopy slid back.

A helmeted head rose from within the bowels of the machine.

John Rourke unzipped his parka.

He had made his decision.

His life was changing, and he would change with it.

The figure from within the aircraft stepped out onto the wing stem, then dropped easily to the snowy ground. At first hesitantly, then as he opened his arms, very quickly, the figure ran to him. The helmet was tugged away, brown hair cascading from within it, instantly swept up in the wind, brushed back with a gauntleted hand.

John Rourke's hands went to his coat and he opened it wide.

The pilot of the aircraft came into his arms and he closed both arms and coat around her. "I've been thinking, Emma Shaw. That I love you."

"John," she murmured, barely audible over the keening of the wind as his mouth came down over hers and silenced all speech with a kiss . . .

Tim Shaw had made his decision. The three men were, indeed, following his tracks in the snow and gravel, were searching for him, were bad guys.

By way of rationalizing killing them, he reminded himself that there were three men and he had only one set of handcuffs and no flex cuffs with him.

It was a job for the .45, the .38 in his left hand, there for "just in case."

His right first finger squeezed against the .45's trigger as the sights settled on the throat of the furthest away of the three men. It was always better to shoot the one furthest away with the shot that had the longest preparation time, the best potential sight picture. He shot the man in the thorax, the man's body flopping back into the brush, assault rifle spraying air.

One of the two remaining men wheeled toward the sound of the shot, a riot shotgun coming up fast, but not faster than Tim Shaw could swing the muzzle of the .45 on line with the man's center of mass and pull the trigger. This wasn't bull's-eye marksmanship, and squeezing the trigger would have been at once unnecessary and too slow. The second man spun ninety degrees left, hands clasping his chest as he tumbled, the shotgun falling to the ground.

The third man was firing. But Tim Shaw was rolling left, following the natural, downward contour of the ground, the third man's bullets tearing into the brush and rocks behind which Shaw had only a split second before taken concealment and cover. Shaw fired, a double tap, at least one of the two bullets catching the man in the throat, near the carotid artery. The man stumbled to his knees, but kept firing, spraying his weapon across the ground.

Shaw tucked down as low as he could, bullets whining off the rocks near him, dirt and gravel kicked up, pelting his face and hands, making further shooting impossible.

The gunfire stopped.

Tim Shaw raised his head a few degrees and peered toward the third man. The man still knelt, the gun in his hands, but resting across his thighs. His head was bent forward.

He was dead.

Chapter Twenty-Four

Emma Shaw could hardly concentrate on what she had to say, because John Rourke had told her that he loved her.

She started to light a cigarette, consciously steadying her hands, but John beat her to it with his battered old Zippo windlighter. She watched his eyes across its blue-yellow flame for an instant longer than needed, then forced herself to look away as she exhaled. The plotting table in the captured Nazi briefing room was the only source of light now, casting shadows on all the faces, masking all the eyes. What did Annie Rubenstein think of her? And Natalia Tiemerovna, for God's sake?! Was she the scarlet woman in their eyes, the homewrecker?

But, Emma Shaw didn't care.

As John had held her in his arms, he whispered to her, "If Sarah's alive, she'll be leaving me. I don't have any right to ask you to love me, and I'm not made to cheat, so we can't—not now—"

"I understand," she'd told him, just feeling him

holding her, his arms and his coat all wrapped around her, making her feel little and vulnerable like she hadn't felt since she was a very young girl. She didn't understand, not really, except that John was possessed of an inner morality which was more than a personal code; it was the very fibre of his being. As such, it was inviolate. And, she would abide by it, even if she'd had another choice.

Now, she wanted him lying beside her, holding her, coming on top of her, penetrating her; she didn't want to be talking about wars and airplanes and all the things around which she'd built her life.

But, she had to.

"The remaining aircraft in my squadron are landing, one at a time, for refueling. The Nazi fuel is a little rich, but we can handle it. The availability of fuel reserves increases our potential for operational capability considerably. Our mission was initially designed for a punitive strike against enemy forces here as a backup to your ground operation. If that proved unnecessary, for either of the obvious reasons, we were to hit the enemy, if such still existed and return to base or assist however we could in evacuation of this facility. For that purpose, we have a V/STOL cargo lifter accompanied by four additional fighter aircraft which should be landing within the hour. The evac will be to CSVN 84211, the USS *Paladin*.

"The *Paladin* is a Geronimo Class submersible carrier, with nuclear strike capabilities, should such be required. It's as safe as church, so to speak. And, her flight deck is large enough, when surfaced, to accept the cargo lifters one at a time."

154

"What about this facility, Fräulein Commander?" the German liason officer, Gefen, asked. Commander Washington was predicted to survive, Emma Shaw had been told, but at the present was unable to fulfill his duties. Gefen, as the next highest in rank, was assuming Commander Washington's command function concerning the Allied commando unit.

"This facility, considering that it has been taken by Allied forces and that there are enemy prisoners with which we have to deal, must be held. As it was explained to me, control of this facility could provide some significant strategic advantages for our forces against Eden forces located in the western portion of the continent, where, as we all know, some of the enemy staging for attacks against Hawaii will take place. Colonel Elizabeth Fullerton—" Emma Shaw consulted her watch "—should be hitting the silk over this site in another six hours and ten minutes with two companies of Marine Airborne. We intend to keep this little spot, destroying it only if the tactical situation dictates that we must.

"Until Colonel Fullerton's personnel arrive, however, those who will be left here will require all the help they can get in the event of attack by a strong enemy force. My squadron, under my second-in-command, will remain at ready in order to reinforce your position here in just such a contingency. The enemy gunships can be utilized as well; we've got enough people to man them, I understand. I'm operating under very specific orders as concerns prioritizing the evacuation of certain key personnel

155

from this facility." And, she looked at John Rourke directly.

"I can be of more use here," he told her, his voice very low, almost a whisper holding a hint of anger.

"Allied Command doesn't think so, John. Your value isn't in dispute. But, you're too important a prize to the enemy, dead or alive." John said nothing and she went on. "That goes for the entire Rourke Family. If found alive, my orders were to evacuate to the *Paladin*. From there, I don't know."

John stood up, looked down at her and said, "I'll have to see to Sarah, that she's well enough to travel. Annie?"

His daughter stood up, joining him as he almost marched to the door.

Emma Shaw stared after them for a few seconds, then resumed her briefing.

Chapter Twenty-Five

"I don't like it! He's too good, Father!"

Deitrich Zimmer had always thought that a sense of humor was important to the overall well-being of any individual, and he allowed himself a few seconds of laughter now. Finally, he told his son, "You worry too much, Martin!" Laughing still, he added, "This is all part of a plan I have refined over many years in waiting. Now, it can be fulfilled. This plan upon which we have embarked is the most desperate gamble in all of human history, my son, so you should feel that you are a part of history. Because, whatever the result, the world will be changed forever, whether we win or lose. And, if we win, we will realize the dream of Alexander and Caesar and Hitler, be sole masters of the planet. Such a prize is worth such a risk."

"My mother's programming will not be strong enough to overcome her natural instincts," Martin said definitively. His son was terribly single-minded at times, Zimmer reflected. Martin went on, saying,

"All her adult life, she has not only been John Rourke's wife, but, until the Night of the War, been committed to the principles of nonviolence. And you expect her to kill her husband!"

Deitrich Zimmer's hands rested on his desktop and he stood up, then began to walk across the broad expanse of the low-ceilinged room that was his laboratory office. Beyond the blank walls where no windows could be cut because of the demands of security, there lay one of the most spectacular views on the planet, the Himalayas. This was, indeed, the eternally snow-covered roof of the world.

He was at once its master and its prisoner. With his armies moving across North America and his naval and air forces poised for the death blow against Hawaii and Mid-Wake beneath the sea, all that remained to consider was New Germany itself and the comparatively inconsequential civilizations of Europe, Australia and Lydveldid Island. New Germany would be a formidable opponent, but with the power of the Trans-Global Alliance effectively neutralized, New Germany would fall.

Unless, of course, the nuclear detonations which would invariably ensue did, indeed, precipitate the final destruction of the planet itself.

"You have not read Milton, have you, Martin?"

"Milton who? You know I don't like to read."

Deitrich Zimmer counted himself a failure in the raising of his son, but soon the process of genetic altering could begin. The remains of Hilter, recovered from deep within the mountain community in what had been upstate New York, were even now being brought to him. Still, Martin would always be a disappointment. But, Zimmer loved the boy. "I meant the poet," Deitrich Zimmer said finally, smiling indulgently. "John Milton. His most notable work is entitled *Paradise Lost.*"

"So?"

"Like Satan, I too would rather rule in Hell than serve in Heaven, Martin. Do you understand that?"

Martin didn't answer, but that was as Deitrich Zimmer had expected. He said, "Martin, consider the following. With the medical technology that I possess, you and I are essentially immortal. When these bodies which we wear," and Zimmer gestured across his own body, "begin to decay, they can be replaced by cloned bodies already waiting for us in cryogenic sleep. The electrochemical impulses which inspire our minds with what is called memory and thought, are constantly recorded, so even a sudden death will not bring death. The dream of immortality is ours, yet we are not its slaves. Should either of us at some time in the distant future truly tire of life, we can leave it. This is the ultimate freedom, the ultimate power. We will be like the ancient gods, Martin, but unlike them we shall not fade from memory, shall not perish except by our own hands, by our own wills. This I have given to you, and you doubt that I realized that your mother would almost certainly so resist her programming that she would not kill your father? It was even more obvious to me than it is to you, and I do not share her genes. She will go so far as to attempt the act, and your biological father, John Rourke, will be forced to kill her and thus be destroyed or be forced to submit to me so that I will free her.

159

"And, his submission will be total, Martin! Total! John Rourke will be the slave of my will, of your will. Think, lad! He will be the visible leader of the Earth until the time is right that he should be replaced—by you, son! Trust to my plan."

Deitrich Zimmer returned to his desk as Martin, silently, sullenly, walked from the room. Martin was ill-prepared for greatness, however Deitrich Zimmer had tried to raise the boy. Martin was self-indulgent, petulant, dulled by excess. But that would change, too.

Chapter Twenty-Six

The *Paladin* was as magnificent as it was enormous. Sharing the V/STOL fighter's cockpit with Emma Shaw, John Rourke was truly in awe at such a magnificent example of man's domination over nature as was this undersea vessel they now approached.

Larger by far than twentieth-century aircraft-carrier surface ships, its upper deck was of sufficient length that a Concorde, the fastest passenger aircraft of that century, could have landed in perfect safety. But, beneath this deck, there were tunnels, themselves the size of World War II carriers it seemed, the tunnel mouths opening and closing with and against the seas surrounding them, opening for takeoffs and landings of fighter aircraft and larger fighter bombers, then closing again, the water within returned to the sea, becoming safe environments for the boarding and disembarkation of aircraft, servicing maintenance, all the necessary functions. During battle, the elevators within the decks could raise and lower from airlocked chambers below, inserting fresh and already-manned aircraft, retrieving damaged aircraft or injured personnel. Refueling during combat was accomplished by remote robotics.

The aircraft themselves, such as the V/STOL flown by Emma Shaw, were capable of operating as minisubmersibles or fully combat-worthy fighter planes, their pilots equally as at home within the sea or in the air.

These submersible carriers and the aircraft which called them homebase comprised the most versatile fighting machines ever devised, and they were designed for the maintenance of peace, the prevention of war.

And, although John Rourke felt in awe of the technology represented here, he felt greater respect for their mission. With such machines, a world could be taken. But that was not their mission. And Deitrich Zimmer and his Nazi followers knew that, which was why Zimmer had opted for the use of nuclear weapons. Otherwise, his forces would not have had a chance.

The water rushed over and around the V/STOL's fuselage, the sensation of motion wildly exciting, like that of a roller-coaster, and John Rourke realized that his hands were clamped to the arms of the copilot's seat. For a moment, he could imagine himself careening through the galaxy in some space-opera film, but rather than star fields, schools of deep-sea life—fish and squid in a wild pageant of color—surrounded him.

"John? Would you like to take the controls for a few seconds, just to feel that you've done it? It could only be for a few seconds. It flies just like a regular aircraft when the controls are on manual."

"Are you sure?"

"It'll be all right."

John Rourke's hands reached out to the yoke, grasped it, his fingers flexing over it.

"Ready, John?"

"I think so."

She laughed. "On three it's yours. One . . . Two . . . Three!"

There was suddenly power in the yoke and as Rourke's hands closed more tightly over it, the aircraft's nose dipped slightly, the school of translucent fish which had already been fleeing the approaching craft vectoring off in response to his slight course change, swimming madly, but effortlessly, it seemed.

"Ha! This is wonderful!" Rourke almost shouted.

"Hold her steady, John, just like an aircraft. Don't think water and fish. It's just heavy air, okay?"

"Okay, Emma." He felt like a child, or as best John Rourke could remember being a child, a sense of freedom and wild wonder filling him, like the first time he'd soloed a conventional jet aircraft so many centuries ago. "Magnificent! I envy you getting to do this! I really do!"

"When there's time, I can get you the instruction you'd need. With your flying skills, it'd be a snap for you."

"I don't know about that—the snap part! Take the controls back before I get us into trouble, Emma."

"On three, then. One . . . Two . . . Three!"

And the power left the yoke beneath John

163

Rourke's hands and he sagged back into his seat, the smile on his face still something he could feel . . .

James Darkwood waited in the observation deck, his eyes riveted on the fighter squadron homing in on the *Paladin*'s landing bays. And, even though he was aboard what was perhaps the most powerful war machine ever on earth, he felt naked without a sidearm. Nearly as uncomfortable as he did in khakis. He had worked in Naval Intelligence as a part of Trans-Global Alliance Intelligence for so long that it seemed like forever, and shaking the habit of constantly being on guard, even had it been possible, would not have been prudent. This was his first sea duty in years, and would not last long. He was here for a conference and nothing more, then he'd get his new orders and return to the trenches. If the Nazis escalated their use of nuclear weapons, the world would be a battlefield sooner than he cared to consider.

His illustrious ancestor, Jason Darkwood, had helped to eliminate a nuclear threat over a century ago, John Rourke beside him, the entire Rourke family, too, and, of course, the almost legendary Sebastian, Jason Darkwood's sometimes cryptic black first officer and lifelong best friend.

Perhaps it was the fate of the Darkwoods to fight beside the Rourkes. James Darkwood did not know. But he did know that this would, somehow, be the fight for the future of the world. He felt that in his bones, as a stirring, a shiver along the length of his spine.

"Commander?"

He hadn't worn the rank that long and, for a moment, Darkwood didn't realize that it was he who was being addressed. After a second, though, he turned around, already seeing the seaman's face reflected in the viewing port. "Yes?"

"Begging the commander's pardon, but Captain Mallory requests that you join her when she welcomes General Rourke, sir."

Darkwood smiled, saying, "Let me tell you, son, if the Captain addresses John Rourke as 'General,' she'll be getting off to a start on a sore point. He may be a general, but he prefers 'Doctor' or just 'John.' Dr. Rourke isn't one to stand on ceremony and he seems to abhor titles of rank. So, give yourself an edge if you get to meet him. Trust me, he won't put you on report if you call him 'Doctor,' but he won't let you in on his good side right away if you call him 'General.'"

"Aye, sir."

"I'll be along directly, sailor."

"Aye, sir."

And Darkwood turned back toward the sea. This was a beautiful planet, and there was a strong chance that it would die. "Shit," he muttered, shaking his head at his own reflection as he donned his cap and started walking.

Chapter Twenty-Seven

Sarah Rourke's eyes squinted shut against the brightness of the light, and her stomach felt uneasy with the fresh surge of motion. Where she was made absolutely no sense at all. She'd seen clouds and water and faces peering down on her with great feeling, but she was lost.

And she was confused beyond any similar feelings she had ever had before. Was she Almost-Sarah, or was she Sarah Rourke? Inside her, like something deep and dark and hidden, there was a purpose. And, she knew the purpose. For some reason, John had shot in the very moments after she'd borne their third child, a son. She remembered the fire and the shooting and she remembered a face peering down at her and the face was vivid. It was John's face, but somehow different, in a way she had never seen his face before. There was a momentary flash from the muzzle of his gun and everything after that was gone until she awakened.

Were these her memories, or memories of the real

Sarah Rourke? Were they one in the same. If she were Almost-Sarah, she shared each and every one of the real Sarah's memories, because she was as much the real Sarah as the real Sarah. If she was Almost-Sarah, her body was genetically identical to that of the original because she was a clone. If she was Almost-Sarah, her mind bore the same memories. The brain, after all, was an organ, like any other, its functions vastly more sophisticated in their way. And the input to the brain was what made memory, what determined judgement, and the input to her brain was that of Sarah Rourke. Whether she was the real Sarah or only Almost-Sarah, she was Sarah.

And John had shot Sarah in the head, all but killing her. For some reason, she thought the reason for his uncharacteristically horrible deed was his wild passion for Natalia. But, it was hard to imagine Natalia condoning such a thing, nearly as hard to imagine as John doing it.

But John had done it. She learned later, from Dr. Zimmer, who had saved her life through his miraculous surgical techniques, that John had attempted to kill the original Martin, her son, and John's, whom Zimmer had raised as his own child. It was odd to imagine Zimmer, a Nazi, being capable of such kindness. It barely made any sense at all. She puzzled over that as she was wheeled along a hospital corridor. But, unlike those in any hospital she had ever seen, the corridor walls were of steel, gleaming and bright, more like an operating theater might be than any ordinary corridor.

But John had killed one of Martin's clones. That

168

was bad enough. Dr. Zimmer said that Martin had uncovered what had been done to her, and by whom. Perhaps John had been seized by some momentary madness, Dr. Zimmer explained. Whatever the reason, killing the clone of Martin was an attempt to disguise the truth, which of course was also terribly uncharacteristic of John. To John, truth was the greatest passion, and from that passion sprang every other passion of his life.

The most telling of Dr. Zimmer's arguments was when he admitted to her who he was. "I was the man responsible for the attack on the hospital. It was a murder raid, of course, the intent to kill your husband. But after your husband shot you, he in turn was critically injured by one of my men. I found this baby whom I named Martin, your baby. You will hear many evil things of me in the world outside, Sarah, and they will almost all be true. I am the Nazi leader, I plan for war, I intend to achieve world domination or perish in the attempt. Perhaps my motivations for saving your baby and eventually restoring you were the inverse of the terrible deed committed by your husband, John Rourke. There is a saying, which I'm sure you know: There is a little bad in the best of us, and a little good in the worst of us.

"Your life and the life of your son, Martin, are my 'little good,' as it were. I feel, at least, that my little good was of greater import than anything I have done that is evil. So, perhaps someday, if you view my record as a man, you will find the same compassion for me in your heart which I found for you in mine."

169

These memories were real, but were they hers, or implanted into Almost-Sarah? Did that make a difference?

She remembered John shooting her. That was undeniable. And, she had nearly as concrete proof of his killing of the man he'd thought was their son, Martin. If he did not deny killing Martin's clone, then it was certain that his intent was to kill Martin and just as certain that he would attempt to do so again. He could not be allowed to do that.

There was only one way to assure that he did not kill their son, his sworn enemy. And that was to kill John. Her life was in ruins, but with John dead perhaps Martin could be made to feel safe in the world away from Dr. Zimmer's control, so that he would come away with her, learn that the Nazi ideology—which Deitrich Zimmer freely admitted teaching Martin—was wrong. Perhaps Martin, through his knowledge of both sides of the conflict, could bring about peace, allaying the relentless momentum toward war. It would be a war from which the human race might never recover.

And, that might only be possible if she killed her husband.

Her head ached with a terrible fury and she felt tears welling up in her eyes. As she closed her eyes, she saw John's face as he stood over her, gun in hand aimed at her head.

170

Chapter Twenty-Eight

"I am all right, really," Wolfgang Mann announced as he eased himself into a chair to John Rourke's immediate right. John clapped him on the shoulder, nodding approvingly.

Emma Shaw felt very much like a little mouse who had scurried out of her hole in the baseboard and suddenly found herself transported through some freak of time and nature to the most momentous moment in history.

Everyone was here. Aside from Captain Mallory, commanding the *Paladin*, there was Admiral Thelma Hayes, commander of United States Forces and, only hours ago, elevated to Supreme Commander, Trans-Global Alliance. There was Field Marshal Heinrich M. C. Krause, commander of the forces of New Germany. Marine Corps Lieutenant General Thomas Wilson, chief of Allied commando operations lit a cigarette. Doctor Thorn Rolvaag, the scientist who claimed that the world might end, drummed his fingers softly on the conference table.

James Darkwood, whose reputation as the most intrepid agent in Allied Intelligence must have preceded him everywhere, merely surveyed the faces at the table. His own face seemed identical with that of his illustrious ancestor Jason Darkwood, whose picture hung in the main entrance of the Naval Academy at Mid-Wake alongside that of John Paul Jones. James Darkwood looked incredibly handsome without being pretty, his wavy hair, the well-defined bone structure, the intensity of his eyes. It wasn't uncommon to see a young female Midshipman standing in front of Jason Darkwood's picture there at the academy, the thoughts running through her mind obvious.

And the entire Rourke Family, except for John's wife, Sarah, was present as well—Michael, Annie, Paul and Major Natalia Tiemerovna. Why she herself—Emma Shaw—was here was a mystery. She had nowhere near the rank required.

As if her senses were not sufficiently reeling, only moments before entering the *Paladin's* conference center she received a message that her father, Tim Shaw, had been injured in battle with terrorists in Hawaii, but had made it to help, was now hospitalized and expected to fully recover. A second message came seconds after the first, from her brother Ed, confirming that their father was "banged up" but expected to be back to duty within a couple of days. There was also a request: "When you get the chance, Emma, try to talk some sense into him, huh? He could've had a SWAT Team with him, but he went after this Nazi asshole all alone and almost bought the farm. But he nailed the guy and then got

172

the three triggermen that were there to back the guy up."

She left the vid-booth, ordering that the messages be erased, then proceeded to the conference center, wiping imaginary moisture from the palms of her hands along the sides of her skirt before she shook any of the offered hands.

She was looking to stand by a bulkhead somewhere, out of the way. There were electronic name locaters at each chair along all sides of the table and hers was to the left of John Rourke. Was she officially recognized as his woman, a part of the Family? If that was the only reason she was here, she was not happy for it, although being John's woman was her ultimate joy—or would be. But, she was her own person. John knew that, respected that.

Emma Shaw would wait and see.

Admiral Hayes called the conference to order, not standing, merely clearing her throat and beginning to speak. "Several potentially cataclysmic events confront us, and they are all interlinked. Their outcome could affect the future of life on this planet. General Wilson, give us an update."

"Yes, ma'am." General Wilson stood. He was a small man, just a hair under Emma's own height, but he was burly chested, powerfully built. His voice veritably boomed as he spoke. "We confront several rather disturbing possibilities. In order of occurrence, the allies of our Nazi enemies, Eden, have perfected several variants of deadly biological agents. Thanks to Commander Shaw—" Emma was stunned that General Wilson had mentioned her name, even knew her name, "—much of the bio

173

threat has been, at least temporarily, neutralized with the destruction of Eden City Plant 234, this only made possible by the intelligence work of Commander Darkwood and his associate from New Germany, and the work of many others who shall remain unsung, I know. Given time, however, like all bad pennies, the Eden bio effort will resurface and come back to haunt us." He tapped a chocolate brown finger alongside his bulbous nose. "The bio effort's destruction will only slow down the time-table for one of the crises facing us.

"Next," General Wilson continued, "came the discovery by Dr. Rolvaag, which has been confirmed by scientists all over the free world, that there is a volcanic fissure opening in the ocean beneath us, spreading inexorably it seems toward the Pacific coast of North America. It is Dr. Rolvaag's considered opinion, on which he will soon elaborate, that this fissure can only be stopped—and then it's only a gamble, not a certainty—by the employment of a large number of nuclear weapons, their explosive force to close the fissure.

"Thirdly," General Wilson went on, "is the immediate nuclear threat posed by the detonation by air burst of a tactical thermonuclear device. This escalates the as yet undeclared war, by higher stakes than we would have thought possible less than twenty-four hours ago. And, I believe Dr. Rourke has some news that is equally alarming."

Emma looked at John. He'd said nothing to her of anything like this. He squeezed her hand under the table, then leaned back. "Will it bother anyone if I smoke?"

"Not at all, sir," Admiral Hayes responded.

John reached to Natalia's cigarettes on the table, saying, "May I?"

Natalia nodded. John took a cigarette, fired it in the flame of his antique windlighter. As he exhaled, he spoke. "Paul and I discovered something quite alarming, just prior to the death of Wolfgang Mann."

Some of the men and women about the table audibly sucked in breath.

John went on, looking at Wolfgang Mann as the Generaloberst stared in amazement at John. John smiled, saying, "Relax, old friend. The man who died was *almost* Wolfgang Mann. He was a clone, a nearly perfect duplicate—"

"A clone!" Dr. Rolvaag murmured in astonishment.

"Yes. Almost perfect, and I suspect a preproduction model, as it were, somewhere along the prototype chain. Because Dr. Zimmer arranged things so that we would realize the counterfeit Wolfgang Mann was just that—counterfeit. I have substantial reason to believe that Dr. Zimmer has duplicated not only my entire Family, but more importantly to the general interest of the war effort, himself and the man he calls his son, Martin Zimmer, the leader of Eden. I further have reason to believe that Dr. Zimmer has perfected the means by which to effectively record the electromagnetic impulses of the brain—record thought and memory, then download that data into a recipient, a clone. Zimmer has essentially made himself immortal, unkillable."

"Explain, Doctor," Admiral Hayes said, her face expressionless, her eyes pinpoints of light.

"Certainly, at least within the limits of my abilities. Cloning as we know, is based on the theory and practice that each cell of a living organism contains the entire genetic fingerprint. A cell from a finger, or almost anywhere in the body, for example, if grown under appropriate laboratory conditions into an entire organism could reproduce the host in complete detail. In my day, it was done with frogs and organisms less complicated than man, but was theoretically possible, in fact the subject of some excellent science fiction. I believe that Dr. Zimmer has perfected this process. Considering his skills, considering the time elapsed since my day and this, and the enormous medical and scientific strides taken, it's hardly out of the question at all. At the least, my Family faces a personal crisis. In all likelihood, Zimmer and his self-styled son have placed themselves in a position where they will effectively never die. In a worst-case scenario, Zimmer might well have battalions of fighting men who were the subject of special genetic engineering, perfect warriors, each identical to the next and none indispensable because each could be replaced with his own carbon copy."

"Carbon?" Admiral Hayes repeated.

John smiled. "An ancient means by which copies were made. A duplicate, identical in virtually all respects to the original."

"What you're proposing would alter the course of warfare for all time," General Wilson suggested.

"Indeed. With his latest scientific weapon, if

176

Zimmer wished, he could mount a war which destroyed the planet to the point where life could not be sustained, then through cryogenic Sleep—which we all know, my Family especially so—and his cloning process, he could awaken in some distant future and go on forever, merely giving armies time to commence growing two decades before his own awakening. He would win, ladies and gentlemen. Zimmer would realize the dream of every conqueror since the dawn of time. He would rule the world and stay around forever to run it, never having to leave it. When one body became worn or diseased, he'd merely download his latest recording from the brain into a waiting body kept in some type of stasis and, in the most literal sense, be born again."

Chapter Twenty-Nine

"You're thinking that's what has happened to Sarah, aren't you? That she's been cloned?" John smiled, shrugged his eyebrows, sipped at his drink. The small bar in the officers' mess was more elaborate than some of its onshore counterparts where Emma Shaw had shared a drink with a man, but no man like this. John Thomas Rourke was as much the stuff of preposterous tall tales and fact-based legend as Kit Carson, Wild Bill Hickok or Buffalo Bill, as much the heroic historical figure as George Washington, Daniel Boone or Teddy Roosevelt. When he didn't answer her question about Sarah's being cloned, Emma Shaw tapped him on the shoulder and he turned and looked at her. She looked him right back, saying, "Don't you?"

John's fingers played with a thin, dark tobacco cigar, his lighter beside his drink. "Yes."

"Isn't there some way you can tell?"

"Yes, at least I think so," he answered.

"Go ahead and light the cigar. You've smoked

them around me before."

"You're sure you won't mind?" John asked her.

"I won't mind your smoking the damned cigar! But, will you just tell me what's happening? Please, John?"

John shrugged his shoulders under the elbow-patched black military sweater he wore. Even though Emma Shaw saw no evidence of the fact, he would, of course, be armed; but, he always was. She was armed as well, which was strictly against regulations, of course. Only with a knife, a switch-blade her father had given her, which she kept regularly in a pocket of her flight suit and now carried in the purse that was on the barstool beside them.

"So, what do you think?"

"About what?"

"About Sarah! How would you tell, I mean?"

"Very simple, really," John answered, smiling indulgently at her, his high forehead furrowing just slightly. "If she's Sarah, regardless of any programming that Deitrich Zimmer might have inflicted upon her, she won't kill me. If she is a clone, she'll possibly kill me. Either way, she'll try. Zimmer wouldn't have let us get her so easily otherwise."

"Easily!"

"Emma, he's probably got a half dozen of each of us—Sarah, me, Annie and Paul, Michael and Natalia. And Wolfgang. If you'd been with us in cryogenic Sleep in New Germany, he'd have a few spares of you lying around. Trust me on that. I'm learning how the man thinks. And, he thinks very well, however twisted his purposes. Either way, though, I suspect he's counting on the fact that Sarah or her clone won't succeed, but that I'll be convinced enough that she is Sarah that I'll come to him for a deal."

"Would you?" Emma Shaw asked him pointedly, picking up his lighter, opening it awkwardly, rolling its striking wheel under her thumb. She fingered the instrument as she closed it, thinking how smoothly, how effortlessly John made the thing make fire for him every time.

"Yes—go to him, I mean. What I said to you earlier, about loving you. I meant that. And whoever the real Sarah is, she'll leave me. You see, I'm convinced that the real Wolfgang Mann is the Wolfgang Mann with us. I had him scanned. There aren't any microprocessors in his head, or at least nothing we can detect. The same for Sarah. And Wolf is too much like Wolf to be anyone else but who he is. It's a gut-level feeling that I can't really explain. Forgive my lapse from logic."

"Forgiven."

"Thank you. But, there is some logic at work. In order to reinforce the idea that Sarah is Sarah, so I'll trust her and walk into Zimmer's trap, Zimmer gave us the real Wolfgang. I think the assumption is valid. And Sarah might really be Sarah, or might not. Either way, when she attempts to kill me, and hopefully fails, I'll have no choice but to go to the scource of her programming. He'll try to take me, download my mind into one of the clones, at the same time programming the clone to behave with a certain set of responses which will make the clone obey Zimmer's will. Then kill me, of course."

181

"Oh! Of course," Emma Shaw said, nodding, not knowing what else to say to someone who so matter-of-factly discussed his impending death. "Then what?"

"Well, I'd be dead, and he'd have the fake John Rourke run the world for him for a time, I'd suspect. Only logical, if one thinks like Deitrich Zimmer. But, you have to admit that it's an interesting hypothesis. Would I still be me, only different, with a duplicate body and all of my own memories and thoughts and ideas, just a few extras added? And, if one discounts the extras, would I be me, truly me? Would Zimmer undo his own plans by recreating me?"

"You lost me somewhere in metaphysics."

John laughed, sipped again at his drink, asked, "Sure the cigar's not bothering you?"

"It's not bothering me."

"Anyway, it's not all that into metaphysics. It's merely advanced biology. I had a friend in the days Before the Night of the War who spoke about cloning sometimes. He was convinced that once we could find a way of dealing with the morality and dealing with the mechanics of recording the brain—and any sort of taped recording is nothing more than the capturing of electromagnetic impulses, which is what the brain runs on, of course—that cloning would eventually bring man immortality. He was right, my friend, that is."

"But what about the clones? Don't they have rights as people instead of spare parts?"

"If the brain is allowed to grow in a stimulation vacuum, it's rather like a battery fresh from the

182

factory. The old kind of storage battery."

"I know what you mean—about the batteries," she added.

"Fine. The battery doesn't really do anything, nor does it have any capabilities—not even potential energy—until it's charged. Once it's charged, then it's capable of a wide range of activities, depending on how it's employed, for good or bad."

"But, they're still people."

"Well, exactly, but Zimmer doesn't have to worry about questions like what's moral, what's immoral, because he's amoral, and he has the technology to do what he wants. So, he has clones."

"And you think that no matter how he programmed the real Sarah, he couldn't overcome her natural better instincts?"

"No, not really. Sarah's killed in self-defense. I imagine that Zimmer would have worked up some sort of scenario where I'm out to kill Martin, our son. Something like that, giving Sarah a morally acceptable reason to kill, in defense of her child. She'd have to be convinced that somehow I slipped a trolley—"

"Slipped a trolley . . ."

"Old expression—that I wasn't playing with a full deck, had a few screws loose, like that?"

"Right."

"Anyway, God only knows what Zimmer would have told her, but it would have to be something he planted in her as a memory, not just a story, so something wrapped around real events, not faked ones, just seen from a different point of view. He could have dragged Natalia into it, anything.

183

Anyway, the thing about the real Sarah—and maybe a clone, too—is that I can read her moods, her body language well enough that I'll have a little advance warning and be able to react in time to stop her. Whether she's really Sarah or the clone, who, in a way, is really Sarah, too. I mean, if there is a soul—"

"Metaphysics!"

"Right," he nodded, smiling, "then it would stand to reason that the soul would accompany intellectual awareness. So, maybe both people would be Sarah."

"One soul in two bodies."

"Hmm—odd idea," John said, nodding his head again. "Either that, or the clone wouldn't have a soul, or the clone would have a different soul. Then, where did it come from? Where did it enter the body? In the petri dish, as it were? Lots of tough questions, both philosophically and morally, represented by the mere concept of cloning. And, if you add the idea that a clone would be kept as a nonsentient spare-parts bank, well, then there's really a moral dilemma.

"And," John continued, his eyes apparently riveted to the glowing tip of his cigar, "there's another interesting idea. What if two distinctly separate but perfectly identical beings having the same cognitive experiences, etc., were able to function as one? They ever do a remake of *The Corsican Brothers?* It was an old film with Douglas Fairbanks, Jr., I think."

"I don't think so, but I know the story. You mean like that, in the movie?"

184

"Not quite," John told her, his eyes not yet abandoning the study of his cigar's tip. "But a shared consciousness. If there's truth to the idea of mental telepathy and similar phenomena, which I know for fact there is, since my daughter seems to have cornered the market on it, then it would only make sense that two identical beings would be able to communicate in such a manner. And that is how we should be able to defeat Deitrich Zimmer, with any luck."

Emma Shaw admitted it. "You've lost me completely."

One nice thing about John was that although he was utterly intelligent, he never rubbed it in. He didn't now. "Let's say that Deitrich Zimmer and I have one special thing in common—we both believe that it pays to plan ahead. Whatever he'd call it, however he'd phrase it, the idea is the same. Whether I have the real Sarah or a clone, there's another Sarah available to him, up and running, fully programmed, all dressed and ready, just in case. Like carrying spare magazines for a pistol, a spare flint for a lighter, be ready for whatever contingency arrives by anticipating it in such a fashion that an appropriate response can be instantaneous. Good, common sense. He has common sense, no morality, no decency, but good common sense. And, so do I."

"So you could use Sarah, or her clone, as a telepathic link to Sarah or her clone or another clone, if it wasn't Sarah in the first place or Sarah were—" She shut up.

"Dead," John said very quietly, but not matter-of-factly. "Yes. Communicate with that, that—that

185

Almost-Sarah and reason with her, tell her the truth about whatever lies she's been fed and gain her help from inside against Deitrich Zimmer. You see, to kill Zimmer, which I must do, the only way is to kill the clones—"

"Oh, God—just taking innocent lives like that—"

"I don't see any choice, God help us, and not just his but—"

"You couldn't, John. I know you."

"I may have to kill the clones of Sarah and the children and Natalia, and even myself. Without the cloned recipient, even if Zimmer were to be able to download a recording of the genuine article's mind, he wouldn't fool anyone. And, without the recordings, the clones would be fully grown infants. I don't know," he added, taking a swallow of his drink, then another, draining the glass.

"Aw, John . . ."

"But the only way to stop Deitrich Zimmer from eventually ruling the world and employing his Nazi concepts of racial purity and totalitarianism, evil winning, the only way to prevent that is to destroy the original, the clones, the recordings of the mind. For that, I'll need help inside. I'll go to him, bring the real Sarah or her clone, whoever she is, making him think that despite my best efforts, he's won, then get him. That's why I shouldn't have told you."

"I don't understand, John."

"It wasn't fair to tell you that I love you, because if everything worked out so that I survived, then fine, I could have told you then. But there's a solid chance that I'll die, and I mean really die. Taking the clones of myself with me. They have to be destroyed if

186

there's any chance that Zimmer could triumph. And, I'd have to go. With me dead, he could clone away to his heart's content and he wouldn't have my mind, wouldn't have me, wouldn't be able to bring about what I'm sure he's planning. That's the trouble with making people more important than they really are. All I ever wanted to do was ensure the safety of my family. I had no aspirations toward acclaim, statues like that God-awful thing on top of the Retreat back in what used to be Georgia and is now so vilely called Eden. There's nothing special about me and there never was. I just happened to be in the wrong place at the right time, and because of that, people think I'm something—"

"Just a second. Just one damn minute, John Rourke. You are special, damn it! You're the bravest, the best—"

"Come on, huh? I thought you really understood who I am and—"

"I do. You're the one who doesn't, John. I'm no student of history, but I know enough about it to know that in the last half of the twentieth century, if there were real heroes, nobody ever learned about them. And there had to be firemen and policemen and teachers and soldiers, men and women who did what they had to do whatever the cost to themselves. But, it was an age when everyone with any power in the media—the dissemination of information—pushed the idea of collectivism, denied that individualism was anything at all, even existed. And, if you tell me that you're not a hero, John Rourke, then I'll tell you that you're full of shit. Because you'd be believing the crap. They're starting to push it again

187

today, for God's sake! That individual effort doesn't count, but collective effort does.

"My father," Emma said, starting to light another cigarette, John lighting it (effortlessly) for her, "is a prime example. He just nearly went out and got himself killed doing something by himself, and he's going to do it again. And I'm not going to try to stop him. My brother wants me to. Eddie's telling me, 'Gotta get the old man outa thinking he's a friggin' one-man army' and shit like that. Nuts to that! Things don't have to be decided by committees as long as there's a human brain around, and individualism isn't only the basis for all genuine achievement, it's the damn basis for all thought! Don't tell me you aren't a hero, John. The world needs heroes, like you, because you're real, and if you can't look at what you've done in your life with any degree of objectivity, I can.

"Twice, not just once," she told him, tapping her nails on the bartop for emphasis, "you almost single-handedly saved all of humanity from totalitarianism, you survived the end of the world—twice! That damn statue of you on top of your mountain, back in Georgia, John. Whether you like it or not, whether it embarrasses you or not, you really did that! You shot down the last enemy helicopter with a damn .45 automatic! And the American flag was flying in the breeze behind you because you put it there because a friend of yours, a man who was another hero, died trying to do the same damn thing a thousand miles away when you destroyed the enemy's chance of surviving the fire in the atmosphere! You're history, living fucking history, John. When you touch me, I

188

have a hard time not fainting! And I'm not the damn fainting type, John. Grow up, huh? Accept yourself for what you are, and realize what you mean to others.

"If you go and get yourself dead," she told him, her fists balled up now, her cigarette burning in the ashtray beside his cigar, "I'll be a fucking widow before I've ever been—before I've ever been fucked, damn it! I love you and so does your Family and you can't just go off—" And then she shut up. She had to, because he was just what she said he was, a hero.

John Rourke swallowed hard—she could see his Adam's apple move. He stubbed out her cigarette and put his cigar into his teeth. "There's more than an hour before the briefing resumes. I can't agree with your exalted opinion of me, however flattering it would be, but I see a point you made."

"Which one?"

"About becoming a widow before you've ever been—"

"Fucked."

"Yes."

"And?"

"Let's correct that situation, Emma."

"Do—you—do you—" Her hands were suddenly folded in her lap and she looked down at her hands, not at him. "You—but what about?"

"If I were a hero, I'd have a good answer for everything, wouldn't I? Hoist on your own petard, as it were, hm? If I were a hero, I wouldn't—"

She looked up at him as she told him, "Oh, yes you would, John Rourke."

"I love you. I've said that to three women in my

189

life, in the way I mean it now. To Sarah, to Natalia, but never to either of them in the way I'm saying it to you. I love you, Emma Shaw."

"Then let's do . . . My cabin or yours?"

John laughed; and, for a moment, she didn't know what to think.

He told her, "Rather stuffy fellow that I am, right now I think I'd be perfectly willing to do it right here."

Emma Shaw, her voice so soft that she could barely hear herself, said, "I'm yours. I always have been."

John Rourke leaned toward her from his barstool and kissed her lips and she felt she would melt.

Chapter Thirty

It had never been like this, making love.

The touching of two bodies, hands against parts of the flesh where hands except one's own never touched.

It was feeling, in its most literal and at once figurative sense. His fingertips caressed her breasts, his lips her nipples, his body enveloping her own, invading her, bending her to his will in a way she had never known before.

"I love you," he whispered.

"And I love you," she answered. "It's funny, but I think I've loved you since the first moment I saw you. But you were married and—"

"I know. Be quiet and kiss me," he told her.

She obeyed, and inwardly laughed at herself. Obeying a man! My God, how far she'd come, but was it regression or progression? He touched, she responded, but she wanted to. So, was that obedience, was that submission, or fulfillment?

There had never been fulfillment like this, so deep,

so powerful, and fulfillment was merely a thought, his body so wonderfully laboring above her, making her body move in rhythm to his. The roughness of his skin, the force of him made her pulse, made her body vibrate uncontrollably. She had lost control, and she had wanted to lose control all of her life but one could not give up control; it had to be taken, then surrendered because there was no choice to do otherwise.

"You will marry me."

"Yes."

"Do you love me?"

"Like I've never loved," she whispered, meaning it with all of her soul.

His body seemed to devour her, and his eyes consumed her when she could keep her eyes open.

Open.

Sarah Rourke opened her eyes, but Wolfgang Mann was only a dream.

Chapter Thirty-One

She had already determined that if, for some reason, he couldn't because he was still technically— but, as he undressed her, Emma Shaw abandoned any worries. "Oh, John!"

"Be quiet," he ordered.

She obeyed, but that was what she wanted to do. Her jacket he placed neatly over the back of the chair near the foot of her bed. "You'll be needing this in a little while."

She only nodded, tempted to speak so that he could tell her once again to be quiet.

His hands moved to the zipper of her skirt, zipped it down. She moved her hips. The skirt fell around her ankles. He touched her waist and she moved her feet and he picked up her skirt, setting it neatly over the chair back.

There was this silly little tie at the collar of her shirt and he undid it, didn't remove it. His fingers moved against the buttons of her shirt and Emma Shaw thought that she would scream.

She raised her hands in front of her and he unbuttoned her cuffs and she almost died.

He slipped her shirt from her shoulders, down along her arms and held her against him, kissed her. His fingers undid the hook-and-eye clasps at the back of her bra and she bent her shoulders forward and it fell away, the straps caught in the crooks of her elbows. The synth-wool of his sweater was scratchy against her nipples and she screamed softly and John kissed her quiet again.

His hands moved along the bare curve of her back, into her panties, thumbing them down over her hips. She moved her legs and they fell.

She still wore stockings, and her panties were down around her ankles and her arms were caught up in the straps of her bra and she wanted to be his more than anything she had ever wanted in her life.

Would the damned phone ring?

Would the enemy attack?

Would she know or care?

Without being asked, she reached to the bottom of his sweater and pulled it up. He bent forward and she pulled it over his head, throwing it down to the deck.

Inside the waistband of his trousers, one on either side of his waist, were two pistols, worn without holsters. He took a step back, removed them, set them on the deck at the right side of the bed, then touched her again, behind her now. Emma Shaw closed her eyes, feeling his mouth as it moved along the curve of her throat, to her shoulder, his fingertips touching nipples that only a moment earlier had been pressed against the roughness of his sweater.

She turned around, eyes still closed, feeling his hands almost circumferencing her waist. He had big hands, she thought, almost laughing. His lips touched at her throat again, moved downward, touched at her left nipple, then touched at her lips and she wanted to scream again. "Tell me to be quiet, John."

"Be quiet."

"Yes," she whispered. She opened her eyes, her hands (which had been limp at the ends of her arms at her thighs) starting to undo the garrison-width belt at his waist. Men hid behind these things, she reasoned, the buckles enormous, the leather thick and heavy. She started to pull it out of the trouser loops, realized she didn't have to, started to feel for a zipper. There was none, only buttons, and she undid these starting at the top one, working her way down lower than she needed to, feeling the swelling of him with the knuckles of her fingers and actually screaming a little, very softly.

He kissed her, harder than he ever had before, and she understood more things than she had ever known in the world in that same instant . . .

John Rourke looked down at her face, her eyes closed. In a fraction of a second, he would enter her.

Deep inside him, he realized that what he was doing was right. For everyone.

And he did.

Chapter Thirty-Two

They were not late for the meeting, and planning ahead had nothing to do with it. Their arrival time mere chance, John Rourke walked into the conference suite, Emma Shaw at his side, on time to the second, for the second session of the meeting to start (according to the black-faced Rolex on his wrist).

They sat down, Rourke holding Emma's chair for her.

Admiral Hayes said, "Our first order of business in this second session is Dr. Rolvaag's summary of the crisis concerning the vent."

Thorn Rolvaag stood up, walking toward the far wall, a remote video control clutched in both hands. Rourke could see the man's fingers playing the device's buttons, like the fingers of a musician over some well-loved instrument.

The size of modern video screens still amazed John Rourke. Utilizing a liquid-crystal technology, they could cover an entire wall, picture-reproduction perfect in its clarity.

The pictures began, very well-resolved underwater video of the vent beneath the Pacific which was the cause of such great concern. Volcanic lava showed, the yellow-edged redness gleaming like some forbidding view of hell itself. A scale appeared at the bottom of the screen, as a size measure. The width of the vent seemed nearly a quarter mile. Rolvaag began to speak, "There, ladies and gentlemen, is what might well be the scar from which our planet will not heal, the surface scratch which reveals the horrible illness within. Without closing this vent—and this video is quite recent, only a few hours old—I feel that our planet is doomed." Had this been a film of some sort, all of the personnel attending the meeting aboard the *Paladin* would have begun to gasp, there would have been murmurs of disbelief, perhaps muted screams. There was none of that, because what Rolvaag said was nothing new, but bitterly established fact instead. "The problem is not controversial, only my projected solution to it, namely the use of nuclear weapons to reroute the vent, dissipating the force of the volcanic flow. But, whatever the remedy, without remedy this vent will relatively soon reach the easternmost edge of the Pacific plate, and strike the westernmost edge of the North American continental plate, precisely where, during the Night of the War, the shock waves from the bombing caused the cataclysmic rupturing of the San Andreas fault and other tributary fault lines, precipitating the collapse of the easternmost edge of the Pacific plate into the sea. As you may recall from history books, and as the Rourke family doubtless recalls from experience, the resultant cataclysm

198

caused everything to the west of the San Andreas to collapse into the sea. How many millions of persons were killed, we will never know. But the cities of Los Angeles and San Francisco, and everything above them and below them and in between them ceased to exist in a matter of minutes. The resultant tidal surge swamped almost all of the Hawaiian Islands' land mass, the coast of Alaska, etc.

"This disaster which awaits us, if it cannot be prevented, would make all of what has gone before pale by comparison. As you no doubt know, but I must emphasize again, what could very well happen is the linking of all the 'jewels' in the 'ring of fire' which surrounds the Pacific basin. In other words, the vent would slam against the North American plate and split. In itself, that might seem desirable, because its energy would be dissipated. However, that energy would follow along the path of least resistance, as energy does unless forced to do otherwise. It would follow the plate boundary, activating volcanic activity to the north and to the south, gathering momentum and energy as it moved, fed by the volcanic areas which it touched.

"Soon, ladies and gentlemen, very soon, the vent would effectively encircle the entire Pacific Basin. Once the encirclement was complete, the eruptive force would be of such strength that an event unlike any other perhaps in the history of the solar system would occur. The eruptive force would blow out the Pacific basin. Then, one of two events would occur, and there is no way to tell which—either the entire planet would implode or the planet would be launched out of orbit. I lean toward the second

199

theory. As a scientist, I find it ironic that if we cannot prevent the vent from reaching the North American plate, I'll never know which theory was correct. In the instant that the ring of fire is completed, the explosion of the Pacific basin will begin. Any life surviving the rain of volcanic ash, the darkness which will by then have consumed the planet, will be instantly destroyed. So, neither I nor any of my colleagues will ever know whether the planet will cease to exist as anything but gigantic pieces of rocky debris in an orbit once held by a planet or become a dead nomad, ejected from the solar system into space. Or, the planet might be caught in the gravitational field of the sun and drawn into it."

James Darkwood, the nature of the remark somewhat flippant sounding, but the tone of his voice conveying deadly seriousness, asked, "Is there any more to your good news, Dr. Rolvaag?"

Thorn Rolvaag summarized. "If we cannot stop the spread of the vent, it means the end of all life on this planet forever."

John Rourke lit a cigar, not asking if the smoke would bother anyone. The problem of secondhand smoke seemed somewhat less than significant at the moment. "Dr. Rolvaag," Rourke began. "Your proposal is to utilize nuclear warheads as strategically placed charges with which we'll divert the vent, dissipate its energy."

"Yes, Dr. Rourke, along the lines of the theory you proposed shortly after the eruption of Kilauea. We can create a system of canals or channels, as it were, thus dissipating the force of lateral movement within the vent, blowing off energy into these canals, harmlessly essentially, in the hope that the vent will lose sufficient force and stop of its own accord. That is, as far as I can see, our only hope. Other scientists agree that ideally we should discover some means of relieving the volcanic pressure. It's my methodolgy which scares them. And, in truth, I can't say that I blame them."

"Why does it scare them, as you say, Doctor?" Admiral Hayes asked.

"For the simple reason that nuclear detonations are what probably brought about this crisis in the first place. The earth is looked at by most of us as a giant object that we can abuse however we like. And, I'm not talking about the echo system, here.

"Let's take an example that everyone should readily see," Rolvaag went on, caught up, it seemed, in the analogy he was about to make. "In the Lydveldid Island of my ancestors, policemen commonly carried swords, as a badge of office. But my ancestor, Bjorn Rolvaag, preferred a staff. His staff—my family still possesses it, passed on through the intervening generations—was made for him by a retired scientist—"

"Old Jon the swordmaker," Michael supplied.

Thorn Rolvaag smiled, nodded. "Yes. The same man who made the knife you carry, as I understand."

Michael nodded, adding, "Like your forefather, Old Jon was a fine man, Doctor."

"Thank you, sir." Rolvaag cleared his throat, then went on. "That staff was designed to be used for every conceivable function for which a staff might be needed—as a weapon, a climbing assist, whatever. The staff looks as perfect today as it did in Bjorn

201

Rolvaag's day. Because it was cared for properly and only used, not abused. If this mighty ship, the *Paladin*, had existed in Bjorn Rolvaag's day, and he had set about beating at its hull with the staff, he would doubtless have done some minor damage to the hull of the *Paladin*, but in the process would have mutilated his staff. Rather than using the geology of the planet, we have abused it. And, perhaps, beyond any hope of repair. Any object, if it is constantly abused, will eventually deteriorate. Nothing, except perhaps our own concept of the Divine and for those of us lucky enough, love, lasts forever. This may be the end of the species, which must come someday to be sure. But I feel that the impact, the repeated battering, of the multimegaton thermonuclear devices used over six centuries ago is bringing about this termination prematurely.

"The evidence is overwhelming," Rolvaag said, his voice obvious in its passion, "that the destruction of what was the West Coast of the United States was brought about by the impacts of the bombs and missiles. The fault line created within the Gulf of Mexico and extending outward into what was called the Bermuda Triangle, the fault which shortly after the Night of the War precipitated the cataclysmic earthquake which collapsed peninsular Florida, destroying it utterly—this was clearly precipitated by the pounding of the nuclear weapons against the Earth's mantle.

"You'll notice, if you study the history of the thing, that Florida's collapse occurred several weeks after the Night of the War. Archives from the Chinese Second City indicate that there were

202

cataclysmic earthquakes over the period of time immediately following the Night of the War, and even in the five centuries between the Great Conflagration and the return of the Eden Project, earth tremors nearly destroyed the Second City, the civilization at New Germany in South America, etc. Lydveldid Island was, itself, nearly destroyed, the Hekla community devoured only to later be rebuilt, this latter by volcanism on an unprecedented scale. This is all a pattern which has been developing for centuries, thanks to the folly of mankind."

John Rourke interrupted. "The folly of mankind in the days following World War II isn't in dispute, Doctor. And, it wasn't confined to the proliferation of nuclear weapons. What was lacking was the resoluteness to risk all for what was right. On the global level, this translated into the superpowers feinting at one another, playing a game of death. One night, the game got out of hand. The Night of the War was the result. It was essentially inevitable, given the nature of mankind, not that there'd be warfare but that something would go wrong resulting in catastrophe. And, by that, I don't mean that we, as a species, are evil or stupid. Far from it. Philosophy may seem out of place here, but I tend to think that there's never been a better time for it.

"Man desires peace, basically, to be left alone to live out his days in the bosom of his family and friends, as it were—normal man. But there have always been those for whom the pursuit and capture of power was the reason for living. For some of those others, the pursuit, however vigorous, was, if not to the benefit of mankind, not overwhelmingly to its

203

detriment. Many of these men achieved what we call greatness. A far smaller percentage achieved infamy. Life was always precious, but to an increasingly great number of people in the twentieth century, especially those living beneath the umbrella of Western civilization as it was so euphemistically called, the desire for continued existence overwhelmed all other motives. If there was a chance to survive while hiding from what was wrong, take it. We took that chance, as a species.

"In the closing decades of the twentieth century, ladies and gentlemen, there was a virtual litany of abominations. From the close of World War II onward, evidence strongly suggested that the United States abandoned some of its POWs and MIAs because of political expediency. This was unconscionable. Totalitarian regimes flourished, making the lives of all whom they controlled hell on earth. And we, as Americans, or British or any of the other major Western powers, let those regimes essentially do what they wanted so long as we were not affected. The torturing of political prisoners by foreign powers, the erosion of order in public education giving rise to heightened juvenile delinquency, the proliferation of dangerous drugs under the umbrellas of legal loopholes and uncaring citizens, the sweeping horror and incalculable cost in human suffering brought about by pernicious disease, such as AIDS. Racism, sexism, things that by rights should have died of their own weight, or been brought to book by the righteous, were allowed to spread, to continue, to entrench themselves in society because society was too apathetic.

"We have a choice now," John Rourke said, after a long moment, his eyes studying the glowing tip of his cigar. "We can either summon up the courage we need as a species in order to meet the crisis at hand, or die. Therefore, if Dr. Rolvaag's solution seems only to be the lesser of two evils, that'll be nothing new. That's how we elected presidents for years, after all, and not always choosing the lesser of two evils at all. We have a clear-cut choice presented to us. Either take a wild gamble which may result in our death as a species or our survival as a species, or don't gamble, just wait and die. What real choice is there if we are to call ourselves human beings?"

And, John Rourke was suddenly embarrassed, because everyone at the table stood and began to applaud his words.

Chapter Thirty-Three

Wolfgang Mann sat down with a drink in his hand, his complexion pale and his carriage a little wobbly, but he had been ill and was still, it seemed, not fully recovered from his ordeal.

But John Rourke was still confident that this man was, indeed, Wolfgang Mann.

The *Paladin*'s officers' mess was essentially deserted, the ship on a modifed alert status and few personnel having the luxury of not needing to be present at a duty station or sleeping.

Emma was sleeping. Their cabins had adjoining doors and he could come to her, she had told him, asked him.

The meeting had ended for the day, to be resumed in the morning. John Rourke, too, was tired, needing sleep. But some things took precedence over sleep. Nothing had yet been resolved at the meeting concerning the war strategy and the strategy for fighting the growing volcanic vent beneath the Pacific.

But something would be resolved at the meeting scheduled for early the next morning or John Rourke would stop wasting time with meetings.

The thing which had to be resolved now could not wait even until tomorrow. He had seen Sarah; she slept soundly, sedated slightly. By tomorrow, she would be fully awake, fully restored—and their marriage, which had lasted more than six centuries, would be ended.

That was certain.

And so was the answer to the question which he was about to ask Generaloberst Wolfgang Mann.

"Are you in love with Sarah?"

"John, it is not—"

Any doubt which John Rourke might have retained concerning Wolfgang Mann's true identity vanished. The man was cut from the same cloth as he. "Please speak frankly, Wolf."

"I cannot, because you are my friend, and friendship is something too precious—"

"But you have no choice but to be honest with me, because you are my friend," John Rourke countered.

"Yes—to both. I am sorry, John. I did not mean for it to happen."

"I know that, old friend," Rourke said honestly. "Nor did Sarah. I would assume you agree, that she is in love with you, as well."

"She has never—"

"I would never have thought any different, of either of you, Wolf. I, on the other hand, realized some time ago that Sarah's and my marriage was ended. It was when I caused the death of Martin, or

208

Martin's clone—he was still our flesh, hers and mine, whether clone or the original. Before the Night of the War, our marriage was collapsing from its own weight. The War itself merely postponed what was inevitable. Had everything worked out after the defeat of our old enemy, after she and I set up the hospital clinic at what's now Eden City, well, perhaps we could have immersed ourselves in the rebuilding of the world to the point where we could have coexisted and stayed married, happiness be damned. I still love her, and I know she loves me. But, we were never friends. Do you know what I mean, Wolf?"

"Yes. And I feel for you. My late wife was my best friend, and I had thought I could never have such feelings again with a woman, both love and friendship. But, I found them in Sarah, God help me. God help us all."

"Yes," John Rourke said, "God help us all. I'll give her a divorce, uncontested. And God bless you both."

"John?"

"Yes?"

"What will you—"

John Rourke exhaled, slowly, his eyes leaving Wolfgang Mann's eyes, settling on his own hands. "The events in which we are embroiled may well cost me my life, Wolf. I decided that what little time I may have left should at least in part be spent in happiness. That's understandable, I think. I, too, have found a woman who is both lover and friend to me."

"The female pilot—"

209

"Emma Shaw, yes. I'll ask you a favor, if I may. Should I die, do what you can for Michael and Annie, and Natalia and Paul, of course."

"And Emma Shaw?"

John Rourke smiled, saying, "As with the others, I'd expect no less of you for her."

They shook hands and John Rourke stood, leaving his drink untouched. He had made love to Emma Shaw for two reasons: he had wanted to very badly and known that she wanted him to and he loved her; and, the self-knowledge that he had done such a thing while Sarah still lived would force him to do what had to be done and set Sarah free of him. Forever.

He turned his thoughts elsewhere as he left the lounge behind, entering one of the main companionways which would take him to his quarters, on the same level.

Something which had not been discussed at the meeting was the reality of the rift within the Nazi Party. According to James Darkwood's reports, Croenberg (whom Michael had met and fought with while attempting to carry off an impersonation of Martin Zimmer) had aspirations to his own power base and was working to unseat Martin Zimmer in Eden as well as Deitrich Zimmer in the Nazi hierarchy, as its leader.

John Rourke recalled the remarks of Sir Winston Churchill concerning an alliance with Stalin, that to defeat Hitler he would, in fact, make a pact with the devil. Making a pact with Croenberg might well be possible, and certainly politically expedient. It was morally wrong, however, and to win at the cost of one's integrity was not to win at all.

John Rourke stopped in his tracks, stood, shook his head, said nearly aloud, "My God, John Rourke, you're an anachronism!"

Laughing a little, he continued on along the corridor. He would bring up the matter of Croenberg, as a possible means of exploiting a rift within the Nazi infrastructure, but if anyone suggested an alliance, secret or otherwise, he would pick up his ball and go home.

He would not make a pact with any devil.

Chapter Thirty-Four

It was the best of good luck, having John Thomas Rourke himself aboard the USS *Paladin*. Not only would Dr. Rourke be vulnerable, but Dr. Rourke's death (if he survived to take the credit for it) would doubtlessly advance him.

The *Paladin* was one of the few United States warships whose on-board scientific work demanded the ongoing employment of civilian employee professionals. As a Nazi sympathizer on land in Hawaii, he was able to attend clandestine meetings, deface synogogue walls, contribute occasionally to the propaganda effort and do little else except wait for the glorious day of liberation when troops of the New Fatherland would march unmolested up from the beaches and those who had been loyal to the party these many years would be rewarded with positions of power and influence.

As a Nazi sympathizer here aboard the *Paladin*, he had been able to smuggle out a steady stream of Naval secrets to Nazi intelligence personnel located in various ports of call around the world. But now, it was as if the old gods had selected him, chosen him because he had been loyal, rewarded his all-but-infinite patience.

The ultimate target awaited him.

And, even should he die in the process of killing John Thomas Rourke, he, Elwood Brooks, would be immortalized. Like the Horst Wessel song, named after a courageous young party member in the Third Reich who had given his life for his beliefs, so would songs be sung to his memory as well.

Elwood Brooks had whipped together a plan in a matter of hours which other, lesser men would have required months in order to prepare.

To that end, he knocked on the door of the cabin belonging to Commander Emma Shaw.

When she opened the door, he fired the gun.

Chapter Thirty-Five

John Rourke stripped away his sweater and turned on the television set. The *Paladin's* cable system had several channels and he selected the one which carried nostalgia television.

These were electronically remastered programs from the mid-twentieth century, televison's so-called golden age, and films from the post-World War II period up until a short while Before the Night of the War.

One of his favorite Westerns was playing, and while John Rourke began to clean his guns, he watched it. It was an adaptation of one of Louis L'Amour's most famous novels, starring John Wayne. There was Indian trouble, but John Wayne was ready to the task, of course. John Rourke had always liked the story, because aside from being a rousing tale, well-acted and well-photographed, the characters, Indian and white, functioned within the framework of their own personal honor.

His mind on the film (or, at least he tried to keep it

there), John Rourke attacked the Lancer reproductions of the SIG-Sauer P-228s. He liked these guns quite a bit, identical in every way to the originals, the original 228s among the few 9mm Parabellum pistols that he ever liked Before the Night of the War. In that small group of 9mm Parabellums, he also included the SIG-Sauer P-226, the Taurus PT-92, the Browning High Power (although the older ones frequently needed polishing for proper feeding of hollow points), the Interarms/Star Firestar, the somewhat old but nevertheless outstanding Walther P-38 and Heckler & Koch's unconventional SP-89 pistol, this latter the same size as one of the HK submachine guns, but minus a buttstock of course.

As fond as he was of the SIG 228s, however, and as much as he realized how these new additions to his battery of fighting handguns would be a tremendous asset to him, nothing would ever take the place of the twin stainless Detonics Combat-Masters. He had carried the little .45s, usually in their double Alessi shoulder rig, ever since the guns first became available, his first Detonics a blued gun that he'd had Metalifed by his old pal Ron Mahovsky.

The little Detonics pistols had never failed him.

The array of handguns John Rourke relyed upon, although rarely all at once, was considerable. He had been asked often why he utilized so many guns instead of just one or possibly two. Indeed, in the days prior to the Night of the War, when circumstances permitted his being armed with conventional firearms, he carried only the two Detonics Combat-

Master .45s, and occasionally a revolver as a spare gun, either the little Colt Lawman MkIII snubby .357 Magnum, one of the most rugged compact revolvers ever built, or when a gun could be carried openly, as in the field, his Metalifed and Mag-na-Ported Colt Python.

For all the hype other calibers received, .357 Magnum was perhaps the most effective manstopping handgun caliber there was. .44 Magnum, in proper loadings, might essentially equal it, but didn't really surpass it. He had switched over to a .44 Magnum revolver in recent times for one reason only: personnel he encountered these days might well be wearing bullet-resistant clothing. Full-charge 180-grain, .44 Magnums could penetrate that, as well as armorless sheet metal of the type used in conventional vehicles.

Rourke finished cleaning both the SIG 228s, the Detonics CombatMasters and the full-sized ScoreMasters, setting to work on the two revolvers he now regularly carried, the Metalife Custom Model 629 .44 Magnum and the little .38 Special Smith & Wesson Centennial.

The trick to properly cleaning a Smith & Wesson revolver if one desired smoothness of operation was to take the extra time and trouble to remove the crane screw, then slip the crane and the cylinder out of the frame, cleaning in the area where the cylinder rotated around the crane. With ammunition leaving behind it substantial powder residue, this was extremely important. A gross accumulation of debris in this area could bind a cylinder to the point where the advancing hand was forced to work unduly hard. This, of course, could lead to mechanical difficulties.

Meanwhile on television, John Wayne had just given away his prized Winchester rifle with the bowed lever.

The film was ending and John Rourke was tired. He finished seeing to his guns, then washed his hands quite vigorously in the basin. The Germans produced the lubricant Rourke used, chemically identical to the Break-Free CLP he'd always stocked at the Retreat.

He stripped, making certain there were weapons properly in reach in the event that he needed them, sitting down naked on the edge of the bed. He called the sick bay, inquiring about Sarah for the night. She was sleeping peacefully and naturally, he was told.

Rourke told the computer which monitored the ship's systems, "Lights out, please." The lights went out.

He lay back beneath the covers and stared into the total darkness. He felt, oddly, at peace. And tonight's sleep promised to be a good night's rest.

Chapter Thirty-Six

Over the course of real time—not centuries spent in cryogenic Sleep—in which Annie Rourke Rubenstein had known her husband, Paul, she had noticed that some of her father's and Paul's best friend's tastes were beginning to rub off on Paul.

While they'd watched a John Wayne Western together, which Annie had almost memorized word for word (the film was one of the tapes her father had at the Retreat and she had watched it dozens of times), Paul cleaned his guns. Since it was difficult to touch anything, either electronic or in book form, when one's hands were covered with oil, unless one wished to ruin the object touched, television (either a video or broadcast programming) was the obvious answer in lieu of conversation.

She'd opted for a bath, a luxury she enjoyed and in which she rarely indulged. While sitting in the tub, a facial mask drying, she could hear the film and the occasional comment from Paul as he cleaned not only his guns, but hers. Her mind was generally elsewhere.

She was about to become the child of a broken home. Her father's and mother's marriage was doomed. If she were inclined to take sides in the thing, Annie would have been at a total loss as to which side she should take. Living with someone who was as nearly perfect as a human being could be would be frustrating beyond belief or endurance. Yet, her mother's inflexibility Before the Night of the War had been the major contributing factor to the discord which would soon culminate in divorce. Sarah Rourke had refused to even consider her husband's point of view concerning geopolitics. And, as he strove to be the embodiment of the philosophical objectivist (the only endeavor in which John Rourke was vastly less than perfect), Sarah Rourke was a liberal.

Her father, Annie knew, try as he might, was too soft-hearted, an admittedly odd way of looking at a man who had fought his way across more than six centuries. But, instead of realizing that the oil and water of his world view and his wife's would never mix, he had tortured himself by trying and trying and trying some more.

Philosophically, Annie Rubenstein was more aligned to her father, and over the course of time since the Night of the War, her mother's liberalism had taken some cruel blows. Sarah Rourke discovered that guns weren't evil, because they were only inanimate objects. Guns could be used for good or ill, and without guns and other weapons available to them, the good people would be the victims of the bad people, having no recourse for self-defense. Sarah Rourke had learned that liberalism in its common interpretation (as opposed to true, classic liberalism), of the type which ushered the United States government and other nations of the world into high-priced chaos, was the antithesis of what it truly meant to be human. Altruism, even when it was sincere, was self-destructive. Kindness, Judeo-Christian charity, concern for the welfare of others—all of these were best accomplished by men and women who practiced these undeniable virtues out of the sheer love of practicing them, not out of some warped sense of obligation. To preach weakness and passivity was tantamount to preaching suicide, if not physical (which was sometimes the result at the governmental level), then certainly intellectual.

Her mother had learned, Annie knew, that what her father had believed in all of those years had withstood a philosophical acid test in the aftermath of the Night of the War that her philosophy could not. He had been right; she had been wrong. If blame were to be shouldered—but she ascribed blame to neither of them in any real sense—it was Sarah Rourke's. But, in a larger sense, Annie's mother's guilt rested only in buying the popular lie as some sort of moral and intellectual superiority, when in fact it was neither moral nor intellectual at all to deny reality and then refuse to realistically try to change reality's nature.

She stood up, the drain plug out, the water from her tub running down the drain—into the bilges?—as she turned up the shower. A bath was relaxing, luxuriously sensual, but a terribly inefficient way to get clean, stewing in one's own dirt. She showered vigorously, washing her hair twice, conditioning it, soaking her body under the warm water while the conditioner did its work.

The Western was long since over and Paul had come into the bathroom, washed his hands and, by now, was probably reading.

Annie shut off the water, toweled herself dry, wrapping a towel around her head for a time as she slipped into her nightgown and brushed and flossed her teeth. The towel had done as much as it could. With a blow dryer, she finished the job, finally brushing out her hair. Her hair was almost to her waist when she left it completely down. Natalia had trimmed away a few inches of split ends for her a short while ago and Annie had decided that this current length was as long as she would let it grow. Shorter might be nice, but she liked the things she could do with her hair at this length and Paul liked her hair long.

She thought about Paul as, again, she brushed her hair. In this modern age, Paul could have taken a series of injections which would have restored his well-thinned hair completely. He elected not to, self-conscious about the idea. Paul was sweet. He genuinely considered himself totally unattractive. He wasn't, certainly, the sort of man who would be some entertainment idol. But, through her admittedly jaundiced eyes, he looked handsome beyond description, with thinning hair or otherwise.

As she went to set down the brush, she dropped the brush, sucked in her breath so fast that it sounded like a scream, then almost collapsed.

"Annie!" Paul was kneeling beside her, his journal

and a pen going to the floor beside her knees. Her knees were cold, bare against the tiles of the bathroom floor, her nightgown billowed out around her. "Annie? What is it, sweetheart?"

It wasn't the sort of vision that was really clear, just a feeling, and the visions that were strong feelings were usually the worst kind. She licked her lips, trying to catch her breath.

"It's Daddy. Something wrong—"

"Can you see where he is?"

"No—but—he's sleeping, I think. Paul?"

"I'm on my way. Lock yourself in after I'm gone. Your guns are on the writing desk."

And Paul was gone.

Annie knelt there.

The door slammed.

She closed her eyes, trying to force herself to have the strength to stand and lock the cabin door.

Chapter Thirty-Seven

Paul Rubenstein's guns were in his hands as he ran along the companionway.

He should have told Annie to—to do what? Arouse her father from his sleep? But that might only hasten whatever danger John was in. Call Michael and Natalia, even Emma Shaw? Annie'd probably do that, anyway.

He ran past a knot of sailors. "Mr. Rubenstein? Sir! What's the matter, sir?" He ignored them, kept running. Shirtless, shoeless and sockless, Paul Rubenstein was quietly amazed that he'd remembered to pull on a pair of BDU pants. They were buttoned, but his belt was flapping open. He must have looked like a wild man, a pistol in each hand, cocked and locked, half-naked, running. He turned the right angle into the section of companionway along which John's cabin was situated . . .

Elwood Brooks watched Commander Shaw as,

at last, she stirred. He carried two gas pistols, improvised here aboard the *Paladin,* as were the cartridges which they contained. The pistol he had fired at Commander Shaw when she opened her cabin door was loaded with what would generically be called knock-out gas, a combination of chemicals which induced instantaneous unconsciousness without causing permanent damage. Not that that mattered, but he needed her alive so she could scream.

The second pistol was loaded with cyanide gas. During the Cold War between the superpowers centuries ago, cyanide gas pistols had been extremely popular as a means of committing murder. This was his intention now. Ideally, according to what Elwood Brooks had read, the subject should be ascending a staircase when the cyanide was fired, so that the conditions of a massive coronary occlusion, which the gas simulated, would be further substantiated by the activity of the deceased in the instants prior to death.

There was no staircase at hand, but that would be all right. It was doubtful that anyone would believe that Dr. John Thomas Rourke, the living legend that he was, had succumbed from something as mundane as heart failure. But, the murder could not be provably linked to an assailant.

Brooks's hands were double-gloved, guarding against laser detection of partial fingerprints through ordinary gloves. The gas guns were made from a plastic with a low melting point and would be destroyed.

Both guns were loaded now with the cyanide gas

in the event that one burst should not be enough to bring down the powerful Dr. Rourke as instantaneously as required. And, Brooks had spare cartridges. One of those would be used to kill Commander Shaw. But, he needed her awake for now, so that Dr. Rourke would come rushing through the connecting doorway between their cabins when she screamed.

And, she would be screaming in just another few seconds.

In order to get a seasoned combat veteran to scream for help, Elwood Brooks had considered various possibilities. There were a few laboratory animals aboard the *Paladin*. He could have employed the most potentially objectionable of these laboratory animals, of course. Would she have screamed if she awakened with a rat sitting on her face? Probably, but Elwood Brooks disliked rats in the extreme.

He elected instead to utilize something with which he was considerably more familiar: acid.

He removed the vial of acid from the container in which it was carried under his sweater.

The instant Commander Emma Shaw awakened, he would begin to use the acid on her face. She would scream.

John Rourke would enter hurriedly.

By that time, Elwood Brooks would be waiting beside the door and fire the gas pistol. Then he would kill Commander Shaw and leave.

The scream would be heard, but there should be time to escape into the anonymity of the ship's company. Should John Rourke kill him as Rourke went down, so be it. No sacrifice was too great for

227

the cause of National Socialism.

Elwood Brooks stood over the bound form of Commander Shaw.

He uncorked the acid vial.

Her face was very pretty in a real sort of way, nothing artificial about the woman.

He would pour the hydrochloric acid onto the left side of her face, at the cheekbone, near her left eye.

She would react.

Dr. John Rourke would react.

Then, Dr. John Rourke would cease to exist.

Elwood Brooks started, ever so slowly, to tip the vial.

Chapter Thirty-Eight

Paul Rubenstein reached John Rourke's cabin door. If someone were inside, about to kill John, knocking on the door might only speed up the process.

Paul Rubenstein made his decision.

He stepped back from the cabin door, the safeties downed on his High Powers, fourteen rounds loaded in each.

Taking a deep breath, Paul kicked out with his right foot against the cabin door's lockplate, the technique for the kick taught to him by Natalia.

The lock splintered away from the synth-wood door jamb and the door swung inward as Paul Rubenstein went through.

John, naked, was already rolling out of the bunk where he'd slept, the little Centennial .38 Special in his right hand. "Paul?"

"It was Annie—she sensed that you were in danger and—"

There was a scream from the cabin next door.

"My God," John rasped, grabbing up one of the twin stainless Detonics pistols from the nightstand beside him as his body went into motion. The Centennial was in his other hand. He was moving toward the adjoining door, Paul two steps behind him, John making a wheeling barefoot kick with his left foot, knocking the adjoining door off the jamb, the door slamming inward.

Emma Shaw, trussed up hand and foot with strips of bedsheet, lay on her back in her bunk, smoke rising from the pillow under her head.

There was a puff of smoke inches away from John's face. There was the sound of a gunshot, from John's .45.

John began collapsing into a heap.

There was a blur of motion, the dark shape of a slender man.

Paul Rubenstein fired both Browning High Powers simultaneously, double tapping both 9mms, the man-shape spinning round, hurling something toward Paul Rubenstein's face.

Paul threw himself right and down, over John's body to protect his friend from whatever it was.

The strange figure fell to his knees as Paul stabbed the pistol from his left hand toward the man and fired again, spraying it out into the spinal cord, killing him.

The carpet beside Paul's right hand smoked. There was broken glass there and Paul realized what the substance was which had been inside the vial: acid.

Emma Shaw shrieked. "He killed John!"

Paul Rubenstein rolled up to his knees, turning

John over onto his back, away from the acid. There was no pulse in John's neck and his eyes stared up at the overhead light.

Paul Rubenstein stumbled back, shook his head, got to his feet. Throwing the emptied pistol onto the bed beside Emma Shaw, safing the still-loaded one and dropping it into the deep pocket at his right side, he reached for the woman with one hand, the bedside telephone with the other.

The pillow beside her head smoked and it looked as if a little of her hair had been touched by the acid; otherwise, she seemed unharmed.

Paul shouted into the receiver. "This is Paul Rubenstein. Full cardiac team to Commander Shaw's cabin on the double. John Rourke may be dead!"

He slammed down the receiver, dropped to his knees beside his friend's body and started CPR.

Chapter Thirty-Nine

No bra, no panties, no socks, wearing only a sweater, a pair of fatigue pants and her track shoes, Emma Shaw hammered her fist against the bulkhead.

The pharmacist's mate had cut away about two square inches of her hair on the left side and pronounced her whole and well. She'd had split ends there anyway.

Meanwhile, the ship's doctor had worked to revive John.

Already inside a portable heart-lung machine, he was wheeled out the door and gone.

The dead man, a civilian science worker named Elwood Brooks, was body-bagged and taken away on a stretcher. Paul Rubenstein was joined by Natalia and Annie and Michael Rourke, Annie and Michael and Paul following after John to sickbay.

Natalia righted the cabin's overturned desk chair and sat down. Wearing a baggy white sweater with the sleeves pushed up past her elbows, a loose-fitting, nearly ankle-length full skirt of navy blue cotton, little white anklet socks and blue ballet flats, Natalia looked lovely, as she always did, despite the hour and the circumstances. "Get dressed, Emma Shaw. You belong in sickbay with your man."

"But, they—"

"If you were good enough for John, you'll be good enough for them. I learned that six centuries ago. The Rourke Family—and that includes Paul, of course—doesn't pull punches. If they didn't like you, you would know about it by now. Resentment about Sarah? There is bound to be that, but Sarah's ultimate goal in life was never to make herself a saint. If that's Sarah alive down there in sickbay, she'll understand. If John had realized years ago what he apparently realizes now, well—" And Natalia laughed. "I would have killed you if I'd had to, but in a fair fight, of course." She stood up, walked over to where Emma Shaw stood beside the bed and embraced Emma, then kissed her on the cheek. "Just pull something on and let's go, all right?"

"All right."

"Good."

Emma Shaw pulled something on and went. Major Natalia Tiemerovna was the sort of woman who could pull anything on and look as if she'd stepped out of the pages of a fashion magazine after spending hours achieving the perfect look. Emma Shaw had realized when she was just a teenager that she was not that kind of person. When she just pulled something on, it looked like she'd just pulled something on.

Natalia sat beside Michael, her head against his shoulder on the long bench along the bulkhead opposite the doors to sickbay. Annie, wearing a long robe over a long nightgown, fuzzy slippers peeking out beneath its hem, sat on the bench along the opposite bulkhead. Paul, one foot resting on the bench, stood beside her.

Emma Shaw felt very alone and very responsible.

There was no word from the doctors, which evidently meant that John had not been pronounced.

"Sarah!"

It was Paul Rubenstein's voice which Emma Shaw heard. She turned around, looking back along the corridor formed between the two benches. A uniformed Navy nurse was pushing a wheelchair, in the chair sitting a remarkably pretty woman with long auburn hair caught up loosely at the nape of her neck. She was pale, but seemed well somehow.

Annie went to her, knelt at her feet, hugged her. Michael bent over her and kissed her. After a moment, Natalia went up to her, said something that Emma couldn't catch, then leaned over and kissed her cheek. Paul crouched beside the chair, put his arms around her, held her for a moment.

Then, her eyes met Sarah Rourke's eyes and Emma Shaw shivered. This was the woman whose name every schoolchild knew, the woman who had kept her family together throughout all the violence and death in the aftermath of the Night of the War—kept it together only to have her husband stolen from her when her back was turned.

Emma Shaw licked her lips and found them dry.

235

Annie looked at her, smiled.

A man stepped up beside Emma Shaw. When she turned to look at him, she recognized him as Wolfgang Mann. "General—"

"Commander Shaw. You and I have a great deal in common, it seems. Share a cigarette with me, perhaps a cup of coffee. It is only the next room."

"Yes."

She felt his hand at her elbow and let him lead her away . . .

Sarah Rourke wondered if her work had been done for her by some man whose name had been Elwood Brooks? Had he succeeded in killing the unkillable John Rourke?

If not, she would still have to do it.

Chapter Forty

Emma Shaw's coffee had no taste. Neither did the cigarette. But she drank the coffee and smoked the cigarette anyway.

Wolfgang Mann—he'd told her, "Call me Wolf, Fräulein Commander Shaw"—lit another cigarette with the lighter on the table in front of him. "I have a lot of smoking to catch up on, Fräulein."

"Emma, please," she said. "Call me Emma."

"Emma. You and John are—?" He let the question hang on the air like the smoke he'd just exhaled.

"Are?"

He smiled. "You have doubtless heard the rumors that Sarah and I—"

"Yes. I'm very happy for you, if it works out. John told me that he thought you and Sarah were in love."

"We were, one hundred and twenty-five years ago. We never—but, ah—"

Emma didn't know what to say to him. Saying something like, "Well, John and I sure did and it was great!" would have been in terribly bad taste. Instead, she said, "I hope you'll be very happy."

"I had wished the same for you and John. And, you should remember, Fräulein Commander— Emma. You should remember that John Thomas Rourke is an extraordinarily difficult man to kill."

She was doing a good job holding the tears in until he said the magic word, and the tears started flowing in spite of all her resolve to the contrary. She felt Wolfgang Mann's arm moving to hold her at the shoulders and she let him. "I, ah—" But her throat closed up on her.

Wolfgang Mann, his voice soft, almost whispered, "I know exactly how it is that you feel, Emma. My wife, whom I loved deeply, was murdered by the Nazis as a calculated act of terror. I found myself falling in love with Sarah Rourke, and thought that she might somehow have some feelings for me, and then she was essentially killed in the fire at the hospital, when the Nazis, once again, perpetrated an act of terror. I had nothing left. My children were dead, my wife murdered, and the woman I loved— but had told myself I could never possess—was also taken from me. The pain inside is impossible to bear, is it not?"

Emma Shaw was biting her lower lip, nodded her head, her nose running, her eyes streaming tears, her head aching, body shaking.

"I held a brief conversation with the *Paladin*'s chief of security. It was a rather close brush with death that you yourself endured, I understand."

Still unable to swallow, or to speak, Emma Shaw managed to nod her head. She didn't care about

238

herself, only John.

"The weapon used was a cyanide gas pistol, I believe. Before the Night of the War, as I understand it, such a weapon, when properly used, was always fatal. But now, we live in an age of medical miracles, Fräulein! You should take heart. If John were dead, you would know by now."

She shook her head, managing to say, "They could, could still be trying—"

"To revive him? To what end?"

"I—"

Then her world ended, or at least she thought that it did, because Emma Shaw looked toward the door into the waiting room and there stood Natalia Tiemerovna, eyes streaming tears.

Chapter Forty-One

Michael Rourke sat at the far side of the round table. He had selected a round table, he supposed, because as a boy he had read the stories of King Arthur, who had selected a round table so that no knight would assume himself to be more important than any other.

They were not knights at this table, nor would any of them assume themselves more important than the other, but it was a quest of epic proportions upon which they would all soon embark, all of them except Wolfgang Mann, who sat with them as well. He would look after Sarah Rourke while they were gone, for however long that would be.

"Go ahead," Michael," Paul said.

Michael nodded. "All right. Paul and I figured this out kind of quickly, but we figure it's the only way to save Dad's life."

Emma Shaw sniffed loudly, used what was obviously a man's handkerchief and blew her nose.

Wolfgang Mann smiled a little apologetically.

Michael went on. "All of us are part of the Family." Emma Shaw looked pointedly at him and he at her. If he could have read lips, he would have sworn hers silently formed the words, "Thank you." Natalia lit a cigarette.

Michael said, "Our father has suffered irreparable heart damage as a result of the cyanide gas. According to the doctors, the preparation required for the proper adjustment and fitting of an artificial heart would consume a minimum of seventy-two hours. They can only keep him on the apparatus they're using for another thirty-six hours without the risk of brain damage. They caught him barely in time as it was, but all their equipment indicates his brain survived intact. A human donor heart could be found, but considering the time constraints a good tissue match would be unlikely, meaning he'd possibly die anyway. I would give my own heart—" Michael could no longer speak.

Paul spoke then, and Michael listened. "Michael spoke with Natalia and offered to give his own heart to save his father's life. Natalia did not agree, but Michael decided to make the offer anyway. She was sensible. Michael was emotional. We all love John in our own ways. Anyway," Paul continued, "there is one surefire source for a replacement heart that will be a perfect match in every way, identical to the original. If we can get to that source and make ourselves take it, we can save John's life. Otherwise, John'll be dead. I mean, he could be kept alive, but brain damage would set in and the John Rourke we knew would be dead, gone.

"It seems like a clear-cut moral choice, if we've got

the nerve and can get to the heart. John was certain that Dr. Deitrich Zimmer had cloned us all while we were in cryogenic Sleep in New Germany. If John was right, there is at least one duplicate of John Rourke, perhaps several, perhaps dozens, being kept in stasis at Zimmer's headquarters facility, which Allied Intelligence thinks it knows the location of. In the Himalayas. If we can get in there and back here in under thirty-six hours, with the heart, we can save John's life. According to the doctors, he'd be up and around in less than a week, still in time to be of major assistance in the tasks to come—defeating Deitrich Zimmer's Nazis, hopefully finding a way to stop the progress of the volcanic vent as it heads toward the North American plate. He'd be good as new. With the procedures they have for accelerating the knitting together of bones—they have to cut through the chest and lay the rib cage back in order to operate—but they can make the bones heal together, just as they were before. He wouldn't even have a scar. Good as new or dead. Those are the two options we have.

"Now, kidnapping a clone of John Rourke and bringing him here to murder him won't sit well with any of us. If there were another choice, I wouldn't touch this with a ten-foot pole. And I don't know if I'll ever sleep the same after this. But, I know I'd never sleep at all if I just let John die."

"I will do the killing," Natalia volunteered, Michael just looking at her as she said the words. "All of you believe in an immortal soul, and you taught me to believe the same way. But my soul has a great deal more to answer for than any of yours. I will kill the clone."

Michael said to the woman who would soon be his wife, "All of us will do what needs to be done, Natalia. And that's the way it'll be." Then turned to Emma Shaw. "Emma will do the driving, getting us out of Zimmer's facility with the clone or the heart. Whatever." He looked at Annie, his sister. "We'll be air-dropping in the mountains. Get us all the equipment we could possibly need, Sis. Explosives, too. We get in there, we destroy the whole damned thing."

Annie nodded.

Michael said, "Wolf pointed out to Paul and me that there is the possiblity that Mom—Sarah—isn't the genuine article, is herself a clone, and that our real mother, the real Sarah, may still be alive inside Zimmer's headquarters in the Himalayas. If she is, we get her out, too. Any questions?"

There were none.

Paul said, "Be ready to leave in two hours, a briefing in one hour. Michael and I have discussed this with James Darkwood and the Intell people both here and in Hawaii and there's a plan forming. We haven't ironed out all the kinks, and maybe we won't be able to. We'll see."

"What kind of a plan?" Annie asked him.

Paul looked at his wife, then at all of them in turn. "We can't storm our way in, kidnap a clone of John Rourke and shoot our way out. That just won't work. So, we have a lot we'll have to do in preparation for the actual operation. It's looking like a two-pronged attack on the facility, from within and without, almost medieval in format."

And Paul smiled. "Considering we don't know very much about Zimmer's headquarters in the Himalayas, don't even know for sure that it's there, everything's kind of a shot in the dark for now. We should all know more by the time we get to the briefing."

"Until then," Michael said, "get your gear together, everything you think you might need, get ready. After the briefing, it won't be long before we're on our way. The main enemy we have right now is time. We have to fight that harder than anything."

Chapter Forty-Two

James Darkwood—Annie Rourke Rubenstein couldn't help being reminded of Jason Darkwood, commander of the *Reagan* more than a century ago—stood at the rostrum at the front of the *Paladin*'s main briefing room. There were a full dozen Navy SEALs in the room as well. Why some locations aboard a Naval vessel were called cabins and others rooms bemused and amazed her, but she was used to it. One slept in one's cabin, but inspected maps in the chart room.

James Darkwood began to speak. "In order for the Rourke Family to penetrate Doctor Zimmer's headquarters near the pre-War city of Katmandu in the Himalayas in such a manner that they will be free to operate within the structure for a time period sufficient to allow them to locate the clone they seek, they cannot enter by force. In order to achieve that purpose, we have a number of people on line to assist them.

"Michael Rourke and Mr. Rubenstein will be in

full SS field uniform, wearing state-of-the-art makeup in order to disguise their appearance. I'll be with them, since I speak much better German." Darkwood smiled and there was a little laughter. "And, in the Academy, I always liked being in plays, anyway. At any event, the three of us should be able to walk in with the paperwork being created for us even now. Fly in, actually, as we'll be utilizing one of the helicopter gunships taken a short while ago in northern Canada when Zimmer's other base was knocked out. Our faces—Mr. Rubenstein's, Mr. Rourke's and my own—will match the faces of three of the officers who were killed or captured during that battle. Mr. Rubenstein will fly in the chopper.

"The rest of the plan is Mr. Rourke's and Mr. Rubenstein's. Gentlemen?"

Michael looked at Paul. Paul squeezed Annie's hand and stood, walking up to the rostrum which James Darkwood vacated. "Michael and I don't have all the data that we need, yet, and we might not get all we need until we learn it on the ground. But the basic plan is this. The three of us—Commander Darkwood, Michael Rourke and myself—once we're inside, do what we have to do to get away from the intelligence personnel who'll want to debrief us after the battle in Canada which we allegedly survived. We plant the seed that a second gunship should be arriving shortly, with wounded and other personnel."

The SEAL Team Commander, Lieutenant Christakos, raised his hand.

"Yes, Lieutenant?"

"How'd we get there?"

"Doglegging it across Canada to Greenland and so on. More importantly," Paul added, "you should be asking how any of us knew where to go. This is a top-secret base, known only to the high command and those personnel actually stationed there."

Lieutenant Christakos laughed. "I'll bite. How'd we learn about it?"

"From the Allies. We killed an Allied officer, but not before we discovered from him the location of our own base. They can't argue with that, can they?"

"I guess not."

Annie was proud of Paul. "At any event," Paul continued, "when that second gunship arrives, we'll have all the rest of our people inside the head-quarters, we hope. The second party will have as its principal task the taking and securing of the airfield facilities—we hope our intelligence people will confirm the headquarters has them. This is a bastardized way of working out the details for an operation like this, but we won't have the final intelligence data until we reach the naval base located about a hundred miles inland of what in our day was called Bombay, on the western coast of India. These days, it's called Darkwood Naval Air Station, after Commander Darkwood's ancestor, Jason Darkwood.

"At Darkwood Naval Air Station, we'll get handed to us every scrap of intelligence data concerning the Nazi base in the Himalayas, what used to be Nepal. We already have the two gunships en route to the base by the route that actual survivors from the defeat in Canada would have used, just in case they're picked up off satellite or

249

high-altitude observation craft. We'll rendezvous with our respective aircraft in the wastelands in what was once Iran. Then we're into it.

"Once the second gunship reaches the Nazi headquarters and, with any luck, secures the airfield, Commander Shaw will assign who flies what. All of you SEALs have cross-training in fighters and, if you get your tactics straight from Commander Shaw, and follow her lead, should be able to handle enough aircraft to get everyone out. Everyone who's able, anyway. Michael and I will get our hands on something that will blow up and use it to destroy the area where the clones are being kept. Once we rendezvous with the second element, Commander Shaw and Major Tiemerovna will have one function only. Get the clone aboard an aircraft and fly out of there and get back to the *Paladin* as quickly as humanly possible. The other aircraft will be on their own once we're airborne.

"But, we shouldn't have to worry about pursuit. It will be the job of the second element to sabotage anything left behind that can fly, and generally do as much damage to the Nazi headquarters as possible.

"After we're out, an as yet undisclosed number of Marine Airborne, Navy SEAL and German Long Range Mountain Patrol personnel will attack the base. Even if it weren't desirable to neutralize the base as quickly as possible, there's the substantial chance that Deitrich Zimmer might launch additional nuclear missiles as retaliation for the raid. We can't allow that to happen.

"Any questions?"

Chapter Forty-Three

They went together as a Family, asking her to join them. And, she did.

Annie cried. Natalia did not, but looked like she wanted to. Sarah stared blankly.

Michael held back tears, but it was obvious that he was doing that—holding them back—and Paul, beside him, holding to his shoulder, gritted his teeth, jutted his jaw and stared with glassy eyes.

Wolfgang Mann only stared.

Emma Shaw was cried out.

John Rourke lay, unconscious, on a bed behind the glass of the intensive-care ward. Tubes led in and out of him, and a temporary artificial heart—it was a machine which pumped his blood and interacted with a fresh oxygen supply—kept him alive.

She would do this thing; and, if she had to, she'd help Natalia cut the heart out of the clone with her own bare hands if that was what it would take to bring John back among the living.

The man, Elwood Brooks, was otherwise spotless-seeming in his record. He might have been a Nazi, or perhaps just insane. But a little man with a plastic gas pistol had done what armies of enemy commandos of every description had never been able to do: he had killed John Rourke. If the machinery were shut off, John would be dead in a matter of minutes.

Only their action, a raid on a facility about which they knew next to nothing, against odds they could not reckon, stood a chance of saving his life, bringing him back from the dead. John Rourke had survived over six centuries against every conceivable danger and a madman brought him down, using her to do it.

If Paul Rubenstein hadn't riddled Elwood Brooks's body with bullets, Natalia would have found the man in the brig and killed him herself.

Michael cleared his throat. "If we're to do this thing, we have to go."

Sarah Rourke said, "I don't want to lose any of you. If he weren't already dead, he'd tell you that this is madness."

Paul, maybe mad, maybe tired, maybe afraid, dropped to a crouch beside the wheelchair in which she sat and looked at her hard. "What are you really saying, Sarah?"

"I know that he tried killing our son. And, I know something else."

"What, Momma?" Annie asked her.

"That's an academic point now with him dying, dead already, isn't it?"

"What are you saying, Momma?" Annie persisted.

252

"I loved your father, and he loved me. I don't know what happened to him, but I do know what he did, to me, tried to do to Martin. If I could, I'd tell Dr. Zimmer that all of you are coming, so he could prevent you from getting inside. What you're talking about is murder. Killing that clone is killing a human being. And, for what?"

"For—for what?" Michael Rourke stammered. "For him, for God's sake, to save our father and your husband! What should we do? Nothing?"

"John Rourke led a life that will be perceived by everyone as a life dedicated to helping mankind. It should be left at that. With your father dead, Michael, the truth will never have to come out."

"The truth?" Paul demanded. "The truth! What the hell is the truth, Sarah? Come on! You know something we don't, you're saying. What?"

"I know what really happened the night the Nazis attacked the hospital at Eden City, and none of the rest of you do. I know who pointed the gun at my head and pulled the trigger."

Michael Rourke literally staggered. Annie's hands went to her mother's shoulders, turning her around, wheelchair and all. "What are you saying?"

"There's no reason to soil your memories of him. Believe me, I wish I didn't remember what happened!"

Natalia, already dressed in one of her black jumpsuits, inserted herself between Annie and Sarah Rourke. "Are you implying that John shot you, Sarah? And, if you are, you're saying he did it because of me, aren't you?"

"Infer what you like, Natalia. And, I have nothing

253

against you. Maybe John was seized with some temporary madness. I don't know. But he killed the clone of Martin, thinking it was Martin. And, if he'd lived, he would have killed Martin eventually or died in the attempt. You know that."

"Spell it out, Mom," Michael almost hissed.

Emma Shaw realized that her whole body was shaking.

Wolfgang Mann acted as if he were about to speak, but then turned away.

"Spell it out, damn it!" Michael shouted, his voice echoing off the bulkheads. "Spell it out, Mom!"

"Fine. I remember your father pointing a gun at my head and pulling the trigger, God help me. The last word I said before I almost died that night was to call out your father's name." And, Sarah Rourke started to cry.

Natalia, her voice little over a whisper, said, "You were shot with a .38 caliber bullet. The X-rays revealed that. That is verifiable fact. Lots of cartridges—.380, like I carry in my PPK/S; 9mm Parabellum, like Paul carries in his Brownings; .38 Special—have the same bullet diameter. If enough of the bullet that was lodged in your brain was recovered, a ballistician could tell what kind of gun fired it, not just the diameter of the bullet.

"It was probably a 9mm Parabellum. That night, John was carrying his Centennial. If the bullet Deitrich Zimmer took out of your head was a .38 Special, then you'd have proof, or at least a basis for argument, Sarah.

"In those days," Natalia continued, "the only time John ever carried anything in 9mm was when he used that suppressed Smith & Wesson automatic. And he wasn't wearing that gun that night. If it was a 9mm Parabellum that Deitrich Zimmer took from your head, the person who shot you could have been Zimmer or one of his people, or perhaps even Commander Dodd or one of his people. Wouldn't that make sense, since the Nazis were generally using guns given to them by Commander Dodd and the only handguns Dodd had access to were 9mm Berettas, like Michael carries? But, we will never know anything more about the bullet, will we? Will we? Because the man who took the bullet from your head was the man who put the bullet there in the first place and he wouldn't tell you that if he tried making you think that it was John. Would he?"

"Natalia, you can say whatever you like, but my memories are my memories. I remember John standing over me and firing a gun at my head. That's the last thing I remember."

Emma Shaw felt like she was about to vomit.

Finally, without looking at anyone, Wolfgang Mann spoke. "One thing is clear," he said. "Either this woman is one of the clones of Sarah Rourke, or Deitrich Zimmer was able to program her mind with memories that he created for her. In either event, what she says is not the truth."

"Damn you, Wolf!"

Wolfgang Mann's eyes filled with tears.

Chapter Forty-Four

They flew in separate fighter aircraft as they left the *Paladin*. The V/STOL tore upward, crashing out of the waves with a loud crack as Emma Shaw leveled out, skimming the whitecaps in order to stay under scanning until well away from the *Paladin*'s actual location.

In the copilot's seat behind her sat Natalia Tiemerovna. Natalia had requested to be her passenger, and Emma was glad for the company. But, so far, Natalia had said nothing at all. And it would be a long flight without conversation, radio silence necessary as well.

They would bypass Hawaii entirely, already too far north, heading toward the Izu and Bonin Trenches and into the Philippine Sea, over what little remained of the Philippines and Indonesia, then around the horn of the Indian subcontinent.

In the first few seconds of going airborne after a submerged takeoff, Emma Shaw had always found it fascinating to watch the action of the slipstream on the water droplets over the canopy. They were gone in seconds, but when circumstances permitted, observing them was like observing living organisms, tiny things in some terrible hurry, condensing, separating, disappearing.

"It is beautiful, what you see each time you do this," Natalia said through their intraship radio.

"Why did you ask to come along with me?"

"Because you and I have been made allies by circumstance, Emma. Had things been different—and I do not regret my love for Michael—but I would have been John Rourke's love, as now you are. I was fortunate. So are you. I loved John, realized I could not have him, then fell in love again, with his son. On the other hand, John had matured—that's the only way I can put it—by the time the two of you began to have feelings for one another. He was willing to sacrifice his entire life for a woman who wanted to divorce him, because to John the mere consideration of such a thing was out of the question.

"He's changed, but only a little bit. And, you're fortunate that it was just enough. I love Michael now more than I ever loved John, then. You and John are meant for each other. Don't believe what you heard."

"I know John wouldn't do something like she said," Emma Shaw responded.

"Sarah knows that, too—the real Sarah."

"Then she is a clone!"

Natalia told her, "I did not say that, Emma. The woman we spoke with in sickbay might be a clone or might be Sarah. John felt that she was Sarah. If

258

anyone would know, he would, but if anyone could be tricked, he could be. I tend to believe that she is Sarah."

"But—" But what? Emma Shaw thought. Natalia knew more about this than Emma Shaw could ever hope to begin to understand. She let Natalia go on.

"Deitrich Zimmer's success with cloning would be impossible, as John pointed out yesterday, without the ability to somehow record the electromagnetic impulses within the mind in the same way that sound or image is recorded on magnetic tape. If we assume that technology to be wholly viable, then there is no reason to suppose that it could not be utilized for the purest form of what used to be called brainwashing."

"I know the term. The Russians used to—" Emma shut up.

Natalia laughed. "Ancient history. Some of the agencies within the Committee for State Security of the Soviet as well as some elements within the GRU—that was Red Army Intelligence—utilized advanced techniques for extracting information. It was very ugly. Rarely was the attempt made to implant information, and in every case I ever heard of, never was such an attempt successful. The point is, Deitrich Zimmer could have fabricated the memories and downloaded the tape with the artificial memories in the same manner he would download memory into the blank mind of one of the clones. Sarah doesn't merely imagine she remembers John trying to kill her. She really remembers it, even though it never happened that way. She has a real memory of the event happening in more or less the way that she described, and the implanted memory of John being the man who pulled the trigger. And, because the event really took place, only with someone else doing the shooting, she has all the ancillary memory to back up the induced memory.

"The memory is real," Natalia said, "but it is not what really happened. Trying to convince her of that fact would be essentially impossible."

"So, if it is the real Sarah we're talking about—" Emma Shaw didn't know what to say.

"If this woman is really Sarah Rourke, we may be able to convince her that John never did what she remembers, demonstrating to her the technique by which Zimmer implanted the memories that she has. But, even though on a rational level she'll know the truth, her memories will still be there. Zimmer's technique is the most insidious thing I have ever heard of. We could not remove the memory without removing all of her other memories. We are powerless to erase what he has inserted."

"Then even if she realizes on a rational basis that John is guiltless, she'll still remember him trying to kill her."

"Forever. Yes. When the opportunity presents itself, I hope that I am the one to kill Deitrich Zimmer. But, until then, you and I will have to be very strong, Emma, stronger perhaps than you have ever had to be. If Michael or Annie killed the clone of their father in order to save their real father, I have no idea what effect it might have on them. I don't think we can have a doctor remove the heart from one living human being in order to save the life of another, even if the donor is a clone of the recipient. The ethics involved would be staggering.

"I will kill the donor," Natalia went on. "And you may have to—what's the term? Damn! Yes. The football thing?"

"The football thing?"

"Run interference! You may have to run interference for me. The Rourke family tends to moralize quite a bit. Not Annie, really; she's very practical. And Paul would never forgive himself. I will kill the clone just when the operation is about to begin. You may have to help me then. Do you have the nerve for it, Emma, in order to save John's life?"

"You love him more than you'll admit, still," Emma Shaw told Natalia Tiemerovna.

Natalia Tiemerovna said, "Over the intervening years since I first became entangled with the Rourke Family, I've come to believe in the concept that there may very well be someone known as God. If there is, it would only be logical that He doesn't place people into life haphazardly, that we all have some purpose. My purpose now can be to save a marvelous life, a life like no other life. And I alone have the ability to do it, to walk over to a sedated body that looks identical in every way to the body of a man I once worshiped—and still do in a way—and kill. Life on the cosmic scale is very much like life on the most minute scale.

"There are some people whose mission or lot it is to do the things that other, better people cannot do. I'm one of those people, Emma Shaw. Can I count on you to help me?"

"Yes. But John may hate us both for this."

"Hate us? John cannot hate. It isn't part of his makeup. He doesn't have the capacity for hatred. He

261

might never forgive us, though. Are you willing to risk losing the man you love in order to save his life?"

Emma didn't have to think of an answer.

It was nearly time for her to begin to climb, get to cruising altitude and start watching out for enemy aircraft and enemy missiles.

"By your silence, I detect an answer in the affirmative."

"And we can count on Annie if we need someone else to help us?"

Natalia said, "Yes."

Chapter Forty-Five

If his parents could have seen him, they would have rolled over in their graves.

But then, Paul Rubenstein recalled bitterly that they had no graves, would have died with all the rest of the people in Texas with the de facto President of the United States when the sky caught fire during the Great Conflagration.

SS field uniforms were black, and there were collar tabs with the lightning-bolt runes of old. The cap insignia was the death's-head, just as it had been, but set over the swastika.

Paul Rubenstein wore the rank of Sturmbann-führer, equivalent to a major, while Michael was a Hauptsturmführer, his rank equivalent to a captain. Appropriately, since James Darkwood was the only one who spoke acceptable German and, hence, would do most of the talking, Darkwood bore the single starburst of an Obersturmbannführer.

"Boy, if my mom and dad could see me now," Paul at last said aloud.

"They'd be proud of what you were doing, Mr. Rubenstein," Darkwood volunteered.

Paul smiled, looking at Darkwood in the full-length mirror the three of them shared. "Only if I got a chance to get the words out of my mouth before they started to tear me limb from limb," he countered.

Michael forced a laugh. "I'm finding myself wishing I'd insisted that Maria Leuden had spoken German to me instead of using her English."

"Maria Leuden?" Darkwood said.

"A woman I knew, very well, before Natalia and I became—" And he paused.

Quickly, Paul inserted, "Fortunate we had enough uniforms without bullet holes in them."

"Allied Intell has been collecting enemy uniforms since the start," James Darkwood said, buckling on his pistol belt. "And don't think we haven't used them before."

Paul Rubenstein grabbed up his borrowed arctic parka and started for the door . . .

Darkwood Naval Air Station controlled the Arabian Sea, the Bay of Bengal and the Indian Ocean to the west. Smaller than the Naval Air Station itself was Hapgood Naval Base, attached to the Naval Air Station, a facility for servicing submarine craft in the Allied armada. Although other forces had navies, the United States Navy was the only true naval power, and it ruled the seas.

But, with the increased technology of the present, even the deepest diving craft was vulnerable to attack from the air. The possession of air power was not a sole prerogative of the United States.

As the three men walked toward the briefing area, the temperature a balmy sixty degrees, the wind warm off the Arabian Sea, James Darkwood discussed in layman's terms a sketchy breakdown of force tables as the war was about to begin in earnest. "We have them outgunned, of course, between the United States forces and the forces of New Germany, adding to that the other Allies. Most people discount the Australians, for example, but really they have a tough little airborne unit and although they don't have many aircraft, their pilots are good. If it comes to an all-out land war, we'll win. If it's decided under the sea or in the air, we'll win. The only two really effective weapons in the Nazi-Eden Alliance, with the temporary destruction of Eden's chemical and biological weapons facilities are terror and nuclear."

"There's little difference between the two," Michael Rourke observed. "Nuclear weapons are merely instruments of massive terror, brandished for the purpose of terror."

"Oh, you're right there, Michael," James Darkwood said, "but the added factor is that the Nazis have shown us, quite pointedly, that they'll employ nuclear weapons if needed."

"During World War II," Paul Rubenstein mused aloud, "the reason Hitler didn't have nuclear weapons was that he didn't believe in their potential. Imagine, what it would have been like if Hitler's scientists had been able to perfect a V-2 type weapon which could have been launched even from occupied

265

France, to impact the Eastern Coast of the United States, and the payload had been even the most primitive sort of nuclear device. It would have been vastly smaller than the bombs the United States dropped on Hiroshima and Nagasaki in order to end the war in the Pacific, but such a weapon would have turned the tide of the war.

"No one in the United States, even at the highest levels of government," Paul went on, "would have known the exact capabilities of the weapon system, so no one would have known where Hitler could strike next. The demoralizing effect alone could have won the war for him. If he'd been able to field a hundred such long-range rockets armed with primitive, dirty atomic warheads, he would have won the war. What a world it would have been after that." Despite the pleasant temperatures, Paul Rubenstein shivered at the thought.

"We're faced with the same possibility now, really," Michael observed.

"Indeed," Darkwood agreed, nodding his head. "I remember reading in the history books that after World War II there were Nazi groups all over, calling themselves various things, in the United States going under the title of white supremacist extremists and like that. And people didn't really take them all that seriously."

Paul laughed bitterly. "If there had not been a war between the superpowers, if we'd avoided all of that, there would have been a rise in National Socialism again. The population of the United States, because of the baby boom following the war, was aging. By the early decades of the twenty-first century, it

266

would have been necessary to open the United States to massive immigration from abroad for the simple fact that without it there wouldn't be a work force, with half the population over retirement age. That alone would have been all the trigger the Nazis needed to get them rolling with the disenfranchised. It's curious that that Nazis actually needed us."

"Us?" Darkwood repeated.

"Jews. Hitler and his elite needed a scapegoat for Germany's woes following World War I and the onset of the Great Depression. They needed a scapegoat in order to galvanize the emotions and the interests of a country they intended to use for their own purposes. It would have been the same if the Night of the War hadn't interrupted it.

"Nazism is a cancer," Paul went on. "But it can't be cut out, because it's the formalization of race hatred. And that'll always be there with some people. Today we have Deitrich Zimmer and his new Reich. Let's say that we defeat him. Fine. In some future, probably not as distant as we'd hope, there'll be another Deitrich Zimmer and another Nazi movement. It may call itself by another name or use the old name, but the message of hatred will be the same and the desire to kill those who are different will be the same, too. We can cut out a Nazi growth, think we've destroyed the problem for good. But when we least expect it, the growth will be there again, infecting everything it touches with death."

"Sobering thoughts," Darkwood said. "And why do we bother, then?"

Paul laughed again. "You know perfectly well why we bother to fight, don't you? Decent men and

267

women have two choices when confronted by evil incarnate: turn your back and await the inevitable or fight. Mankind has spent thousands of years trying to avoid confrontation with evil, and unsuccessfully, too. We let evil grow to the point where it becomes harder and harder to stop, just hoping against hope that somehow it will fade away and we won't have to fight it. But always, in the end, we have to take a stand. That's always the way."

Chapter Forty-Six

Despite the circumstances, Annie Rubenstein was amused. It was odd watching men having their faces made up.

The three closest physical matches—bone structure, height and frame size—were picked from among the officers killed or captured at the Nazi facility in Canada, then their identity papers taken. The theatrical makeup expert who worked on her husband, her brother and James Darkwood was a veteran of intelligence work. Although her full-time career was in Hawaii in the movies, she freely admitted as she worked that the occasional jobs for Allied Intelligence were both more interesting and more challenging.

Tall for a woman, a little past middle age and exceedingly pretty with short, wavy dark hair with just a touch of grey, her name was Helen Gould.

Natalia was assisting her, cutting a roll of paper-thin bandagelike material into short strips of approximately six inches in length, then rolling each strip. Two containers of water sat on the table beside her. Before Helen Gould began all three of the men had been told to scrub their faces with soap and water then rinse as well as possible. After doing so, their faces were blown dry with hair dryers. Helen Gould talked as she worked. "What I'm doing is using some of the same technology that we employ when we are making a life mask of an actor for a stunt man to use when he's performing something really dangerous that the actor can't do himself but the face has to be seen.

"The problem here that's different from my movie work is that a life mask that I might make for a stunt man only has to approximate the actor's features when seen quickly and from a distance. Cutaway shots that would show a true close-up on the face are filmed afterward and inserted at critical points within the action. So, when you get the chance to see the actor's face for a real close-up, you're really seeing the actor's face and not the life mask.

"So," she went on, "that's why I said a moment ago that these occasional jobs I do for Allied Intelligence are a lot more challenging."

Annie watched as Helen Gould worked soap into the eyebrows of the three men. As she worked she explained, "I have to build up their bone structure subtly, which means I have to do some plaster of Paris work, which means I have to make molds of their faces. If I didn't use the soap, when I remove the plaster of Paris mold, I'd remove the facial hair as well."

"Ouch!" Paul said in mock pain.

Annie laughed and said, "As my husband always

270

said, he doesn't have that much hair to begin with. Why are you making a life mask, though, if it wouldn't stand up to close scrutiny?"

Helen Gould answered quickly saying, "The man that your husband is supposed to be, for example, has a much lower forehead. In order to achieve that effect on your husband's face I have to build up the forehead area. The life mask is a form for me." She began rubbing a substance which reminded Annie of Vaseline into Paul's facial skin.

"Soon, you'll all be beautiful," Natalia said, smiling.

"I think the word you're searching for, Major Tiemerovna, is 'uncomfortable'—soon we'll all be uncomfortable," Darkwood announced.

Chapter Forty-Seven

Emma Shaw's eyes squinted through the magnifier as, frame by frame, she reviewed the video taken by high-altitude observation flights over the now-confirmed site of the Nazi headquarters near what was once Katmandu. The mountains themselves seemed as innocuous as mountains could be. Visual imagery provided no discernible clue that there was anything here but snow-capped granite crags, surrounded by glacial ice and snow, yards deep.

She told the computer, "Add thermal imaging."

The computer responded, Emma raising her head from the magnifier and staring at the frame she'd just examined. There were heat signatures everywhere, some of them barely visible, a few of them quite hot. If Deitrich Zimmer's forces were using an airfield—and they had to be, because the mountain crosswinds would be dangerous for helicopter use, and the only access into the mountains would have to be by air—the aircraft had to be flying in and out

273

by terrain following.

Putting herself mentally into the position of one of these Nazi or Eden pilots, she plotted approach paths to every one of the larger thermal signatures, confirming her gut reaction at last that the largest of these thermal signatures was the access opening into one of the mountains. And, she laughed. Zimmer was running an operation very familiar to her, only translated to land, whereas she was used to the same thing at sea.

The mountain which she now studied in greater detail was like a submerged carrier, like the *Paladin* which she had just left. And, there were access tunnels, the mouths of which opened and closed to admit returning aircraft or allow exit on a sortie. Then, the tunnels were sealed until needed again.

She had seen thermal signatures like these before, but of United States submersible carriers. And the signatures showed the takeoff and landing bays.

With no clearly present airfield, Paul Rubenstein would have a difficult time, and that would be after fighting what would have to be killer crosswinds in order to reach the right coordinates. If whoever monitored access to the landing bays refused access to the solitary Nazi gunship which Paul would be flying, there would be no place to land and the whole plan would have to be abandoned.

This was a dicey plan, dicey beyond belief, but so reckless an endeavor that it was the sort of thing no security force could plan against. That was the only consolation.

As to what was going on inside the mountains, where everything was located, how what she

274

imagined as a series of tunnels could interconnect portions of the complex, she could not hazard a guess from the observation photos beyond the fact that the smaller heat signatures, so faint they were only visible through digitized enhancement, had to be air exchanges.

Again, however, she put herself in someone else's shoes. The air exchanges would be located for maximum efficiency. Nazis had but one virtue, if any aspect of a Nazi could be called virtuous: Nazis were efficient in the extreme. The exchanges would be placed near areas of maximal need. Power-generating facilities, living areas, the aircraft takeoff and landing bays, etc. She began to study the areas she had defined as the landing bays once again.

By ordering the computer to digitally increase pixelization, she was able to make additional educated guesses concerning the landing bays, their size, their structure, their maximum dimensions. Synth-fuel fumes were noxious-smelling, albeit essentially harmless, and would have to be evacuated before getting into the overall air system of the complex.

Calling on the computer for maximum enhancement of the thermal signatures and utilizing a transparent film over the still-framed screen, she was able to construct rough maps of the takeoff and landing bays, deducing that there were three such installations, all located on the north face of the mountain designated on the map underlayment as L-9.

L-9 might not be the central section of the complex, but was, indeed, the business end of the operation. Extrapolating figures based on her familiarity with submersible aircraft carriers, Emma Shaw arrived at a figure for the number of aircraft which the facility might successfully handle. Assuming typical Nazi/Eden V/STOL fighters, each landing bay could house and service one hundred and twenty such craft. The three bays, combined, would accommodate three hundred and sixty fighters. Allowing for squadron sizes and the like, Emma Shaw determined that roughly three hundred V/STOL-type fighter aircraft could be expected to be on hand.

"Aw, shit," she said aloud.

The computer's voice—nothing at all like that of her old automatic copilot, Gorgeous—announced, "The term 'shit' does not compute."

"Is that a fact?" She lit a cigarette, then started feeding her drawings into the computer program so that the drawings could be enhanced based upon everything which was known about Nazi/Eden airfields. With the help of the computer, fuel storage facilities, tower facilities, even pilot briefing rooms and waiting rooms could be filled in with a reasonable degree of accuracy based upon how such facilities had been laid out in the past.

The Nazis were not only efficient and organized, they were also predictable. If an airfield layout worked well for them in the past, it would work again. Eden airfields, of which there were considerably more than Nazi ones, were laid out in the same fashion, because the Nazis, of course, were the ones who laid them out for their allies.

While the computer crunched her data input,

Emma Shaw began working out her escape route from the facility, should they survive long enough to reach that point. The Nazi/Eden fighter aircraft were fairly capable machines, but considerably less maneuverable than U.S. Navy fighter aircraft. So, she couldn't hang around to get into a fight with any of the three hundred or so aircraft which might be on her tail the moment after she took off.

She would have to get to maximum speed as quickly as possible and see as her only strategy the possibility of outrunning her pursuers.

That was a poor plan, but the best she had. If the sky behind her filled with enemy aircraft or their missiles, she would be done for.

And, so would John Rourke.

Chapter Forty-Eight

On those rare occasions when he indulged in a nap, Deitrich Zimmer left explicit orders that he was not to be disturbed except in the event of an emergency. He knew better than to trust anything truly important to his son, Martin.

So, when the buzzer beside his head sounded and Deitrich Zimmer opened his eyes, his first reaction was not anger at being disturbed but concern at what the emergency might be. He wiggled his toes within his socks, starting his circulation, then slowly moved his feet at the ankles, then began to raise his knees slightly as he spread his arms from his torso and moved them, flexing his fingers as well.

This practice consumed only a few seconds, but he somehow felt better for it, more instantly clear-headed when he awakened.

Zimmer sat up.

The cover on the couch was, like the couch itself, black, as were the walls of the little sideroom to his office suite. The furnishings were sparse, the only light a single, green-shaded lamp beside the couch on a table otherwise devoid of anything except for a carafe of water and a glass. The water was changed every hour on the hour unless he was using the room for sleep. The idea behind its Spartan appearance was total lack of sensual stimulation, thus sleep-inducing.

He fluffed his pillow, preparatory to using it again, flung the throw out across the couch so it would not become inordinately wrinkled—he was a neat man and always had been—and walked to the door. He did not lock it, ever. He opened the door now and squinted against the light as he grabbed his sweater from the solitary chair just inside the doorway. He flung the sweater around his shoulders as he closed the door and searched out the cause of his alarm.

It was Rottenführer Hoffmann, his valet. Hoffmann stood at attention just inside the office doorway, about two meters away, at the far end of the vaulted chamber. "Yes, Hoffmann. What is it?"

"Herr Doctor, forgive me for disturbing your rest. But, I was told to inform you that a helicopter approaches the citadel, the occupants claiming to be survivors of the SS Commando unit from the headquarters in Canada. They request permission to land."

"Who are these persons? Who is their officer?"

"They are three officers, Herr Doctor. The Senior identifies himself as Obersturmbannführer Rudolph Gessler."

"Gessler," Deitrich Zimmer mused aloud. "There

is no Gessler who knows the location of the citadel."

"Forgive me, Herr Doctor, but I was told that the Obersturmbannführer related to communication central that the location of the citadel was learned from a captured American prisoner, whom they then killed."

"Hmm. That is plausible, but doubtful. Thank you, Hoffmann. That is all."

"Yes, Herr Doctor!"

Hoffmann made a neat about-face, opened the door nearest him and exited the room. Deitrich Zimmer walked toward the desk, stood beside it for a moment, fingers splayed over it, taking deep breaths as he fully awakened. Three officers in a helicopter approaching the citadel on the basis of information taken from an American prisoner. Most unlikely. He smiled. It was too stupid a scenario for an intelligence operation. The officers were probably quite genuine.

Still—

Deitrich Zimmer raised the telephone receiver and told the computer, "Security."

In seconds, the voice of the security officer of the day responded.

Zimmer said, "The helicopter in question should be allowed to land, the three officers aboard should have their papers checked, then after they have been allowed to refresh themselves, I wish them brought to me. They shall be accompanied by a security detachment wherever they go. Understood?"

"Yes, Herr Doctor!"

"That is all." Deitrich Zimmer hung up the telephone receiver and took a cigarette from the gold box on his black marble-topped desk. He lit the cigarette with an electric lighter and exhaled smoke through his nostrils. He raised the receiver again, telling the computer, "Martin Zimmer."

Martin answered on the fifth ring. "Hello?"

"You are aware, Martin, that a helicopter with three officers aboard it appoaches the citadel. I have given permission for it to land."

"It could be a trick, Father."

"Yes, it could. Then, we shall see what sort of trick, shall we? Shall we have some fun?"

Martin responded, "I don't understand."

"We have lives to spare, do we not?"

Chapter Forty-Nine

Natalia Tiemerovna settled herself into the co-pilot's seat, then bent forward, catching up her hair at the nape of the neck and turning it around her fingers as she flipped the black SS foraging cap onto her head, her hair successfully stuffed beneath it. Since there were no women allowed to serve in other than a menial capacity within the Nazi or Eden forces—women were political and social inferiors—it was necessary that, from a distance at least, she should appear to be male rather than female.

"Ever think how easy we've got it, Natalia?" Emma Shaw asked, taking the pilot's seat and fixing her somewhat shorter hair so that it, too, would be concealed by a foraging cap. "WE can dress however we want, really."

"I had never really thought of that. I suppose you're right. If I wear pants, I'm practical. If a man wears a skirt, he's strange."

"Unless he's a Scotsman and he calls it a kilt. Three minutes before takeoff," Emma Shaw an-

283

nounced, starting to flip switches on the control panel. "Run the check with me?"

"Of course," Natalia responded . . .

Annie Rourke Rubenstein sat with the twelve Navy SEALs in the aft section of the Nazi gunship. Like her, they were all dressed in SS field uniforms, all armed with Nazi weapons, their own weapons concealed beneath their uniforms as were her own weapons.

Several of the SEAL Team personnel were putting last minute touch-ups to the edges of their fighting knives, these as widely divergent as she could imagine. Some carried knives roughly shaped like her father's Crain LS-X, only smaller. Others carried double-edged daggers.

Unlike Natalia, Annie had never been much of a knife person. She carried two knives only, a Cold Steel Mini Tanto dating from Before the Night of the War and an Executive Edge Fazendeiro lock-blade folding knife, this also from Before the Night of the War. On those rare occasions when she could dress as she liked, the Fazendeiro was in her purse. Her father generally favored custom knives, but two of the three knives he carried were not custom knives at all, because in additon to the Crain LS-X knife, handmade for him by Texas knifemaker Jack Crain, he carried the little A. G. Russell Sting IA Black Chrome and a pen-shaped Executive Edge Grande.

Her father had told her once, "Only a snob rejects something because it isn't custom. If something is good it's good; if it's bad, it's bad. It doesn't matter

284

who made it. The Gerber Paul carries, the Bali-Song Natalia uses, the little Executive Edge Grande I carry in my shirt pocket. The Cold Steel Mini Tanto I've just given you. A friend of mine named Glenn Barnes once gave me an Al Mar folding knife. You've seen me use it. Al Mar was one of the finest knifemakers ever, and his work was commercial, not custom. Anyway, remember that a gun can run out of ammo; a knife won't, all right?"

She missed her father, just thinking of him. If they succeeded in bringing him back from the brink of death, she would tell him how much she loved him. He knew it, of course, but she hadn't said, "I love you Daddy" to him in a very long time.

And, if her father survived, she had already decided that she would be as understanding as humanly possible when the time came for her father and mother to separate. Her mother, if the woman she had spoken with, hugged, was indeed her mother, would never forgive her father for something her father had not done—thanks to Deitrich Zimmer's brainwashing techniques, which were beyond measure in their effectiveness. In an odd way, Deitrich Zimmer had solved a problem which had been in evidence ever since Before the Night of the War.

Parents often thought that their children were at once deaf, dumb and blind, that their children did not notice the friction building between father and mother, husband and wife. From her earliest days, she had realized that Mommy and Daddy did not get along, that there was something wrong between them. By the time she was old enough to know what it was, they were into the survival situation the framework of which they had lived with in all of her adult life. And, there was nothing to be done about it.

She had seen the way Natalia loved her father and her father loved Natalia and her father had, intentionally, engineered a situation in which Natalia would become Michael's wife rather than his own. Even though his plans had not worked the way he had intended, eventually Natalia and Michael were thrown together and became lovers. Soon, when all of this was over or there was at least a moment left to them in which to be normal (whatever that was), Natalia and Michael would be married.

But her father, had he not met Emma Shaw, would still have been alone. Once it became clear that Wolfgang Mann and her mother, Sarah Rourke, loved each other, her father could have done nothing else but step aside. Fortunately for him, there was Emma Shaw to go to. If her father did not survive, Annie would always be a friend to Emma Shaw, always treat her with the love and respect that she would have shown, had her father married her . . .

Emma Shaw's mind was always able to function on two different levels, and she imagined that everyone else's mind was able to do the same. With one portion of her consciousness, she checked and double-checked the control panel, making certain that all was in order for the flight which would commence in under sixty seconds now. On another level, however, she reviewed other matters of importance.

She refused to consider that John Rourke would die and she would become a widow before she had become a bride. She would never marry, should he die, because there could be no other man who would be anything like him.

Instead, Emma Shaw considered what her life would be like if John Rourke lived. Technically, she would be Annie and Michael's stepmother, Paul's and eventually Natalia's stepmother-in-law. "Weird," Emma Shaw almost said aloud. Annie was becoming a good friend, as was Natalia.

But, what about Sarah Rourke? Was it the real Sarah Rourke who believed those awful lies about John? What would things be like with her? Emma Shaw knew that she was the other woman, the evil seductress (hard to imagine herself seducing anyone) who had led the faithful husband astray. On one level, she felt it was about time, but on another level she felt guilty.

But John deserved a life, and so did she. John deserved someone to come home to who would not constantly rail at him for who he was and what he was, but love him as he was. When the War ended, she would retire, leave the Navy if John lived, devote her full time to being wife and— She felt her cheeks flushing for the first time since she didn't know when. Mother? Would John get her pregnant? Would she bear his children? What would they be like?

She'd given up on the idea of motherhood years

ago, but her biological clock was running just great and she could do it.

"Do you think I'd make a good mother?" Fortunately, she'd pulled her microphone plug before asking Natalia, rather than announcing it over the entire ship.

"Do you think *I* would?" Natalia countered.

"Yeah! An interesting mother, but a good one, I think."

"I'd say the same about you," Natalia told her. "Are we checked out?"

"Yeah." Emma Shaw plugged her microphone back in, announcing, "Make certain that all seat restraints are secure, this'll be a bumpy ride once we're over the Himalayas. All you SEAL Team guys, put away any sharp objects, huh? Hang on and pray."

"Pray?" Natalia asked her.

"That we get this done and we get out with our skins. Yeah, pray. Okay?"

"All right," Natalia answered,

"Increasing main rotor revolution." She switched to the frequency which connected her with the ground control, a cargo lifter sitting in the middle of a snow-splotched sand dune where six centuries ago the city of Tehran had been. "This is X One Niner preparing for takeoff."

"We have you clear, X One Niner. Good luck and Godspeed."

"Religion is everywhere, isn't it?" Natalia asked, seemingly rhetorically.

"Amen, sister," Emma Shaw said, smiling, then changing rotor pitch and starting lift-off. "There

288

used to be a saying, about how there were no atheists in foxholes."

Natalia laughed. "I like what Shakespeare said even better. 'To thine own self be true and it follows as the night the day thou canst not then be false toward any man.'"

"Touché. You think we'll make it?"

"The plan is so horribly bizarre that no miltary mind could even accept its being a plan. We are walking into a totally unfamiliar facility and we intend to kidnap someone—the clone of John—and then kill and destroy as much as possible while attempting to escape in relative safety. It is just insane enough that it might work, simply because Deitrich Zimmer would never expect such a thing. Maybe we should both pray."

They were airborne.

Chapter Fifty

Michael Rourke made a last-minute check of the two Beretta 92Fs under his SS officer's field tunic. The pistols and a half dozen spare magazines were as hidden as he could get them and still have any sort of access. Because some of the Nazi field uniforms were made from a bullet-resistant material, the guns were loaded with cartridges incorporating armor-piercing bullets. His father recounted to him once how the antifirearms rights forces so prevalent during the last half of the twentieth century had manipulated the general public into believing that armor piercing rounds were "cop-killer bullets." In an age when many professional criminals wore body armor as well, the description was hardly accurate, his father had said. However, John Rourke invariably refrained from using what he called "trick cartridges," preferring instead to rely upon a proven-performance round and correct shot placement in order to accomplish the task at hand.

Interrupting Michael's thoughts, Paul announced,

"We're cleared by control. We're going in." He didn't use the intraship frequency, merely speaking loudly enough to be heard over the mechanical noise. There was a chance, James Darkwood had pointed out, that the Nazis might be able to monitor intraship frequencies with long-range electronic surveillance devices.

Ahead of them, Michael Rourke saw a granite doorway sliding away and a gleaming, red-lit hole appeared within the face of the mountain before them. This was it, and his father's life depended upon the outcome. And, perhaps also his mother's sanity. If the woman purporting to be Sarah Rourke really was Sarah Rourke and not her clone, the only person who would have a prayer of convincing her that the memories she recalled so vividly were implanted rather than real would be his father. And the chance for success was slight.

James Darkwood said aloud, rather than across the intraship radio, "I understand that Jason Darkwood played it a lot by the seat of his pants."

Paul laughed. "He did indeed, James. He was an interesting man. I seriously doubt he did anything by the book in his life. That was why Jason Darkwood and Sebastian made such an interesting pair. Sebastian was his direct opposite, Jason Darkwood's. Sebastian researched every detail, whereas Jason Darkwood just sort of winged it as he went along. In some men, that's brilliance. It was that way with Jason Darkwood. John has often said that Jason Darkwood was possibly the most talented tactician that he'd ever met. All tactics is, is advanced problem solving. When you couple that with innovation, you have the brilliance I mentioned. He had that, Jason Darkwood."

"He's been a tough act to live up to," James Darkwood admitted.

Michael laughed, saying, "Well, no one could accuse the three of us with tactical brilliance with this plan. God help us, because that's the only way we're going to even come close to pulling this off."

Paul Rubenstein said, "May He help us indeed," as he started their stolen Nazi gunship into the tunnel mouth; or, Michael thought, was it the valley of death?

Chapter Fifty-One

The door to the takeoff and landing bay was about one hundred feet high and three times that across. It slammed shut, the reverberations echoing along the entire length of the enormous, vaulted room.

James Darkwood's eyes followed the door as it closed. Someone would have to get to the controls for the escape and make certain that the doorway stayed open until they were through.

The landing bay generally followed the largely guesswork diagram which Emma Shaw had originated via Darkwood Naval Air Station's computer. So far, so good. The takeoff and landing bay was cut from the natural rock, the ceiling uneven, piping, conduit, even a passenger and freight monorail moving across it from side to side, emerging from far smaller cuts in the living rock, perhaps passing from one takeoff and landing bay to another. They would have to investigate that.

The technique for the cutting of the chamber was something which would have been unknown in the days of the Rourke Family's past. The enormous retreats of the old mountain civilizations had been blasted and hacked into existence, originating around natural caves and fissures. This would have been lasered from the living rock, much faster, much more precisely and, almost certainly, more economically.

Darkwood stepped down from the gunship's portside fuselage door and onto the tarmac, straightening his uniform blouse beneath the arctic parka as he did so, careful not to dislodge his weapons. For compatibility with Paul Rubenstein and Michael Rourke, he left behind his familiar .45 automatic and opted, instead, for borrowing two 9mm Parabellum Lancer reproduction SIG-Sauer P-226s from Darkwood Naval Air Station's armory. The SIGs were carried by high-altitude observation pilots as part of their personal-defense weapons package. He had no chest holster for either of the two guns, so they were tucked into his waistband.

Paul Rubenstein and Michael Rourke emerged from the gunship, taking up positions slightly to his rear in their roles as junior officers.

An armed SS detachment—an officer and four men carrying assault rifles—approached them where stood. The officer, only an Untersturmführer, analogous to an ensign in the Navy or second lieutenant in the Marine Corps, stopped several paces away from them and saluted, saying in German, "Good afternoon, Herr Obersturmbannführer. On behalf of Herr Dr. Deitrich Zimmer, allow me to welcome you and the other officers to the facility. I am Untersturmführer Wilhelm Leitz, at your service."

Darkwood returned the salute. "I am Obersturmbannführer Rudolph Gessler. Allow me to introduce Sturmbannführer Liebnitz," and Darkwood nodded toward Paul Rubenstein, "and Hauptsturmführer Gerber," or Michael Rourke. "As you no doubt are aware, Untersturmführer Leitz, these officers and myself have undergone quite an ordeal. We must, as quickly as possible, be debriefed. But, I fear, we first require the opportunity to, ah—" and Darkwood gestured across his uniform. The trousers were wrinkled, the boots no longer gleamed. He rubbed his left hand down along his cheeks to his chin, the universal symbol for needing a shave.

"I quite understand, Herr Obersturmbannführer. Such preparations have already been made. A formality, first, however, Herr Obersturmbannführer." Untersturmführer Leitz held out his right hand, gloved palm up.

"But, of course," Darkwood responded, producing his papers from beneath his tunic, holding out his left hand palm upward for Paul Rubenstein's and Michael Rourke's papers. He passed all three sets over to Untersturmführer Leitz.

"I shall return these as quickly as it has been established that they are in order, Herr Obersturmbannführer."

"Very good, Untersturmführer. And now, we wish to refresh ourselves."

"But of course, sir."

The Untersturmführer fell in beside and a half pace behind Darkwood, directing him as they walked along the portion of the takeoff and landing bay's enormous length, toward a caged elevator. The makeup Darkwood wore in order to match the appearance of the man in the papers whom he was replacing was a little itchy. The reference he had made to shaving was, indeed, becoming necessary, but his beard under the makeup was the problem, and one which could not be remedied . . .

Michael Rourke's palms sweated within his gloves as the elevator began to rise. He spoke and understood German rather well, but not well enough to get away with more than a few phrases without being detected as a non-German. He was in the heart of the enemy operation and sooner or later— probably sooner—the fact that he was not who he claimed to be, that all of them were impostors, would be discovered.

As the old aphorism went, time was—indeed—of the essence . . .

Paul Rubenstein followed James Darkwood out of the elevator into a small corridor, the corridor nothing more than a guard station and two parallel banks of elevators. Beyond and to the left were tunnels, stations situated there for accessing the monorails. Paul's German was not very good, but he could follow along generally with the sporadic shots of conversation exchanged between Darkwood and the young Nazi officer who was their guide. The four stormtroopers accompanying them, with assault rifles held at port arms, were what really worried him.

If his identity were discovered, he would be dead, or else soon be wishing that he were. Among the SS, as he had heard through intelligence sources, he was considerably talked about. It was rumored that somehow, single-handedly, his survival after the Night of the War had reintroduced Jews into the world population. And, although these days the Nazis had more pressing interests, their lack of fondness for Jews had not diminished.

They would never take him alive if he could help it, and he would take as many of them as he could with him. Killing Nazis was, after all, a service to humanity. Paul forced himself to relax a little, to stop fantasizing about drugstore stands against hordes of SS men bent on his destruction.

There was the matter of kidnapping the clone who would become the donor of a new heart for his progenitor, John Rourke. The matter of killing a living human being in order to make the heart available was a difficult one. And, he had determined that, as much as the thought of cold-blooded murder repelled him, he was the one who should do it. He'd live with what guilt there would be, better by far than living with the thought of his best friend's death on his conscience or inflicting the murder of the clone on someone else. That was the sort of guilt he could not endure.

Their guide, Leitz, waved them past the guard station, into another bank of elevators.

Paul kept his hands as close as he could to the pistols beneath his tunic, just in case. Officers in the Nazi army rarely carried anything but a pistol, so he had no assault rifle. The Nazi pistol at his belt would be the first thing looked for if a trap lay in store for them.

They entered an elevator, the four guards taking a second car.

James Darkwood said in German, "There will not be a better chance."

Untersturmführer Leitz started to turn around.

Paul already had the full-sized Gerber knife out from under his tunic. He stabbed the knife into the throat of the SS second lieutenant, Michael catching the man with one gloved hand going over the fellow's throat.

Paul stood shoulder to shoulder with James Darkwood as the elevator stopped, lest anyone standing on their destination floor by the elevator doorway should see the body.

But, the corridor was empty.

This was clearly a residential section to which the car had brought them.

"Guards are fifteen seconds behind us," James Darkwood advised.

Michael already had his knife from beneath his tunic. Darkwood's hands were busy screwing a suppressor onto the muzzle of one of the SIG-Sauer 226s. Paul Rubenstein positioned himself on the far side of the doors for the second elevator car, Michael switching off the elevator they had just vacated.

The doors for the second car started to open.

James Darkwood stood in the corridor, hands behind him, feet spread apart, looking the archetypical SS officer in every way.

As the first of the four guards—a young, red-haired Rottenführer—exited, James Darkwood said in perfect-sounding German, "There has been an accident. Quickly! Attend to your officer!"

The Rottenführer and a Sturmmann right beside him started into the first car.

As the two remaining guards left the car, Paul

300

grabbed one, Michael the other, Paul's knife hammering down into the man's chest over the heart.

There were two muted pops, like the sounds of suppressor-fitted pistols in twentieth-century movies. But these were live rounds being fired and not blanks and the suppressor really worked.

As Paul lowered his dead man to the floor, he glanced into the first elevator car. The other two guards were dead, each with a bullet in the neck.

Michael was talking rapidly as he dragged his dead man into the first car. "They'll be wise to us the second somebody looks into this elevator car. We could leave the bodies somewhere else, but the bloodstains would betray what happened anyway."

"Agreed," Paul said.

James Darkwood was holding the second elevator car for them. "Back downstairs. I caught what level it was where we entered. Best shot at finding the area where they keep the clones."

Paul glanced at the Nazi-issue wristwatch he wore. "In about ten minutes, the others should be arriving. We'll have to keep these bodies out of sight until then."

"I'll stay with them. I'm the logical choice since my German's next best. Meet you guys when the shooting starts," Michael said. "Be careful."

Michael was taking the greatest danger onto himself, because he would have to babysit the dead men until the second chopper arrived, assuming it was allowed to land. Michael passed back their identity papers, presumably taken from the dead Untersturmführer's body.

"Agreed?" Darkwood asked, looking at Paul.

"What choice do we have?" Paul responded, grabbing two of the assault rifles, one for himself and one for Darkwood. As made sense, the rifles were energy weapons, considering the enclosed area in which the guards worked. But, they would have to do.

Michael switched on the first elevator car, looking down at the five dead Nazis, saying, "We're all going for a ride, guys! Now, no talking huh." He shot a wave toward Paul and James Darkwood as the doors closed.

"Shit," Paul observed, resheathing his knife as he entered the second car and James Darkwood worked the elevator buttons, already starting to fix a suppressor to his second pistol. Paul, in addition to his High Powers, had borrowed Natalia's suppressor-fitted Walther PPK/S. The suppressor was recently refitted with current, state-of-the-art baffles which, unlike the original suppressor's, never needed replacement or cleaning. The decibel rating was such that the most noise came from the operation of the slide, she'd told him.

He was, evidently, going to get the opportunity for grueling field testing of it.

The energy rifles were both slung to Paul's right shoulder. How he would explain them to anyone was another matter, but if anyone started to seriously question them, that person would have to be silenced at any event. In the final analysis, the presence of the energy weapons really didn't matter.

The elevator stopped and the doors started to open.

Paul Rubenstein took a deep breath and tried to think in German.

302

Chapter Fifty-Two

James Darkwood stepped from the elevator, Paul Rubenstein beside him. The guard on duty there looked up at them.

Darkwood told the man, "We are personal agents of Herr Dr. Zimmer. You must obey my instructions to the letter, Rottenführer, if you value the future of the Reich and your own life."

"Yes, Herr Obersturmbannführer!"

Darkwood looked at Rubenstein, nodded, then walked closer to the guard. "There is a plot against our führer's life. Various Allied agents have infiltrated themselves into this complex for the express purpose of assassinating Deitrich Zimmer, even at the cost of their own lives. They could only have succeeded in reaching this facility and penetrating it successfully, as they have already done, with the cooperation of certain key officers within the staff here. We alone know the identity of the leader of this group of saboteurs. Tell me, Rottenführer, as you undoubtedly have great familarity with the facility, what is the most expeditious route to the laboratory where Herr Doctor Zimmer performs his biological experiments, but a route which would be least subject to scrutiny for a team of armed men?"

The young corporal thought for a moment, then looked up into Darkwood's eyes. "The monorail would be the best way, Herr Obersturmbannführer."

"The controls for the monorail system are—?"

"Each car is independently controlled, Herr Obersturmbannführer, and can take the appropriate siding."

"Which siding would these men exit from, so they would be nearest to the laboratory facilities?"

"Siding fourteen, Herr Obersturmbannführer."

"Is there anything else of which we should be made aware, Rottenführer? Remember! Your name will figure heavily into my personal report to the führer. Think, man!"

"There are always two guards posted at the laboratory doors. Herr Obersturmbannführer. It would be impossible for such men as you describe to pass these guards. I have been assigned to that post many times, and the standing orders are to shoot to kill anyone who is not recognizable as a member of the laboratory staff, Herr Obersturmbannführer."

"Yes, one would think such precautions would be adequate. But! They are not! Some of the conspirators are, in fact, involved in Herr Doctor Zimmer's laboratory experiments, Rottenführer." Darkwood started walking the corporal toward the monorail station, over his shoulder noticing that Paul Rubenstein was in a perfect position to command fire over both elevator banks and the service elevator from the takeoff and landing bay below them. While Darkwood had this cooperative young man at his disposal, he wanted to verify the monorail controls, make certain that he could operate the gondola. "You must remain vigilant here, and refuse to be taken in by contradictory orders, Rottenführer. That is clear?"

"Yes, Herr Obersturmbannführer!"

The wonderful thing about the Nazis was that their system was founded on paranoia, and appealing to this paranoia—secret plots, hidden agendas, classified orders—was invariably a way of getting cooperation. The dumber the Nazi, the more cooperative. He would almost feel sorry to kill this seemingly good-natured man, but when one served the cause of an evil totalitarian government, one had to expect to be counted among the enemy.

Overlooking the gondola controls and satisfied that the machine was powered up and could be used, Darkwood slipped one of the suppressor-fitted 9mm pistols from beneath his tunic, placing it against the Rottenführer's chest, then pulling the trigger.

The corporal collapsed to the floor. Darkwood hissed, "Come on!"

Already, Paul Rubenstein was running toward the gondola.

Together, they hauled the dead man into the gondola with them, pulling down the gullwing-style canopy opening. The gondola automatically powered up.

Darkwood sat at the control panel. "Station fourteen it is."

Paul Rubenstein was already going through the

dead man's pockets for anything useful—maps, papers, general orders.

Soundlessly, the monorail gondola glided away from the station, pausing automatically as another car passed on the main line, then switching onto the main line.

They came out of a small tunnel, passing through free space. Below them, the true vastness of the takeoff and landing bays could be seen. Darkwood judged that the one through which they had entered the complex was the furthest west of the three, this the center one. What he saw before him on the control panel only served to confirm that.

There was an illuminated diagram, or map, set into the control panel, the panel itself merely consisting of emergency controls, the operation of the gondola entirely automated it seemed, once the destination station was entered into the memory. Station fourteen was beyond the third bay. A lighted diode moved along the representation on the control panel, showing their position relative to the monorail route.

The gondola entered a small tunnel, traveling past a station identical to the one at which they had boarded, then leaving the tunnel, passed over the third takeoff and landing bay. As in the one through which they had entered the facility and the one over which they had just passed, there were more V/STOL fighter aircraft here than James Darkwood had adequate time to count.

Behind him, Paul murmured, "About a hundred planes or so."

"Yeah, more or less. And we've gotta figure a way

306

to keep them from getting airborne after us."

"I think I know what we'll have to do. We can't sabotage all the aircraft themselves. We'll have to destroy the opening and closing mechanisms for the doors. The doors themselves will be bombproof, and there should be emergency controls away from the main control stations, unless these people are imbeciles. And, I wouldn't count on that."

"Neither would I. So, you mean we destroy the actual mechanism for opening and closing."

"Exactly," Paul Rubenstein told him. "I watched how they run. It looks to be a series of levers and the levers are exposed on the interior side of the doors. If we can sabotage just one of the joints, the doors will be jammed shut until repair parts can be brought in. That should give us enough time to get out of here."

"What about the takeoff and landing bay we use for our escape? Think we can screw with the aircraft in there?"

"I don't know," Paul Rubenstein told him. "We'll have to cross that bridge when we come to it, see what Natalia and Annie and Emma Shaw and the SEAL Team guys are able to do before we get there. They'll have plenty of explosives, but not plenty of time to use them."

Darkwood's eyes followed their course on the control panel map. The gondola was nearly at station fourteen . . .

Realizing that the liberated Nazi gunship could never get them out of the facility into which they would hopefully soon be entering, Emma Shaw,

Annie Rubenstein and Natalia Tiemerovna had decided on a means by which the gunship could still be utilized. With the SEAL Team personnel assisting them, before getting their craft airborne, they wired explosives into the fuselage, the explosives linked to the synth-fuel tanks, the weapons systems, everything which might explode.

Natalia Tiemerovna had wired the system into the aircraft's control panel herself. If all went well, she could remotely detonate the explosives, to at least partially seal the takeoff and landing bay after them. If they were attacked by a superior force the instant that they landed, either she or Emma Shaw could flip a toggle switch beneath the forward control panel and the explosives would instantly detonate. Emma Shaw had called it a dead woman's switch.

Chapter Fifty-Three

Three minutes remained before the second gun-ship should be requesting permission to land over the Nazi distress frequency. When Paul Rubenstein had begun landing the gunship he'd flown here carrying Michael and James Darkwood as his only passengers, he had advised the tower that a second ship, carrying injured survivors of the battle for the headquarters complex in Canada, was close behind them and should be admitted.

If the dead bodies he, Michael and James Darkwood had left behind them so far weren't discovered, there was a very good chance that Natalia or Emma (at the time the first gunship left, it had not been determined who would be pilot and who would be copilot) should be able to land and the second and most important phase of the plan—to their own survival at least—would be under way.

Natalia's suppressed Walther PPK/S in his right hand, behind his back, Paul Rubenstein exited the monorail gondola after James Darkwood at station fourteen.

Beyond the confines of the station itself lay a guard post and elevator banks similar to those where they had boarded the gondola.

There was a Sturmmann on duty here, a little older-looking despite his one-grade lower rank than the Rottenführer who had proven so helpful to them. This man would have to die as well.

It had been different, fighting the Russians. There had been good and bad among the Communists, men and women trapped into a fight not of their choosing who, under other circumstances, might have been worthwhile persons, perhaps still were. But the Nazi forces, because the Nazis had no real country, their only true ally Eden itself, was an all-volunteer force, the sons and grandsons and great-grandsons of Nazi sympathizers from New Germany, and Eden as well to a lesser degree. Each man in the SS, the Nazi's only military arm, was a volunteer and a Nazi Party member, hence embraced their cause.

Within the SS there were several areas of responsibility, the modern equivalent of the Luftwaffe, or air corps, and commando/shock troop forces.

The divisions within each group were broken down according to race. There were ethnic German units and there were units comprised entirely of personnel who were not ethnic Germans.

The commandos, the highest-ranking divisions within the SS, wore the distinctive Totenkopf skull-and-bones symbol originally associated with the Third SS Panzer Division.

James Darkwood spoke to the Sturmmann on guard, saying, "Tell me if you have seen any armed men passing this way."

310

"I have seen none, Herr Obersturmbannführer. Papers please. Access to unauthorized personnel is restricted beyond this point." The man's weapon was held at high port.

"Certainly, Sturmmann." Darkwood began fishing in his uniform tunic and Paul Rubenstein's eyes drifted to the passive alarm visible on the guard's right wrist. Passive alarms were sensible devices, cued to the wearer's body orientation and pulse rate. Any radical change in either—such as might be precipitated by a sudden fall—would trigger the alarm. The person wearing the alarm had fifteen seconds to deactivate it before the alarm was broadcast into the receiving net.

Paul Rubenstein did not know if Darkwood had noticed it or not. There would be a code which had to be punched into the alarm in order to prevent its being broadcast. Without the code, the alarm could not be neutralized.

There was only one way around the system. Paul took it, walking up to the guard very quickly and sticking the muzzle of the suppressor to the man's temple. "Move and I will kill you. Cooperate and you have my word that I will not. What will it be?" He had stretched his German near to the breaking point.

Darkwood's pistols were out as well, pointed at the guard.

The guard's tough demeanor vanished.

Darkwood snatched away his rifle.

Paul told Darkwood in English, "We have to get him slowly to the floor, then tie him so securely that he can't activate the alarm. He can't be killed, either."

311

"Shit. All right."

Darkwood pulled off his foraging cap, secreted within the turned-up ear flaps, the modern equivalent of plastic flex cuffs. Darkwood moved the Nazi guard's wrists slowly around behind the man, then bound them together.

Once this was accomplished, Paul still holding the pistol to the man's head, Darkwood similarly bound the fellow's ankles. If someone arrived at the monorail station, a shooting war would begin on the spot, but there was nothing else to do, and no more rapid pace could be trusted to succeed. Darkwood reached into the pocket of his parka and produced a syringe kit. He told the guard in German, "This injection will not kill you, merely put you to sleep, I promise that the needle is clean."

Paul looked at Darkwood for an instant, asking, "This won't slow his pulse too much?"

"It shouldn't, unless he has a reaction to the drug."

"Go for it." Darkwood wiped the man's neck with an antiseptic pad, then used a disposable syringe to administer the drug. By the time Darkwood had removed the needle, the guard was beginning to go under.

Together, they caught up the fellow's body, lowering him slowly, gently into a reclining position, then carrying him into the sentry station, resting him on the floor within the enclosure, out of sight unless someone looked into the enclosure. "He'll be missed," Darkwood supplied.

"In another few minutes, there'll probably be an alert anyway." Paul looked at the watch that he wore. The second helicopter gunship should be touching down almost to the instant.

312

Chapter Fifty-Four

The SEAL Team commander announced, "Is everybody ready?"

Armed personnel were moving toward the gunship as it touched down on the pad to the far side of the takeoff and landing bay. Emma Shaw could see the first gunship, recognizing on the fuselage the serialization which she had memorized. It was good luck that they had been allowed to land in the same bay.

Medical personnel were standing by some distance away from the pad, so at least the story that there were wounded Nazi commandos aboard the gunship was partially believed.

Natalia ordered, "Make every shot count. There are vastly more of them than there are of us. We need to be clear of the helicopter before the shooting starts in earnest," she reminded. "Don't forget!" Then Natalia turned to her as they unbuckled their seat restraints, saying, "Stay close to me. Annie will be with me, too. This isn't your usual kind of fighting. Remember, the idea is to put someone

313

down. You're good with a gun. Don't get frightened by what's going on around you. Keep your purpose in mind. Remember, the three of us will stay together."

"I understand."

"Get ready to use your guns, then," Natalia advised her.

Natalia started aft, Emma at her heels, Annie already standing beside the fuselage door, a Nazi assault rifle at high port. Like Natalia's and her own, Annie's hair—considerably longer than theirs—was stuffed under a black SS foraging cap.

Half of the men from the SEAL Team would exit the gunship first, Emma and the two other women mixing in between these men and the other six.

"It should take all of forty-five seconds for us to get some distance between ourselves and the aircraft. But for those forty-five seconds, it is important that we are the most arrogant and convincing SS commandos we can be. Remember," she warned. "Forty-five seconds. Critical. Critical," Natalia said again.

The lock mechanism on the portside fuselage door was released and the door was open. A dozen SS commandos reinforced by six men wearing the insignia of SS/Luftwaffe police waited for them, guns at high port. They were all energy rifles, Emma Shaw noted.

Her mind focused on the pistols beneath her uniform blouse, a brace of Lancer SIG 226 copies borrowed from the arms lockers of Darkwood Naval Air Station. To a person, each of their pistols was 9mm Parabellum rather than any of the modern caseless rounds or energy weapons.

Six SEAL Team members stepped down onto the tarmac, their assault rifles—Nazi—slung in such a manner that using them would hopefully appear to be the last thing on any of their minds. Three of the men had theatrical blood on their faces and one of the men wore his left arm in a sling and was helped by another. Within the sling, he carried a pistol for his right hand and a knife for his left. She'd seen him checking the weapons in the instant before the door was slid open. Annie, Natalia and Emma Shaw jumped down, two more SEAL Team men flanking them, the last four behind them.

The leader of the guard detail, a Hauptsturm-führer with a nasty look in his bright blue eyes, was arguing with Lieutenant Christakos, the SEAL Team leader, wearing Hauptsturmführer's rank as well. Emma Shaw knew next to nothing in German—a few phrases of profanity she had picked up—and couldn't understand what was going on. But Natalia, who spoke German perfectly, seemed to be perfectly calm, her blue eyes fixed on the Haupt-sturmführer.

Natalia, also wearing officer's rank, started away from the gunship, edging some of the men around her along with her.

Two of the guards, enlisted men, moved to block Natalia's path. Natalia's right hand moved ever so subtly. There was a clicking noise, barely audible beneath the aircraft noises around them, and the nearest of the two men stood stock still, his eyes going rigid.

Natalia walked past him quickly.

The guard started to collapse.

The second guard turned to look at him.

Natalia quickened her pace, Annie falling in at her left, Emma at her right. Christakos punched the Hauptsturmführer in the face.

Natalia wheeled around, the knife in her right hand still dripping blood as she sliced it across the carotid artery of a Nazi staff sergeant, or Scharführer, unfortunate enough to be standing within her reach.

Knives flashed everywhere around Emma Shaw, Annie swinging her Nazi assault rifle forward on its sling, Emma Shaw doing the same now.

Natalia kept walking, the rest of the personnel from the gunship falling in behind and on either side of her.

The men who had greeted them at the gunship were all dead on the tarmac, but so far not a shot had been fired.

Their grace period would only last for a few seconds longer, Emma Shaw realized, but the further away they got from the gunship and the closer to the control center, the better their chance.

Natalia strode purposefully ahead, her knife disappeared from her right hand, instead a pistol there, another SIG-226, held almost casually along her right thigh. There was an identical pistol in her left hand, held the same way.

An Untersturmführer approached them, shouting something.

His eyes moved past them.

He stared.

Emma Shaw knew at what.

316

And, she realized, so did Natalia.

The Nazi officer began shouting at the top of his lungs.

Natalia wasn't close enough to use her knife. She raised the pistol in her left hand and shot him dead, one bullet between the eyes. Then she shouted, "Let's go!"

Annie swung her rifle into a hard assault position, spraying it into a knot of SS personnel beside the metal steps leading up into the control center, bringing four men down. A fifth man ran, killed by somebody before he made three steps. Emma Shaw had her own assault rifle to her shoulder, firing short bursts at everything that moved that she didn't recognize as one of her own people. She wasn't good enough to fire from the hip.

She saw Natalia, out of the left corner of her peripheral vision, running for the control-center steps, Christakos and two other SEAL Team members with her. And Emma Shaw remembered Natalia's admonition. She tapped Annie Rubenstein on the shoulder and the two of them started after Natalia.

Natalia was halfway up the steps, a pistol in each hand. Two men wearing Luftwaffe insignia, energy rifles in their hands, appeared in the doorway. Before they could raise their weapons, Natalia's pistols were on line, firing, spraying into their chests and throats. One man collapsed over the railing, the other tumbled back through the open doorway.

Emma Shaw caught a flash of movement on her right side, swung the muzzle of her rifle toward it, the rifle not fully shouldered as she fired. An energy bolt struck the top rail, bluish white light flickering over the metal, as the man who'd just fired took the short burst and crumpled to his knees, then fell back.

To the top of the steps, Natalia inside, Lieutenant Christakos with her, a cacophony of pistol fire as three men—air-traffic controllers, all of them armed with pistols—went down dead.

Natalia, tearing the cap from her head, shaking loose her hair, ordered, "Lieutenant Christakos, get three of your men to hold this control center. Get the door open immediately before they kill power or we'll never get out. And get the explosives set." She was swapping magazines in her pistols as she spoke, stabbing the pistols into her belt, then grabbing up a Nazi pistol and an energy rifle, her assault rifle slung crossbody across her back.

"Let's go!"

And Natalia was running down the steps, Annie right behind her, Emma Shaw at their heels.

Chapter Fifty-Five

An alarm began sounding, at first from a great distance, but in under a second the alarm's origin was lost, because alarms were sounding everywhere, there in the corridor fronting the biological research labs the alarm so loud as to be deafening.

Paul Rubenstein shook his head to clear it as he followed James Darkwood at a steady, controlled pace toward the two armed guards flanking the doors leading into the laboratory.

"Halt!"

Both guards went to high port. Paul Rubenstein reflected that they had poor training. They should have gone to assault positions. There was nothing to discuss, really. Paul sidestepped left and ducked as he swung the suppressor-fitted Walther PPK/S from behind his back and on line with the nearer of the two men, the hammer thumbed back so the shot would be fired single action.

The bullet struck the man who had ordered them to halt, hitting the throat near the Adam's apple, the man's body slamming back against the doorway.

The second man was already going down, James Darkwood putting him there.

Paul Rubenstein used the Walther's safety as a hammer drop, then upped the safety into the off position again, shifting the pistol to his left hand, his right hand grasping for the pistol grip of one of the caseless Nazi assault rifles he carried. The energy weapons would be used only in a pinch, not nearly as effective because they were not nearly as precise in shot placement.

Darkwood took the right side of the doorway, Paul Rubenstein the left side.

Darkwood, keeping low, reached across to the door handle, gave it a twist and pushed. The door swung inward.

Paul Rubenstein went through first.

There were about a dozen technicians standing at work tables, dazed looks on their faces, the alarm sounding still, all eyes on the muzzle of Paul Rubenstein's rifle.

As Paul was about to summon up his best German to order them to raise their hands, Deitrich Zimmer and Martin Zimmer stepped from their midst.

"Holy shit," James Darkwood hissed.

Paul Rubenstein was on one knee, his assault rifle to his shoulder, the Walther in his belt. Across the sights of the rifle, he stared at Deitrich Zimmer. "You speak English, Doctor, and so does Martin. We want one of the clones. Give us a clone of John Rourke and you might get out of this alive."

Deitrich Zimmer only laughed.

Martin Zimmer said, "You will both die. As to the

320

commando operation going on in Aircraft Bay One, the personnel involved are as good as dead. Surrender your weapons now."

"Eat me," Darkwood responded cheerily.

Paul Rubenstein slowly stood, the rifle still to his shoulder, the sights still on Deitrich Zimmer's chest. The natural action of the rifle's recoil would cause the muzzle to rise slightly as he fired, the bullets lacing upward along the chest and into the thorax, the throat, the head. "You'll be dead, too, Doctor. I came for one of John Rourke's clones. Take us to where you keep them."

Deitrich Zimmer said, "You do not realize, do you. I am a clone!" He drew a pistol from the pocket of his lab coat.

Paul Rubenstein pulled the trigger.

Chapter Fifty-Six

The sirens sounding throughout the complex were almost a relief, because Michael Rourke was becoming physically ill from riding up and down in the elevator car with the five dead bodies. The propinquity to the late SS men was not what bothered him. Although he had never been motion-sick in his life (discounting a ferris wheel ride he'd had when he was a very little boy after trying to digest one too many items of junk food), he was feeling motion-sick now.

When he at last stopped the elevator on the level where he had first entered it, he swallowed, breathed a sigh of relief and leveled an energy rifle in each hand toward the elevator doors as they opened.

Men raced past him along the corridor, but no one seemed to pay attention to him. He used a knuckle on his left hand to hit a floor button—the top floor—and stepped through the doors as they began to close. The bodies were headed up. He was headed into the snarl of humanity around him. There was gunfire, the sounds of energy bursts and the sirens were even louder than before. Commands were being shouted everywhere.

Michael Rourke let one of the rifles fall to his side on its sling as he grabbed out for a young Unterscharführer passing him, almost slamming the man against the corridor wall in order to get his attention. "What is happening, Unterscharführer?"

"Enemy commandos, Herr Hauptsturmführer, have penetrated Landing Bay One. Everyone has been called to duty there."

"Thank you," Michael told him, shoving him away.

The explosives belted around Michael Rourke's waist were the next order of business. Elevators were opening, disgorging armed men into the corridor. And, Michael had a flash of inspiration. He stepped into the first open elevator, let the door close, the car empty except for himself. As the car started up, Michael opened the panel and took manual control, stalling the elevator at the next highest level. He removed one of the explosive charges from his belt, peeled away the backing and clamped it to the panel—it was treated with self-stick adhesive. He set the timer for sixty seconds, reactivated the floor controls to bring him down, stepped through and at the same time hit the switch and pushed the button for the top floor.

There was another empty elevator going up just across the corridor from him. Bulling his way through a knot of enlisted SS personnel, he entered the empty elevator, let the doors close then repeated the process he had carried out with the first car. The explosives were powerful enough that they would destroy all the elevators on each side, once they detonated.

Mentally ticking off the seconds, he set this charge at forty-five seconds, so it would detonate fifteen seconds after the first one. He returned to the level where the Landing Bays were accessed and left the elevator, activating the explosive charge and hitting the top-floor button at the same time.

He wore four more explosive charges and was determined to put them to good use, walking as quickly as he could to the monorail station. After a few seconds, an empty car came, returning from depositing men summoned from the other landing bays.

The first explosion came from the elevator banks, shaking the surface beneath his feet, the walls vibrating with it. There was always the slight possibility that he might be causing the deaths of his friends by sabotaging the elevators and the monorail gondolas, but it was standard operating procedure in something like this to avoid any such mechanical means of traveling from one area to another because of the risk of being stuck between floors, or, in this case, between stations. Paul and James Darkwood would likely adhere to the dictum. He hoped.

Alone in the car, he programmed for the next station, set an explosive charge and, when he reached the next station, left, activating the charge. He'd felt the second detonation in the elevator banks.

He would have to go down to the takeoff and

landing bay below him on foot or use the elevator cage—he opted for the former—then somehow find a way into the first landing bay. There would be mechanical access ports, he was certain. And, he had three more charges to use up.

So far, so good.

Chapter Fifty-Seven

Martin Zimmer was a clone, too, of course; Paul Rubenstein realized when he had been suckered.

Darkwood held all the lab technicians at bay against the far wall and Paul Rubenstein, with the clone of Martin Zimmer in tow, stood before the vault door leading into the chambers beyond where the clones were kept.

And, he made a bet with himself.

That this Martin Zimmer, if a clone was truly identical once the mind of the original was downloaded into its brain, would be just as cowardly as the original. Paul shoved the muzzle of the suppressor on Natalia's Walther against the Martin Zimmer clone's nose. "Do you want to die?"

There was no answer, except in the eyes.

Paul glanced at the locking mechanism for the vault door. "Will your handprint activate the lock?"

"Only Deitrich Zimmer's handprint will do that. And he is not here! You lose."

Paul Rubenstein smiled. "I don't think so. You

know who I am? I'm the Jew, Rubenstein. And I'm going to find it especially nice to leave you alive, if you cooperate, so you can tell everyone how Deitrich Zimmer screwed himself."

There was a look of panic in the Martin Zimmer clone's dark eyes. "What do you mean?"

"A clone is physically identical to the original, right?"

"Yes, but—"

Paul Rubenstein looked again at the hand-shaped panel on the locking mechanism. "Even if Deitrich Zimmer isn't here, his hand is."

Paul Rubenstein jerked Martin Zimmer away from the vault door and back into the main section of the laboratory . . .

Lieutenant Christakos's SEAL Team personnel were holding both the control center and the main access into the hangar bay. Battle-dress utilities used by the Nazis were equipped to be converted into chemical-biological-radiological warfare protection suits, once a hooded mask, gloves and overboots were added, and the SEALs as well as Natalia, Emma and Annie Rubenstein were so outfitted. It was only a matter of time before the Nazis would employ gas, of course, and the commando team was already using it.

Nerve agents were not held in the Allied Inventory, on moral grounds, but knockout gases of various types as well as chemical irritants and smoke were available.

Despite the protection of her suit and her hooded

mask, Annie Rubenstein felt strange, moving about in clouds of gas and smoke. While the twelve members of the SEAL unit held, she planted explosive charges on the aircraft in the takeoff and landing bay. These, coupled with the heavier explosives wired into the gunship in which they had arrived, would not only destroy the entire hangar area, but damage the bay next door and, with any luck, destroy the complex's entire electrical system.

The gas and smoke situation was one-sided. Although the Nazis would eventually employ it, unless the enemy was able to rig blowers, it would do no good. The takeoff and landing bay door opened to the north wind across the Himalayas, all of the gas and smoke utilized was being blown toward the rear of the takeoff and landing bay and into the access area surrounding it, only these rearmost sections of the bay itself affected.

Annie glanced at the Nazi wristwatch worn over the wrist of her left protective gauntlet as she set the timer on the latest explosive package. Unless radio detonated sooner, the charge would go in ten minutes, leaving about nine minutes or a little more than that for them to get airborne, leaving eight minutes or so for her husband, her brother and James Darkwood to get back with the clone.

"Damn," she murmured under her breath, her own voice sounding odd to her within the confines of the mask.

She started for the next-nearest aircraft, taking out her last charge and stripping away the self-adhesive back . . .

*   *   *

It was the most grisly act Paul Rubenstein had ever been forced to commit, but he did it. Wearing goggles and gloves and using an electrically operated surgical saw, he cut off the right hand of the dead clone of Deitrich Zimmer.

Wrapping the bloody stump in plastic or something like it, he pulled off the goggles, then set down the hand to remove the gloves.

Martin Zimmer stood speechless in front of the laboratory technicians. "Lucky it wasn't your handprint we needed," Paul told him. "Come with me. James, get the knock-out gas ready for our friends here as soon as we're on our way."

"Right," Darkwood responded, then raised his voice, saying in German, "I want everyone to move into the office there on your left. Slowly, hands still raised. Any false moves, and I will shoot. Understood? Move, then."

Paul Rubenstein stopped at the vault door, the severed hand of Deitrich Zimmer's clone in his right hand, Natalia's pistol in his left hand, the pistol aimed at Martin Zimmer.

He set the hand against the panel, pushing the stiffening fingers into position.

The panel lit.

The door opened.

When he looked beyond the doorway, he understood the concept of hell . . .

Emma Shaw had placed her last charge and, well

330

enough away from the swirling gas and smoke, she climbed up onto the wing stem of the Nazi/Eden V/STOL she had chosen for herself and the clone to ride in.

She looked at the Nazi wristwatch she wore as she climbed down into the cockpit. Five minutes remained for Paul Rubenstein, Michael Rourke, James Darkwood and a clone of John Rourke to arrive. In three minutes, eight of the SEAL Team personnel (one to pilot Darkwood, one for each of the Rourke Family, and one each for the remaining SEAL personnel, since the aircraft were two-seaters only) would break off from holding this position against the Nazis and go to their predesignated V/STOLS. She had selected, quickly checked for readiness, then assigned eight planes in the first moments after the seizure of the control center. All the other aircraft were sabotaged with explosives.

She started warming up the engines of the V/STOL, Natalia and Annie instructed on how to do it as well, each of them warming up another aircraft. Between the three of them, all nine aircraft that would be needed would be readied for takeoff . . .

The explosive charge he had set aboard the monorail gondola exploded overheard, bodies and parts of bodies, some of them aflame, tumbling out of the granite "sky" which was the interior of the takeoff and landing bay. Michael Rourke had found what he hoped was an access door into the next bay, and the fact that a dozen Nazi commandos were huddled near it in protective CBR clothing only seemed to confirm his supposition.

A dozen men, all heavily armed.

He had energy rifles and he had his two Beretta pistols.

He knew what his father would have done with a dozen men blocking his path.

And, Michael Rourke smiled.

He picked his way across the rail tracks separating the main portion of the landing bay from the access doorway and the twelve men. The men had turned around briefly, glancing toward the origin of the explosion above. If there had not been panic in the takeoff and landing bay from all the activity in the bay next door before the explosion, there was now. Men ran everywhere, emergency equipment converged on the area of the burning wreckage. Several aircraft were in flames, the debris having set them afire.

In another few seconds, two of his three remaining explosive charges would detonate, taking a synth-fuel storage area up, hopefully without consuming the entire bay and killing him.

Near the access doorway, there was what appeared to be a massive electrical junction box. If he could blow that with his last charge, he might prevent any pursuit at all, sabotaging the means of opening the takeoff and landing doors. Because, unless someone else had found the means by which to sabotage the doors, nothing had been done to them. He could not reach the door here and he had not been in the third takeoff and landing bay.

As Michael Rourke neared the access door, he let

332

both rifles fall to his sides on their slings, taking his pistols in his hands, safeties off, the hammers drawn back to avoid wasting the time necessary for the longer, heavier double-action pull on the first shots.

About fifteen feet from the twelve men, Michael Rourke stopped.

The explosion came, nearly throwing him to his knees, the granite beneath him shaking, the sound of the explosion deafeningly loud.

He said nothing. No other sound but the echo from the original explosion and the sounds of the smaller explosions now coming in rapid succession could have been heard.

The men turned toward him, almost as one.

Michael Rourke smiled.

The nearest of the men started to swing the muzzle of his assault rifle on line with Michael's torso and Michael fired, stabbing the pistol in his right hand toward the man's throat. A man shouted something, but Michael could not hear the words. The gun in Michael's left hand fired once, into the man's chest.

The others were raising their weapons.

The first finger of Michael's right hand twitched, then the first finger of his left, then his right again, then his left, then his right, then again his left.

Bullets and energy bolts whizzed past him. Michael kept firing, emptying the twin Beretta 92Fs into the remaining men until, at last, all twelve men were down and the slides of both pistols were locked back open, the guns empty.

Michael Rourke quietly said to himself, "At last I have the knack."

Chapter Fifty-Eight

White as ghosts because the sun never touched them, eyelids shut, the spectres of himself and his wife and his brother-in-law and Sarah Rourke and John and Wolfgang Mann and even of Deitrich Zimmer and Martin Zimmer were suspended in what looked like spider webs, hung like meat ready to be devoured, each inside a cryogenic chamber of evidently advanced design, swirling clouds of bluish white gas surrounding them.

Indeed, some of the clones were only partially whole, missing limbs, one of them—a clone of Deitrich Zimmer himself—missing an eye.

This was an organ bank, a place where replica human beings were kept in cryogenic Sleep, their minds blank slates upon which Deitrich Zimmer could write at will, and whatever he wished.

With the walking, breathing, already sentient clone of Martin Zimmer beside him, Paul Rubenstein stopped before one of the chambers. It was marked, "John Thomas Rourke #11" and within it was an exact duplicate of John Rourke at his present age, every detail—the greying hair at the temples and in the sideburns, the greying hair on his chest—everything perfect.

"You are devils, or your progenitors are, I suppose," Paul Rubenstein told the clone of Martin Zimmer. "Help me get him out of here."

"You will never reach Landing Bay One alive, Jew."

Paul Rubenstein told him, "We had a variety of possible plans in mind before we came here. Each of us is carrying sound and light grenades, each of us carrying knockout gas, each of us has a gas mask, we're heavily armed. We have explosives. But, aside from the CBR gear as a precaution, I think all we'll need is you. You see, I know who you are, or what you are, but the SS personnel between us and Landing Bay One, as you call it, don't. Do they?"

"I don't know what you—"

Paul Rubenstein put the gun to Martin Zimmer's head again. "Get the picture?"

Then he stepped back and Martin Zimmer's clone began to open the cryogenic chamber.

Paul had promised himself that he would destroy everyone here, and he would, but he would not sleep quite the same again.

Because, as his eyes moved over the bodies waiting here in stasis for Deitrich Zimmer's whims, his eyes rested on a clone of his wife, Annie. Just as beautiful, with just as much potential to be warm and brilliant and funny and wonderful and loving and inspirational.

And, he was going to kill her.

336

While Martin Zimmer worked with the cryogenic chamber holding John Rourke #11, Paul Rubenstein peeled away the self-adhesive backing for the first of the explosive charges he would use . . .

Michael Rourke set the last of his charges on the interior of the junction box. This was a nexus for what were probably miles of cable, and through this junction box, the power between this and the takeoff and landing bay beyond flowed.

He would end that in—he checked the Nazi wristwatch he wore—forty-five seconds.

He tried the door, made certain that it would open, pulled down the mask and the hood, sealed the mask, popping the cheeks, then flipped the timer switch.

With a caseless ammo assault rifle in each hand and two more strapped to his back—courtesy of the men he'd just killed—Michael Rourke stepped through the doorway . . .

James Darkwood ordered the laboratory technicians, "To the floor. Pack everything over you that you can. Chairs, cushions from the chairs, get under the desk, the tables there, do anything that you can to protect yourselves. I will be using a type of harmless knockout gas. Then there will be a series of explosions. If you obey me, you will probably survive. If you do not, you will surely die."

The technicians began scrambling for cover. Darkwood fingered the knockout gas grenade in his left hand . . .

*　　*　　*

John Rourke #11 was barely conscious and Martin Zimmer's clone supported him on one side, Paul Rubenstein pulling the clone's right arm across his shoulders to support him from the other side.

The timers were set for the explosions to start, in under ninety seconds.

When they reached the doorway, Paul Rubenstein did not look back.

He could not.

"Stop here," Paul ordered, then pointing the gun still at Martin Zimmer's clone, he got John Rourke #11 over his right shoulder in a fireman's carry, rising to his full height, Natalia's Walther unwavering on its target. "We're on our way."

They walked through the doorway, Paul Rubenstein ordering Martin Zimmer's clone to close the vault door behind them. He told the clone, "Think of it this way. You'll be the only clone Doctor Zimmer will have left. You'll be important." He waved Martin Zimmer's clone across the laboratory, James Darkwood lobbing the gas grenade into the office enclosure the moment his and Paul's eyes met.

"Let's go!"

"You've got Martin Zimmer's clone, here. He's our shield." At least, Paul Rubenstein hoped so.

Chapter Fifty-Nine

Natalia Anastasia Tiemerovna fired over the barricade toward the Nazi position, energy machine-gun fire from that position getting increasingly heavy. The Nazis were massing for an attack, she realized, and in a matter of two minutes, if she and all the rest of the assault force were not in their aircraft, ready to go airborne, they would never clear the takeoff and landing bay before the explosions started.

There was enough aircraft-grade synth-fuel here to incinerate them.

And, there was still no sign of Michael. Her stomach cramped with the thought, and her palms sweated within her gloves. She loved Michael like she had loved no other man in her life, even his father.

If she lost him to death, she herself would crave death.

But she would not accept it. She would go on, dead only in her heart and her soul.

Beside her, Lieutenant Christakos told her what she already knew. "About two minutes, Major Tiemerovna, then if we're not out of here, we're not getting out."

"I know that. Order your pilots to fall back. You and I can hold this position for as long as we've got left."

"Yes, ma'am. Pilots! Fall back to your aircraft. We're getting out of here!"

A cheer rose for only a second, and then the eight SEAL Team personnel began crawling away behind cover, until it was safe for them to make a break to their planes.

Where was Michael Rourke?

There was an explosion on the near wall, between this takeoff and landing bay and the next one over, massive chunks of granite flying up into the air toward the cavern ceiling, and all electrical power went out. The only light came from emergency, battery-operated units placed at intervals along the walls and from the open doorway at the mouth of the takeoff and landing bay.

There was an enormous amount of concentrated automatic-weapons fire, a few bursts from energy weapons, a few isolated automatic bursts from projectile weapons, then several puffs of smoke from gas grenades.

She was about to fire as a figure vaulted over the enemy's barricades, but the shape of the body beneath the uniform and the hooded CBR mask stopped her. "Michael? Michael?"

"I'm on my way," she heard him shout.

And, Natalia was suddenly mortified, and at once

340

grateful that she wore the CBR mask. Because her eyes filled with tears . . .

James Darkwood looked at the watch on his wrist. If they were not in Landing Bay One in a little over a minute, they would be done for. And there was no electricity and the monorail line, even if someone hadn't blown it up (and someone probably had), wasn't running because there was no power.

Paul Rubenstein still carried the clone of Doctor Rourke.

The only light was from their small flashlights, the rest of the corridor near the monorail station in total darkness.

James Darkwood pointed one of the suppressor-fitted pistols he carried into the face of Martin Zimmer's clone. "So, how do we get out of here to Landing Bay One? Or, do you prefer to die? If we're not there rather quickly, die is exactly what you'll do."

"I'm just a clone! I don't—"

"You know everything the original knows." Darkwood thumbed back the pistol's hammer for dramatic effect.

"There's a way. I just thought of it."

Darkwood smiled. Too bad Martin Zimmer's clone couldn't see it.

Chapter Sixty

Paul Rubenstein's right shoulder was alternately numb and throbbing, depending how he moved, but he could not have changed the position of John Rourke #11 if he had tried. The metal-runged ladder down which they climbed through a tube about the diameter of a twentieth-century manhole cover would not have allowed it, nor did the time.

Paul was ticking off the seconds. Even at a dead run, they would not reach Landing Bay One in time.

Martin Zimmer's clone had told them as they started down into the tube that this was a waste-disposal chamber below them, designed to accommodate water and synth-fuel runoff from the landing bays. There were gratings built into the landing-bay floors at regular intervals. Once they were beneath one of the ones with a ladder access, all they had to do was climb up and they would be in Landing Bay One.

If Martin Zimmer's clone lied, Paul had already decided—he would kill the man himself . . .

*   *   *

Emma Shaw sat in the cockpit of her aircraft, counting the seconds remaining. She had always resented the term "cockpit," but there were more important things on her mind.

She spoke into her radio on the ship-to-ship frequency as she watched the timepiece's second-hand sweep to the twelve position. Emma glanced over her right shoulder, seeing Lieutenant Christakos firing a signal flare, calling off the SEALs who were holding the control center, signaling that they should evacuate to their assigned aircraft.

Emma Shaw said over ship-to-ship, "This is Evac Leader to all Evac personnel. At your assigned time, commence takeoff. My aircraft will not—I repeat—will not be taking off. Out."

But Annie 's voice came back to her. "I'm not leaving either. I'm waiting for Paul. I tried talking my pilot out of it, and the other one, but—hell—Over."

"We can't get everybody killed. You and your pilot stay, then. I can fit two in the co-pilot's seat and so can you. Evac Three—do you copy that? Over."

"I can stay, Evac Leader."

"Negative."

"This is Michael. Come in."

"Before you say it, Michael," Emma Shaw responded, "if we don't get out of here, Paul and Annie and myself with that clone, then someone's going to have to do whatever else can be done to save your father's life and take care of your mother. You and Natalia seem like the ones who've been elected.

344

You're flying out of here. I command this end of the operation and you'll damn well do it. Out!"

Emma Shaw looked at her watch. In seventy-five seconds, if they weren't in the air or the next best thing, none of them would have to worry. "This is Evac Leader to all Evac personnel except Evac Two. Get out of here. We'll meet at the rendezvous. I say again, get out of here. Airborne. Now! Out!"

Aircraft started moving across the runway, the nearest to the open doorway picking up speed. V/STOL aircraft could get airborne at slower speeds than standard fixed-wing craft.

Natalia's voice came over the ship-to-ship frequency. "Emma, good luck to you."

"And to you," Emma answered.

The SEAL pilot who waited with Annie Rubenstein waited because he was a hero; SEALs were trained for that. Annie waited for her husband out of love. Emma Shaw waited because she had nowhere else to go. If the clone couldn't be brought out alive, John Rourke was dead. And there was no sense going on living if that happened.

It was better by far to die in combat.

They were past the safe takeoff point.

At fifteen seconds before detonation, she would order liftoff. They wouldn't make it, but at least it wouldn't technically be suicide.

Forty seconds.

As her eyes scanned over the airfield, she thought she saw movement . . .

James Darkwood pushed up just behind Martin

Zimmer's clone.

The grating opened into the center of Landing Bay One.

He looked at his watch. Even though there were two planes on the runway—and just two—there shouldn't have been any.

Darkwood told Martin Zimmer's clone, "Find yourself a place to hide in about the next thirty seconds. This place'll be a firebomb in forty."

Zimmer's clone ran for the wall, stopped, stood there, started running in a different direction.

There was no time to worry about him.

James Darkwood leaned down to help Paul Rubenstein out of the shaft with the clone of John Rourke.

Paul struggled to his feet. "Let me take him."

"No time," Paul insisted, starting to run, his body stooped under the weight of the man he carried.

James Darkwood saw Emma Shaw, out on the wingstem of her aircraft, heard her shouting, "There's no time! Hurry. The other plane, Darkwood!"

"Right!"

He ran, toward the second aircraft, Annie Rubenstein waving him on. He looked to his right. Emma Shaw was on the tarmac, helping Paul Rubenstein with the barely conscious clone of John Rourke. The man had mumbled incoherently, but his mind was a blank page.

Involuntarily, James Darkwood shivered.

He reached the Nazi/Eden V/STOL, clambering up toward the cockpit.

"We'll have to squeeze together," Annie Rubenstein told him.

"No disrespect meant to you or your husband, ma'am," he told her, dropping down beside her as she struggled with the safety restraint—it would never make it for both of them.

The cockpit cowling was already closing, the aircraft already in motion, engines revving. "Like I said," he began again. "No disrespect to either you or your husband, ma'am, but the opportunity to share a seat with you is the nicest thing that's happened to me all day!"

Behind them, James Darkwood heard what he thought was an explosion . . .

Emma Shaw throttled out the V/STOL. If she blew the carburation systems for the engines, she and Paul Rubenstein and the clone of John Rourke would be dead, but if she didn't get up speed they'd be dead anyway. "Hold on to something, Paul!" Emma Shaw ordered.

The other plane was just starting to clear the open doorway into the icy air above the Himalayas. She would not make it in time.

Unless—"I'm firing—aw, never mind. Hang on!"

She flipped the arm switch and in the next instant the firing switches for the aft-firing missile racks, hoping that the added thrust would get them out the door and airborne in time.

The roar from the missiles firing within the enclosure was deafening, the aircraft was vibrating, shaking so badly she could hardly control it.

The helicopter in which they'd flown exploded, the charges there detonating on time to the second.

She looked back through the canopy, across the fuselage, toward the rear of the takeoff and landing bay. A massive fireball was growing, black and orange and yellow, consuming everything in its path, moving faster than her aircraft.

"Oh shit!"

Full throttle, she had to risk going airborne before the marker.

The nose came up, the wheels off the runway. She retracted landing gear.

The fireball was closing on them.

"Have we got a problem here?" Paul Rubenstein called to her over the radio.

"Maybe—tell you in a second." If they lived that long.

The fireball belched toward them and involuntarily she ducked her head as the canopy skimmed only inches beneath the highest point of the door frame.

She looked back, the fireball totally obscuring the face of the mountain now as she climbed the V/STOL into the clouds. "No—no problem, Paul. Why'd you ask?"

Chapter Sixty-One

Paul Rubenstein walked beside the gurney on which the stabilized body of John Rourke #11 rested.

Sedated.

About to die.

Natalia walked on the other side of the gurney, her eyes shifting from the body to the people surrounding the gurney.

They had not spoken about how the clone of John Rourke would die.

The *Paladin*'s chief medical officer had met them as soon as the primary landing bay in which they'd touched down was evacuated of water and pressure equalized.

"There is one very big problem, Major Tiemerovna," he'd told her.

"I know. Trust me," she told him. "It will not remain a problem."

They were on the medical level now, just clear of the elevators. Emma Shaw walked beside Natalia,

Annie beside Paul, Michael behind the gurney, nearest to John Rourke #11's head.

The chief medical officer—a Commander Tierney—had gone on ahead. From what Natalia understood, once the heart was available, the operation could get under way in a matter of minutes.

Natalia had her knife to hand. She would cut the femoral artery on the inside of the right thigh of John Rourke #11, completely severing it so that some misguided person could not somehow save John Rourke #11's life.

This was evil. This was murder. She was fully prepared to do the act.

She touched her fingertips to the butt of the Bali-Song in the pocket along her jumpsuit's right thigh.

She caught Annie's eyes. Then Paul's.

Paul still had her suppressed Walther PPK/S. Was his hand reaching for it under his sweater?

The pre-op area lay about twenty-five yards ahead, the nearest thing to them a vacant intensive-care ward, the door open, the beds turned up and empty.

Natalia watched John Rourke #11's chest as it rose and fell.

John Rourke was a mind, not a body, the body merely the instrument by which the mind could function. She was not killing anything that was even a part of John Rourke.

She started to remove the knife from the pouch on her thigh.

There was a blur of motion from her right, through the doorway of the vacant intensive-care ward.

Sarah, some kind of knife in her hands.

Paul reached for Sarah.

Annie shrieked, "Momma, no!"

Natalia threw her body toward the gurney, trying to protect the heart of John Rourke #11 with her own body.

But the gurney was shoved forward.

Michael was reacting.

"No, Michael!" Natalia screamed.

The knife hammered down in Sarah Rourke's hands, Paul and Annie were grabbing her, wrestling her back.

"I destroyed the heart!" Sarah screamed.

Annie clutched Sarah to her, half fighting to hold her.

Sarah looked over her shoulder, eyes wide, streaming tears. "I had to before he—"

"Shut up!" Natalia shrieked.

And she looked down at the body on the gurney.

John Rourke #11 was dead.

When Michael had moved the gurney so suddenly, Sarah missed. The knife had impaled the clone through the left eye on an upward angle into the brain.

Emma Shaw was already starting to shove the gurney toward the pre-op section, the two uniformed nurses running after her, Emma shouting, "Doctor Tierney! We've got the heart!"

Made in the USA
Lexington, KY
12 May 2015